## Praise for *A Good Mother*

"Bazelon knows her way around a courtroom and unfolds one surprise after another while deftly exploring motherhood and the often crushing expectations that come with raising a family, not to mention the condescending treatment of women in a largely male workplace... A taut, nail-biting courtroom drama."

—*Kirkus Reviews*

"Attorney Bazelon's fiction debut is a powerhouse legal thriller, giving Abby a depth and breadth of backstory rare in first novels. Fans of Tana French, Scott Turow, and Lisa Scottoline will gravitate to Bazelon's tautly paced and richly detailed novel, an exploration of ambition, responsibility, and the sacrifices of motherhood."

—*Booklist*, starred review

"The courtroom scenes are sharp and suspenseful, the twists in the plot are unexpected, and the tension ratchets up until we are truly eager to find out what happens."

—*New York Times Book Review*

"A fast-paced, multilayered legal thriller... This tale of unchecked ambition about one woman's efforts to balance her professional and personal lives will resonate with many."

—*Publishers Weekly*

"A detailed and expert courtroom drama... The legal thrills just keep on coming."

—*Toronto Star*

"Lara Bazelon combines a riveting courtroom thriller with a nuanced and thought-provoking examination of gender, race, and justice. Helmed by an intelligent, complex, and flawed protagonist, *A Good Mother* is a beautifully written debut that kept me turning the pages late into the night."

"*A Good Mother* is a high-stakes legal thriller packed with intense courtroom drama, but it's also a story about the complicated sacrifices and compromises that mothers face. In this impressive debut, Lara Bazelon's talent for both storytelling and the law are on sharp display."

"Sexy, shrewd, and wholly contemporary, *A Good Mother* takes pitch-perfect characters, a page-whipping plot, and themes about marriage, lust, betrayal, and the juggling of new motherhood plus a hard-driving career, and mixes it all into a deeply perceptive legal thriller that made me drop everything else and just READ. Trial lawyer Abby Rosenberg is a flawed and riveting character you won't soon forget. And Lara Bazelon, herself a prestigious defense attorney, is an author to watch. I loved this book."

# A GOOD MOTHER

# A
# GOOD
# MOTHER

A NOVEL

# LARA
# BAZELON

HANOVER
SQUARE
PRESS

HANOVER
SQUARE
PRESS™

Recycling programs
for this product may
not exist in your area.

ISBN-13: 978-1-335-46955-7

A Good Mother

First published in 2021. This edition published in 2022.

Hanover Square Press
22 Adelaide St. West, 41st Floor
Toronto, Ontario M5H 4E3, Canada
HanoverSqPress.com
BookClubbish.com

Printed and bound in Barcelona, Spain by CPI Black Print

This book is for my father, trial-whisperer and fervent believer in the underdog, who always told me I could do it.

# A GOOD MOTHER

2006

**Saturday, October 14, 2006**
**2:51 a.m.**
**Ramstein Air Base**
**Ramstein-Miesenbach, Germany**

"Front desk, Sergeant Jamison."

"He was too big. I couldn't get him off me. He told me I was going to die—[unintelligible]"

"Ma'am?"

"[unintelligible]"

"Ma'am, where are you?"

"1074-B Arizona Circle. Call an ambulance. I need—"

"Okay, okay. I've got the EMT on the other line and the ambulance en route. Where are you hurt?"

"Not me—"

"Ma'am, is that—is that a baby crying? Is that your baby?"

"[unintelligible]"

"Did he hurt the baby?"

"She's—[unintelligible]—the other room. He was going to [unintelligible]"

"Okay, I reported the break-in. We are dispatching—security forces have been dispatched. Where is he now?"

"[unintelligible]"

"Ma'am, where is the intruder now?"

"He was stabbed. Oh, Jesus, oh, Jesus—[unintelligible]"

"What is the nature of the injury?"

"There's so much blood—[unintelligible]"

"Ma'am, I can't—I'm having trouble understanding you. I need for you to calm down so I can tell these guys what's going on."

"[unintelligible]"

"Where is he stabbed?"

"In his chest. He's losing all of his blood."

"The EMT is en route now."

"[unintelligible]"

"Ma'am, could the intruder hurt you or the baby? Are you still in danger?"

"He's not—[unintelligible]"

"Ma'am—"

"—an intruder. He's— It's Staff Sergeant—[unintelligible]"

"I'm having a hard time understanding you, ma'am. Take a breath. Take a breath."

"Staff Sergeant Travis Hollis—"

"The intruder is—he's—he's military?"

"He's my husband. He was stabbed. I stabbed him—[unintelligible]"

"Ma'am, ma'am, are you still there?"

"Travis, baby, don't die on me. Please, don't die."

**Tuesday, October 17, 2006**
**1:30 p.m.**
**United States District Court for the**
**Central District of California**
**Los Angeles**

Climbing the steps to the courthouse at 312 North Spring Street in downtown Los Angeles, Abby Rosenberg surveys the local TV news vans and the small collection of reporters milling about: three women in bright-colored, short-skirted suits, their hair—ash blond, dark blond, caramel blond—perfectly blown out. In consultation with their cameramen, they are setting up for the shoot. Until the hearing is over, there is nothing else for them to do. No cameras are allowed beyond the iron-heavy doors, no exceptions. Inside, the print reporters are lined up, divesting themselves of jackets, shoes, and cell phones as they wait to go through security.

It is seventeen stairs to the top and Abby has to stop and catch her breath. She lists slightly, reaches for the railing, and feels a firm hand on her upper arm. Turning, she sees Shauna Gooden, the prosecutor she'll be up against in court.

Tall, early fifties, Shauna is one of those women who gives no sense that she is invested in her appearance but manages to look good anyway. Her pantsuits are at least a decade out of date but still fit nicely, her jewelry is minimal—diamond studs, a thin gold chain around her neck—but adds just the tiniest amount of sparkle.

"I'm okay," Abby says, and Shauna releases her arm.

They both step back, Shauna surveying her from head to toe with her hands on her hips. "Thirty pounds of extra weight will do that. And what on earth are you still doing in stilettos?"

"Denying reality." Still winded, Abby does not want to risk the embarrassment of a full sentence interrupted by a gulp for air.

"Hide that belly behind a shopping bag and no one would even know." Shauna smiles. "No fat ankles for you."

Abby looks down, but she is long past the point of seeing her feet. Her stomach protrudes, stretched tight as a water balloon under her maternity blouse. She had tried and failed to give it some cover with her jacket, but the days of closing the buttons are long gone. As Shauna has rightly pointed out, the weight is concentrated almost entirely in the balloon, leaving Abby slightly off balance. In moments like these, in public and on display, she is afraid of being pulled inexorably downward until her face is flat against the pavement.

"Thanks," she says warily. "And congratulations on the BWLA award. I heard it was a very fancy lunch at Shutters."

Shauna smiles. "They went all out. Black Women Lawyers of LA, you know, a small but mighty sisterhood." She takes another look at Abby and shakes her head. "There is no way you got this case by accident. And weren't you supposed to pop the little sucker out last week?"

Abby grins. She genuinely likes Shauna, which is saying something. Abby doesn't care for many of the prosecutors in the United States Attorney's Office, particularly the young self-righteous ones who come straight off the assembly line from Stanford or one of the fancier East Coast law schools: conservative suits, conservative haircuts, conservative sense of humor. Which is to say none at all, as far as Abby can tell. Shauna, though, has been doing the job for more than twenty years and has a reputation for being honest and fair. But in court she takes no prisoners.

"I'm due in five days," Abby says. "And yes, random assignment."

Shauna raises an eyebrow. "More like a blatant ploy to get Judge Richards's sympathy. I know Paul." She shakes her head. "The man is shameless."

At this reference to her ever-canny supervisor, Abby grins but says nothing.

"I can just see you now, having contractions at the lectern." Shauna starts laughing, and the heads turn to look.

"Not to worry," Abby says, "I haven't had my bloody show yet."

"Your what?"

Abby smiles. "The red clump of mucus that shows up in your underwear the day before you go into labor? C'mon now, you remember."

Shauna, still laughing, offers to hold Abby's briefcase as they walk inside, an offer she declines. As they wave through security with their badges, one of the security guards calls out to Abby. "Ms. Rosenberg, you need a hand with anything?"

It's Rex James, one of Abby's favorites, a middle-aged,

heavyset guy with a modified salt-and-pepper Afro. Abby smiles, placing a hand gently on her belly. "No, but thank you," she says.

"Sweet Jesus," Shauna says, rolling her eyes as she strides off toward the elevator. But when it arrives, she makes sure to hold the door.

"All rise."

They stand as Judge Richards ascends the bench, Abby feeling rushed. She had hoped to have a few minutes alone with her client. Since Luz Rivera Hollis was arrested seventy-two hours ago on a US Air Force base in Germany and sent back to Los Angeles, Abby has seen her twice in a grimy, glassed-off attorney-client visiting room at the Metropolitan Detention Center. On both visits, they had spoken of nothing but the bail hearing, purposefully myopic conversations trained at the immediate crisis at hand: freeing Luz to take care of her infant daughter while the case trundles forward.

Both times, Luz answered Abby's questions steadily, providing the basic facts requested: the estimated market value of her grandmother's house, the status of the custody dispute that had been launched immediately by her dead husband's mother, the absence in her life of any other act of violence toward another human being. Swimming in her too-large prison scrubs, long dark hair a tangled mess, eyes rimmed with purple half-moons, she looked like a frightened child, which Abby supposes she is. Luz Rivera Hollis is nineteen years old.

There had been no crying, no asking of any of the questions that Abby would expect from someone in her situation. *What is the evidence against me? What are my chances?* There had been no pleading, either. *Please, please*

*help me.* Do everything you can. There had been, Abby realizes now, no curiosity about the legal machine that had
been set in motion. Luz's terror showed only in her eyes,
which were dark and depthless. Midconversation, midsen-
tence even, they would go vacant, causing Abby to have to
repeat Luz's name, loudly, several times. The only thing
Luz had wanted to know was when she could see her baby,
Cristina. That question she had asked over and over.

*You'll see her when I get you out on bail,* Abby had told
her. At those words, Luz's face had lit up. But it is not at
all clear that Abby could get Luz out on bail. The charge
against her is first-degree murder. Abby turns to Luz now,
puts a hand on her back as they retake their seats next to
each other. Luz looks no better today than she had at the
jail the day before. Through the worn material of her jail-
issue jumpsuit, Abby can feel her trembling.

Magistrate judges assigned to hear bail motions get the
smaller courtrooms on the upper floors. Judge Richards's
is packed. There are the usual suspects with their press credentials on lanyards around their necks. The Hollis family is there, too, in force, the victim's mother, gray-blonde,
grim, and gray-faced, braced by her two daughters, all of
them wearing American flag pins. But most of the spectators are members of Luz's church, more than two dozen,
dressed formally, wearing sober expressions. Abby smiles
at them, relieved, but not surprised that they had agreed to
come. Abby, knowing Travis's family would be there, had
intended to pack the other side of the courtroom. That they
had turned out in those numbers will signal to the judge—
especially this judge—that Luz has an important constitu-
ency of supporters.

Judge Richards, fortysomething and wholesome-looking
with a still thick, still brown head of hair, looks down at

them under straight dark brows. Devout Catholic and the father of eight children. Abby glances over at Luz, who is nervously fiddling at the gold cross on the slender chain around her neck.

The clerk calls the case and says, "Counsel, appearances please."

"Shauna Gooden, for the government."

"Abby Rosenberg, Deputy Federal Public Defender, on behalf of Luz Rivera Hollis."

As if on cue, the courtroom door opens, and a priest walks in escorting Luz's grandmother Maria Elena, who holds Luz's baby in one of those pop-out car seat carriers on her skinny wrinkled arm. Asleep, thankfully. They all turn, and Abby notices Judge Richards's clerk, a grandmotherly type herself, giving little Cristina an involuntary pucker of a smile.

Luz's eyes go wide and her manacled hands reach out, jerk the chain, and retract to their default position at her waist.

Shauna looks at Abby and mouths, *Are you kidding me?* Abby, smiling, gives a slight shrug of her shoulders.

Judge Richards clears his throat.

"Mrs. Rivera Hollis, the United States has charged you with the first-degree murder of your husband, Sergeant Travis Hollis. Have you read the complaint detailing those charges and do you understand it?"

Luz's *yes* is barely audible.

"You are here in federal court in Los Angeles today because of a law, recently passed by Congress, which says that civilians who commit crimes against members of the armed forces while outside of the United States shall be extradited for trial in the jurisdiction where they reside. It's called the Military Extraterritorial Jurisdiction Act.

Because your last known residence was within the Central District of California, you are in this courtroom today. Do you understand?"

After another barely audible *yes*, Richards continues, "Alright. It's the government's motion here, so I'll allow you to argue first, Ms. Gooden."

Shauna stands and immediately begins speaking in a voice that carries with it a tone of barely suppressed outrage. "Sergeant Travis Hollis, a decorated combat veteran who served this country bravely in Iraq, found out too late that his most lethal enemy resided in his own home."

Shauna settles her gaze on Luz. "It is hard to think of a more cold-blooded and brutal crime. Upon learning that Sergeant Hollis had been unfaithful through email communications from the—the mistress—Mrs. Rivera Hollis brooded for hours, until her husband came home from a party. Then, wielding a knife, she stabbed him with such extreme force that it pierced through his rib cage and tore open his heart. Despite the heroic efforts of first responders on the army base to save him, Sergeant Hollis bled to death in his own hallway at the age of twenty-three. Mrs. Rivera Hollis robbed Sergeant Hollis's recently widowed mother of her only son. She robbed her own child of her father.

"The defendant planned this. She turned a kitchen knife into a deadly weapon. She is extremely dangerous. She needs to remain in jail pending trial where she can't hurt anyone else."

Luz is returning Shauna's stare, her eyes narrowed in contempt. Abby grabs her just above her shackled wrist and whispers sharply in her ear. "Look down. Look down at the ground."

Shauna has moved on to argue that Luz, facing a mandatory death-in-prison sentence, might escape across the border to Mexico, where she has many relatives waiting to welcome her with open arms. Abby half listens, eyes on her client, who has trained her gaze downward but still looks angry.

When Shauna is finally finished, Judge Richards thanks her politely before turning to Abby. "I'll hear from you now, Ms. Rosenberg." He pauses. "Would you—would it be more comfortable for you to remain seated?"

Abby gives the judge her warmest smile. "No, thank you, Your Honor." She takes her time extracting herself from her chair and walks carefully to the lectern, making sure to give Luz a friendly squeeze on the shoulder as she passes by. Once there, Abby finds she has to hold both sides of the wooden podium, canting her abdomen forward to remain balanced. Shauna is right, she's a fool to be wearing high heels. But that is what she always wears, to add precious inches to her height—on her straightest-backed day, she's barely five foot two. Forgoing the practice isn't just about vanity, although that is assuredly part of it. Choosing sensible flats feels like giving up.

She glances briefly to her left at the marshal on duty; Jared, a friend of Nic's. Lanky and unsmiling, he sits slouched on the front bench, just a few feet from Luz in the highly unlikely event she will try to shuffle off in her leg irons. But Jared is also there to keep an eye on everyone else, including—and maybe especially—on Abby. To make sure she is safe, to guard against the possibility that she might try to do something reckless herself, though God only knows what that might be. Abby knows Nic has arranged it on purpose, as he has with all of her court appearances for the last month, although they do not talk about it at home. Sometimes, Abby has to remind herself that they share a home—what had been her home. A year ago, she hadn't known Nic's last name, just that he was the US marshal who brought her infamous client, Rayshon Marbury, to court every day for the trial. But Nic, as it turned out, had been far more than that. Now, a few unimaginable turns later, they were having a baby.

All of it was unimaginable. Over a year ago, Abby had been just another public defender. Hardworking, and with glimmers of real talent, but also regularly dismissed and condescended to, as many younger female trial attorneys are. But in her third year in the office, she had been assigned to defend Rayshon Marbury, and now she was known as the woman who had proven innocent a man widely considered to be the city's most dangerous gang member, on trial for his life for masterminding the killing of a DEA agent. She had made headlines again and again, humiliating the US Attorney's Office and exposing one of the LAPD's finest as a corrupt racist, then landing in hot water herself over the tactics she had used. Rayshon Marbury's case—and the outsize consequences that came with it—followed her everywhere. Everyone knew who she was and had an opinion about her, for better and for worse.

Abby turns to Judge Richards. "It is all too easy for the government to point the accusatory finger, particularly in a charging document that arranges the facts to their liking and omits the ones that are less convenient. So let me offer a few. Sergeant Hollis was six foot four and weighed 260 pounds. He could bench press his own weight and then some. At the time of death, his blood alcohol level was .26, more than three times the legal limit. My client is five feet tall and weighs less than a hundred pounds. She had given birth two months before the crime."

Abby pauses for a moment to let the contrasting images sink in. "Now imagine for a moment that you are in Mrs.

Rivera Hollis's shoes, forced to confront a very angry, very drunk, very menacing Sergeant Hollis under those circumstances, with a baby to protect." Abby can see Shauna rising and holds up her hand. "We are not here to try this case today," she acknowledges, "but I would be remiss if I stood by and let Ms. Gooden paint my client as a cold-blooded killer without bringing to the court's attention what she was dealing with that night.

"Whether Mrs. Rivera Hollis is guilty of first-degree murder beyond a reasonable doubt is for the jury to decide after considering all of the evidence, a tiny fraction of which the government has provided. Today, there are two narrow issues before this court—" Abby holds up two fingers "—and the standard of proof is far lower. One, would my client likely flee the jurisdiction or two, endanger the community if she were let out on bail? The answer to both questions is no. Mrs. Rivera Hollis has surrendered her passport. She's a churchgoing mother, devoted to the care of her daughter, Cristina, whose christening is next week. To deprive Cristina of her mother so soon after losing her father could be devastating to her emotional development and even her physical health. She is still nursing—"

Judge Richards interrupts, "Is that the child behind you, in the baby carrier?"

"Yes. She is in the custody of Mrs. Rivera Hollis's grandmother, Maria Elena Rivera, who is willing to put up her house as collateral to secure the bond."

"And the house is worth?" Judge Richards is scribbling notes.

"There is roughly $100,000 in equity."

Shauna gets up. "Your Honor," she says, "Sergeant Hollis's mother, who is present in the courtroom today, has filed a petition in family court seeking to terminate the defendant's parental rights and assume sole custody of Cristina—"

Judge Richards continues writing, saying, without looking up, "A petition that I imagine will not be decided until after this case is over."

"Well—yes. But in all likelihood, the defendant will be convicted and Mrs. Hollis will obtain custody. The only other option is, as Ms. Rosenberg said, the baby's great-grandmother, who is elderly, speaks no English, and cannot be expected to properly provide for an infant." Luz's head comes up again, turned once more in Shauna's direction. Abby shoots her a withering look and Luz retrains her gaze on the plush maroon carpet. "And how Ms. Rosenberg has the nerve to stand up here and prey upon this court's sympathy by arguing trauma to the child from the loss of both parents knowing full well that the death of Cristina's father is directly attributable to—"

"Yes, the irony has not escaped me."

"Your Honor, this is a first-degree murder case, the most serious charge the government can bring. The defendant lay in wait for her husband to come home. She premeditated, she planned. If we were in state court there would be no bond. There would be nothing to discuss."

"We're not in state court, Ms. Gooden."

"Apologies, Your Honor." Shauna inclines her head and Abby allows herself a small smile at this unforced error. Even lower-level magistrate judges like Richards—tasked primarily with jobs like determining bail and mediating discovery disputes—don't like to be compared with their counterparts across the street. State court and federal court are two entirely separate realms: one grimy and chaotic, the courtrooms constantly churning, its justice often slapdash and haphazard. The other, with a docket a fraction of the size, is stately, even austere, its courtrooms marbled, the pace sedate. Federal judges pride themselves on decisions that are deliberative and deliberate, the reasoning often set out at some length in writing.

Judge Richards looks out at the people filling the benches, his eyes resting for a moment on the priest before coming back to Abby. "What church does your client attend?"

Luz answers for herself. "Immaculate Heart."

He nods, makes another notation. "What's the age of the child?"

"She is just over two months old."

Judge Richards stops writing momentarily. Without looking up he says, "Priors?"

"None."

Shauna interjects, "That's incorrect, Your Honor. The defendant has a juvenile case."

Abby does her best to stare placidly at Judge Richards as if she, too, isn't hearing this for the first time.

"What juvenile case?" Richards asks.

"It's from 2003, when the defendant was sixteen. We are in the process of retrieving the file."

Richards says, "Because the defendant was underage, the records are sealed, is that what you are saying?"

"Yes—"

Abby interrupts her, "The government knows nothing about this juvenile matter or how, if at all, it might relate to this bail application."

"We intend to find out," Shauna says evenly.

Richards looks at Shauna. "I'm sure you do. And I have to say, it troubles me."

"Your Honor—"

He holds up his hand, and Abby stops talking. "It troubles me," he repeats. "Ms. Rosenberg, anything else?"

Abby nods. She had been debating whether to risk it, but now the choice is clear. "With the court's permission, my client's priest, Father Abelard, would like to address the court." Legally speaking, the priest is irrelevant; the only questions Judge Richards has to decide are whether Luz will hightail it out of town or kill someone else if he releases her. The priest can assuage neither of these concerns because his church is putting up no money and taking no risks on Luz's behalf. A few questions on Shauna's part will suss this out soon enough, but Abby is determined not to give her the opportunity. Not after Shauna just dropped the juvenile delinquent stink bomb.

"The witness will come forward and be placed under oath."

Father Abelard, a small, brittle man, makes his way to the podium. When the formalities are over, the priest begins uncertainly, in a thickly accented voice, "May it please you, Judge. I have known this young lady many, many years. I was the priest at her communion. What happened, only God knows. It is not for me to judge. But I can say, sir, she is a good girl. All her life, she goes to church." He pauses. "I know there has been great suffering and I do not take away from the pain of the brave soldier's family, Mr. Travis Hollis. We pray for them." He nods once, as if to himself. "We pray for them." He turns, gestures toward the silent bundle in the car seat. "But there is also an innocent child in need of her mother. And I know this mother her whole life, and she is a good girl." He nods again. "Thank you, sir."

There is a long silence as the priest takes his seat. Luz moves her manacled hands to wipe clumsily at her eyes with the bottom of her jail-issue shirt.

They all wait while Judge Richards continues to write until he lifts his head again, fingers steepled under his chin. "I am going to set bail." One of the church members whispers in the ear of Luz's grandmother, who claps her hands together and says something in Spanish about Jesus. The priest puts a hushing hand on her arm. Abby watches as Luz's shoulders sag in relief, her head bent nearly to the tabletop.

"Mrs. Rivera Hollis will be fitted with an electronic ankle monitoring bracelet to be worn at all times. Following her release, she will be confined to her grandmother's house except for legal visits, doctor's appointments, and church."

Judge Richards turns his gaze on Luz. "Mrs. Rivera Hollis, if you attempt to flee the jurisdiction, your grandmother will lose her home. And you may well lose custody of your daughter. Do you understand?"

Luz whispers, "Yes."

"Alright, that should take care of the flight risk." Judge Richards taps his pen on his legal pad. "As to danger, the nature of the crime is violent and disturbing. There was, as Ms. Gooden pointed out, the use of extreme force. But we are talking about violence between a husband and wife. A young mother with no criminal history—not as an adult, in any event. We don't know what happened when she was a juvenile. I know that there is a presumption in favor of detention. But based on what I've heard today, I think Ms. Rosenberg has overcome it. I just don't see anything here that shows the defendant poses a danger to anyone else."

Judge Richards pauses. "There's one more thing. The publicity around all of this—" he gestures toward the press gaggle "—is only going to accelerate. But I am not going to let either side throw gas on the fire by trying this case in the media. The attorneys and their respective legal teams are prohibited from speaking to the press. A fair trial is more important than your fifteen minutes of fame. Understood?" Here, he looks meaningfully at Abby.

Abby smiles back as if this were a compliment, rather than a not-so-subtle dig. And the gag order doesn't seem like a bad idea, either. Reporters tended to give prosecutors—rather than her clients—the benefit of the doubt, printing their public pronouncements uncritically and lending them the imprimatur of truth. Depriving Shauna of that megaphone was a good thing.

"Alright. Once the appropriate documents are filed with the court, the defendant shall be released."

"Thank you, Your Honor." Abby turns behind her to look at the furiously scribbling journalists, the wave of smiles spreading across the mostly Spanish-speaking congregation as the news is translated. "There is one more item I would like to address, if the court is amenable."

Judge Richards inclines his head.

"Well—" Abby looks at Jared "—I am hoping that the marshal will allow my client to spend some time nursing her daughter in the witness room following the conclusion of these proceedings."

Jared stands, his faced flushed. Whether it's from anger or embarrassment, Abby can't tell. "Your Honor, that's not part of our protocol. We're law enforcement officers, not—" He stops, out of words. "It's just not appropriate, sir."

"Your Honor," Abby interjects, "there are engorgement issues here, which can be quite serious. Infection of the milk ducts—"

Now Judge Richards is flushing. "Yes, alright." He looks at Jared. "Please have one of your female colleagues escort the defendant and her baby to the witness room." He turns back to Abby. "Anything else?" His expression makes it clear there had better not be.

"No, Your Honor. And thank you for understanding." Abby smiles sweetly.

Shauna stands. "Your Honor, the government is seeking a postponement of the arraignment on formal charges at this time."

Judge Richards raises his eyebrows.

"It is possible that this case could resolve without the need for a trial, if the two sides are permitted time to reach an agreement."

A plea offer. A bit early for that, Abby thinks, particularly after Shauna has gone to great lengths to denounce Luz as a stone-cold killer. But clearly, that had been an opening bid. First-degree murder was a typical government overreach designed to extract an agreement to something nearly but not quite so bad. And Shauna may have real problems. No prosecutor has ever invoked the Military Extraterritorial Jurisdiction Act since it was passed six years ago, in part because it is so logistically difficult to prosecute a crime that took place in a different part of the world.

"Ms. Rosenberg?"

Abby pauses for a moment. Luz will be free on bail. Waiving her right to a speedy trial within seventy days will cost little—no doubt whomever takes over the case when she goes on leave would have to ask for a continuance anyway; it's just too difficult to get ready in that amount of time, particularly when most of the witnesses are overseas.

Suddenly, it dawns on her. She may not have to give up this case after all. Paul had asked her to do the bail hearing for exactly the reason Shauna had said, with the understanding that it would be Abby's first and last appearance on the case. Murder cases in federal court were rare—Rayshon's was an outlier. One with stakes like these—a beautiful young woman, a potential life sentence, an untested law, and the media attention that came with it—rarer still. Paul's plan was pass it off to the new Ken Doll guy they'd hired out of the Army JAG Corps, figuring that even though it wasn't a military law case, it was military enough that his experience counted for something.

But what if Paul couldn't pass it off? The rule in the office was vertical representation—the same lawyer from start to finish—except in the rare instance where that became impossible: a health emergency, a death in the family, maternity leave. If the plea negotiations dragged on long enough and went nowhere, Abby could be back in time to try it. She hasn't been to trial since Rayshon's case almost exactly one year ago. Since she started turning—literally—into a different person with a body and a life that has become in some ways unrecognizable. Pregnant, coupled, domesticated. For the last several months, she has been visited by the same nightmare: she's been buried alive, slowly deprived of oxygen. Each time, she wakes up gasping to the baby's furious kicks, only to realize she had been holding her breath. Now for the first time in months she feels a rush of anticipation, a gust of cool air. She feels herself start to smile—a real one, this time—and bites down hard on her lower lip.

"Ms. Rosenberg?" Richards is looking at her expectantly.

"No objection."

"How much time, Ms. Gooden?"

"Six weeks."

"Ten," Abby says. The federal public defender's office paid for four months of parental leave and she'd promised Nic she'd take all of it, bonding with the baby and saving them the money they would otherwise have to spend on childcare. Well, plans change. This is her case, she can feel it.

"You'll have eight. The defendant will be arraigned on the indictment on Monday, December 11. This court is in recess."

As the rows of people in the gallery rise, there is a thrum of excited chatter in multiple languages, the rustle of gathered papers, the snapping of briefcases and hefting of purses, the flood of murmured *excuse me*s as people in a hurry brush past other slower-moving bodies toward the double doors.

Abby walks back to Luz, remembering the unpleasant surprise about her juvenile record and getting angry all over again. She leans down, her lips to the girl's ear. "I asked you about criminal convictions. I specifically asked you."

"My lawyer told me no one would ever see it." Luz stares sullenly at the floor. "That's what sealed means."

Gently, Abby puts her finger under Luz's chin, lifting her face until they are eye to eye. "Don't you ever fucking lie to me again."

Luz Rivera Hollis arrives in Will Ellet's office twenty-five minutes late, in black skinny jeans and a sleeveless blouse printed with tiny black polka dots, her black hair breaking in loose waves over her shoulders and down her back. She's wearing lipstick that isn't quite orange and isn't quite red, a crimson color that few women could pull off, Will thinks. Luz, though, is among those few. Her fingernails are painted the same color.

It is hard to believe this Luz is the same person Will met last week at her grandmother's house. That Luz had met him at the door in a white high-necked shirt with ruffles at the neck and sleeves, and a long sweeping white skirt, the baby in her arms. It was a look that practically screamed Lady Madonna, particularly given that their brief conversation had taken place in the living room where one of the only decorative features was a wooden cross on the wall.

Will hadn't stayed long that time, though the meeting had been planned in advance to go over the government's written plea offer and the stack of additional documents Shauna had provided to Abby, and Will had driven a good ninety minutes to get to the nondescript ranch-style house, which was situated in a dusty cul-de-sac a few twisting miles off the freeway. Luz had taken her time settling the baby in a wicker basket on the couch before turning to accept the paperwork.

"This is the evidence they have against me?" she had asked, and he felt compelled to answer, "So far."

Then the grandmother had come in, firing indignant questions at Will in Spanish. How could the prosecutors possibly believe that Luz would do such an evil thing? Why hadn't Will gotten the charges dismissed? When would all of this be over? Will waited for Luz to translate, then answered with halting evasions, trying to say as little as possible while not appearing rude. Then Cristina had started wailing and Luz had excused herself. After several minutes of increasingly uncomfortable silence with the grandmother, who was now clearly displeased with him, Will had taken his leave, having learned exactly zero about his client or what she thought should be done with her case.

Today they are on Will's turf, no grandma, no baby. He is firmly in control over the situation. Still, he's irritated by Luz's lateness, which is both unapologetic and nonchalant, as if she's here to discuss a contested parking ticket, not a murder charge that could send her to prison for the rest of her life.

Will says, more heartily than he'd intended, "You can go ahead and close the door. Come over and sit down, please."

Luz closes the door but she doesn't sit, choosing to walk slowly around the room, a shiny black handbag slung over one shoulder, examining his row of framed diplomas, hung perfectly straight and equidistant in a line on the wall. "You have a lot of these," she says. "West Point. Judge Advocate General's Corps." She turns. "You used to be in JAG, defending soldiers?"

"Yes, ma'am."

She nods. "That's why they picked you to take over from her." A pause and then, "Did she have the baby?"

"Um, yes, yes she did." There had been an office-wide email announcement from Jonathan, Abby's closest—and maybe only—friend in the office. Will doesn't know what to make of Jonathan, the only out gay guy in their office whose acidic takedowns—of prosecutors, his own colleagues, and the cruel absurdities of the work they do—he finds simultaneously hilarious and terrifying, knowing he could be next. Not Abby, though. There is a tie between those two, held fast and twisted hard, Will's heard, by what happened in Rayshon Marbury's case.

"A boy or a girl?"

With some effort, Will summons the image Jonathan had attached: a red squished-up face and a tuft of yellow hair. Measurements had been provided, as well as the baby's name, none of which Will recalls. He doesn't know Abby, only of her. She was gone on maternity leave when he started. Not that he would say any of this; Luz is not likely to appreciate that he is new. But only to this job, he reminds himself. It isn't as if he hasn't got more experience under harsher conditions than many of the attorneys who are now his colleagues.

"I don't remember," he admits.

Luz has turned back to the wall, continuing to read aloud. "University of Oklahoma Law School. Summa cum laude." She pronounces it "summer cum loud."

Will feels his face flush, says, "That's just a Latin phrase. They put it there to make it look fancy."

"What does it mean?" She turns, looking at him curiously.

*She has eyes a man could drown in.* Out of nowhere, Will is reminded of that phrase from *The French Lieutenant's Woman.* Not a compliment, the words had been a warning to the protagonist from his friend. *Beware, Charles, of this loose and depraved woman: Sarah Woodruff.* Will had read the novel for a class called Male Images of Women, taken only to fulfill his English requirement, never expecting that what he read would ignite a passion for reading British literature that continued to the present day.

Will's wife, Meredith, liked to tease him about it—the collection of thick dusty books he insisted on taking from move to move; evidence of his otherwise undetectable sensitive side, she said. And she was right; he did hide it. But he identified with those male protagonists: their good taste and gallantry; their quests for self-discovery and elevation of romantic love. Meredith herself did not care much for these kinds of books, her taste ran more to Jackie Collins and Danielle Steele.

Will snaps back to the present. He's thinking too much, wandering around like a man hoping to get lost. The odd combination of cheesiness and high culture he confronts daily in LA is dislocating—the muscle guys and boob-tube-top girls on the Venice Beach boardwalk, the coastal-born Ivy League elites who surround him at work. For the first time in his life, Will doesn't fit. And neither does Meredith, who comes home every day from teaching second grade at an elite private prep school with yet another breathless story about the squad of blonde moms who arrive to scoop up their children at pickup time, with their Uggs, and Juicy

Couture outfits; their lifted, plumped, and lineless skin. Meredith's country-girl cluelessness makes him feel embarrassed, then ashamed of feeling embarrassed. The last thing he wants is a wife with $300 yoga pants and a body sculpted by a plastic surgeon. He feels Luz's eyes on him as she waits for an answer.

"It doesn't mean much of anything," he says curtly. "Just that I did well at school."

Luz has moved now, back to his desk, picking up a framed picture of Will and Meredith on their honeymoon in Hawaii, both of them in bathing suits and leis, holding piña coladas as they sat on lounge chairs by the hotel pool. She puts it back down. "Did the army pay for all that school?"

"They did."

"After you became a lieutenant?"

"A captain. And did three years of active duty. Never deployed, though." Will feels the class chasm opening. Luz's husband would never have been a captain. Had he lived, the guy was staying where he was, an enlisted man.

Will's trajectory was different. The son of a military man, Will had applied himself with a cold fury to everything the army threw at him: forget basic training, he'd run eighteen miles wearing a sixty-pound backpack and spent days alone in the woods, sleep-deprived and without food, to complete the infamous Survival, Evasion, Resistance, and Escape program. When he felt weak or afraid he took care to hide it, just like his novels.

Luz looks at the framed photograph again, then back at Will. "When you smile like that, you look like one of those actors." She snaps her fingers. "The one in—what was it—X-Men?"

Will flushes. He got this all the time. Neither of his parents was particularly attractive, yet somehow he had ended up resembling a guy on a movie poster: square jaw, gray eyes, perfectly chiseled features. At six feet two inches, he is broad-shouldered with a six-pack that, embarrassingly, he does not have to do much to maintain.

Luz takes in his look, then says, "You hate it when people tell you that, huh?"

"Yeah," he says flatly, "I do."

As far back as he could remember, boys on the various bases where Will and his family had lived had taunted him: Adam Levine, Justin Timberlake, name-your-boy-band frontman. *Everyone should have your problems*, his mother told him once, but Will had looked at his father and seen in his face what he already knew to be true. It was far better in the military—and, Will found, life in general—to be rugged than beautiful.

"Men have told me my whole life that I'm beautiful." Luz shrugs. "It's so expected it doesn't even mean anything to me anymore, you know?"

Will nods, trying not to show that her statement, delivered in a matter-of-fact manner devoid of any self-effacing disclaimer, makes him uncomfortable. What woman just outright said things like that? None he'd ever met.

He gestures again toward the chair and Luz finally sits down, crossing her right leg over her left, and exposing the bulky square box of the ankle monitor wrapped around the sharply tapered bottom of her jeans. She sees him looking and says, eyes narrowing, "I hate this stupid thing. And it's making me crazy, being in the house all day, not allowed to go anywhere unless it's here or a doctor's appointment or church. I can't even take Cristina to the park."

"I can only imagine," Will says mildly, thinking that Luz should feel damn lucky that Cristina wasn't nestled in the eager arms of Travis Hollis's mother right at this moment.

Had Abby not managed, somewhat miraculously in Will's opinion, to get Luz out on bail, the only other viable option would have been the child's great-grandmother. It was all too easy to see how Luz could have lost Cristina to her mother-in-law, at least temporarily, and that was assuming the absolute best-case scenario—an acquittal.

He looks briefly at his watch; less than an hour until he has to be in court on another case. "Mrs. Rivera Hollis—"

She looks at him as if he has just said something silly. "Call me Luz," she says.

"Okay," he says, "sure," though he feels unsure, and has in fact never called any client by a first name. "Look, we need to talk about the case. Have you had a chance to go over the discovery—the paperwork—I gave you?"

She bites her lip, shaking her head.

*She's not going to read any of it,* he thinks. Probably ever. Maybe it's better that way, although he had spared her the worst: the autopsy photographs of Travis's chest, sawed open from neck to navel, the ribs snapped like wishbones where the doctors had forced them apart with some medieval-looking device so they could grab his heart in their hands in a final desperate attempt to make it start beating again. If the case goes to trial, he will of course file a motion to keep the pictures out—they are gruesome beyond belief—but he will lose. The government, after all, has a right to put on its case.

"What about the plea offer?" he prods. "Have you read that?"

Her face hardens. "They want me to plead guilty to murder. I won't."

"Manslaughter," Will says.

"Whatever."

Will feels it again, a stab of impatience, that she could

be so obstinate, even juvenile, continuing to reject any attempt on his part to get her to engage in a meaningful way and talking instead about something as banal as people's looks. Then he remembers with a sudden jolt that she is only nineteen. He is talking to a teenager.

"Luz," he says gently. "It makes a big difference. They are offering you a ten-year deal. With good behavior you'd be out in eight."

"Ten years?" She is looking at him like he's crazy.

"I know it sounds like a long time, but if you are convicted you will go to prison for the rest of your life."

"Manslaughter," she says, as if trying out the word. And then, tinkering with it, "Man. Slaughtered." She looks at him. "That's supposed to be better?"

"Yes," he says, realizing suddenly how strange the word is, how bizarre the idea that it might be an improvement. "It's when one person kills another person during a fight. In the heat of passion. There's less blame because it wasn't necessarily on purpose, wasn't, you know, well-thought-out."

Luz appears to have no reaction to his explanation, her gaze has turned away, upward to the window at Will's back with its view of the skyline. For a government office, at a government salary, the view of downtown Los Angeles is unparalleled, particularly at night. But he doubts she is seeing it; her stare is utterly blank, almost as if she is blind.

"There is evidence to support a manslaughter plea," Will continues into the silence. "Furniture knocked over, a broken lamp, and Sergeant Hollis himself, he didn't have his shirt on, his belt was undone, and his pants were—"

"He always takes his clothes off when he comes home drunk," she says. "He always wants to fuck then."

Will blinks, trying not to be thrown by the crude language or the sudden image he has of this reeking, beefy man climbing on top of her. *He was too big. I couldn't get him off me.* Will had known guys like this when he was in the military. Dozens of them. All assholes. "And maybe you, you didn't, and there was a struggle—"

"No." She is still staring at the window.

"Okay," he says, "I'm just—speculating here because you haven't told me. And I know it's hard to talk about, but we have to, Luz. And about your juvenile matter. We still don't have the file from the government, so I'm hoping you can tell me what to expect."

She does not appear to have heard him and again, Will feels his frustration building. "And then there are the emails," he says, plowing on, hoping to provoke her. "I know you didn't read the paperwork, Luz, so I'll just tell you. They searched your computer. They found the email from Jackie Stedman, your late husband's—"

"I know who she is," Luz says coldly.

"Right, sorry." He flushes again. "The government knows that Jackie forwarded you the email chain of messages between her and Travis, the ones you opened while Sergeant Hollis was at the party, just hours before you— before he died. That's motive. That is a powerful motive."

"That's not what happened." She is looking at him now, her expression unreadable.

"That is what the government is going to say happened. That it was planned. An—an ambush."

"No," she says again. Will wants her to be angry but she isn't, she just looks annoyed by his stupidity. Flailing at a guessing game she does not want to play. *Am I getting warm? Cold. Warmer? Colder.*

"We have to talk about exactly what did happen," he says. "You have to tell me." Normally, he would never demand that kind of accounting from a client, believing like most defense lawyers that it is better not to know, or to know only what is absolutely necessary. Normally, he does not call his clients to testify; there are too many unknowns, too many risks. It is the government that has the burden, why help them out by having your client say something really, really stupid, or worse, lie and get caught, which makes the likelihood of conviction and a bad sentence all the greater? But this is not a normal case. The victim is a decorated combat veteran who drowned in his own blood and his client is on a recorded call saying she killed him.

He clears his throat, tries again. "If you turn down this deal, we go to trial. And if we don't have a story to tell the jury, a very different kind of story, you will be convicted."

"I am not pleading guilty," she says. "Never."

The vehemence alarms him. That, combined with her refusal to talk about what actually happened, suggests a high degree of irrationality and denial. "I know ten years away sounds like forever when you have a baby—"

"I won't have a baby if I go to prison. Travis's mother will get custody. She'll take Cristina back with her to Ohio." As if reading Will's thoughts, she adds, "If it comes down to siding between that lady and my grandmother, the judge will pick the white lady who speaks English."

Will nods. It's a real risk. But is that the only reason she is turning down the offer? An answer he would like to hear in response to a question he would never ask. Instead he says, "Alright then. We go to trial."

"Yes," she agrees.

He takes out his notepad and picks up a pen. He considers asking again about her juvenile conviction, still sealed, then decides to wait. Better to go with what is easiest. "Let's talk about your relationship with Travis," he says. "Start from the beginning, when you met."

Luz, ignoring him, has picked up Will's honeymoon picture again, is studying it closely.

"What's your wife's name?" she says.

Will tries not to look irritated at her pointed refusal to focus. What's next, a request to look at the wedding album? "Meredith."

"I feel bad for her," Luz says. "I bet she gets jealous."

"No, she doesn't," he shoots back defensively and then, against his better judgment, "Why would you say that? You don't even know her."

Luz meets his gaze head-on. "Because," she says. "You're so much better than she is."

"That is not true," Will insists, a buzzing in his brain like a fly set loose in a closed room. This woman has no right to speak this way about his marriage. But he feels compelled to protect Meredith against Luz's accusation, and his visceral sense that she might not be wrong. He gives Luz a hard, disapproving stare, pen and notepad forgotten on the desktop. "It's the opposite of what you're saying."

Luz shrugs. "Sometimes," she says, "it's hard for people to see what's right in front of them."

"I'm going back."

Nic takes a pull from his beer bottle. "Back where?"

Abby swallows, pulls Cal more tightly against her. He is a good nurser, had taken the breast from the beginning. Now he is working away quietly, eyes shut tight in concentration, his cheeks filling and emptying as he swallows. She can feel the whisper-fast beat of his heart and louder than that, her own.

"Back to work."

"Right." Nic looks at her quizzically. "When your maternity leave is over. In February."

Abby looks away from him. They are sitting at the kitchen table, the remains of Chinese takeout still in the white boxes, chopsticks protruding like scrawny legs. Neither of them had bothered to transfer the food to plates. Cal was a better eater than a sleeper. Last night he had woken up three times, leaving them both exhausted. But Abby, determined to have this overdue conversation, is pulsing with adrenaline. For weeks now, she's promised herself she would tell Nic, only to put it off. The truth is that she vastly prefers her confrontations in the courtroom, with fixed rules and a referee, particularly when she knows her argument will be an unwelcome surprise.

"I want to go back earlier. To try the Luz Rivera Hollis murder case."

"What are you talking about? They gave it to someone else. The JAG guy." Nic's eyes narrow, cut across her face. Cal's eyes are exactly the same—ocean blue. It unsettles her, the color and the sameness. *Eyes like his won't change color the way most babies' do*, the nurse had told her in the hospital.

"Luz turned down the deal. Her arraignment is tomorrow. I'm going to see Paul afterward. To tell him I'm taking it back."

"Paul."

"My supervisor," she says impatiently.

"Yeah, I know who Paul is. Paul is the reason you didn't get fired for what happened last time." Nic shakes his head. "Now you're going to show up six weeks after giving birth and tell him you want to do it all over again. Why? Come on, Abby, do you really think you have another wrongly accused client who can't live without you, just like Rayshon?"

Abby takes a breath. It still hurts to hear his name. Worse to have Nic use it in this way. Rayshon is her heartbreak, but he is also their bond.

"This is not about Rayshon," she says.

Nic lifts his beer bottle again and their eyes meet briefly. "Be honest."

She feels her face grow hot. "I am. I told you. I need to go back."

"Why?"

"Because." She raises a hand to her throat, running the locket on her necklace back and forth nervously. "I'm not supposed to be here. This was—this was a mistake."

Nic stares at her.

"Not—not, Cal," she says hastily. "Me being here all day, with nothing to do, with no work to do. It's like my mind is eating itself. It is making me crazy that someone else is trying my murder case."

"Your murder case." Nic says the words slowly.

Abby keeps going. "Something like this comes along maybe once in a lifetime, maybe never. This military statute they're trying her with—it's never been used before. There is, literally, no precedent for this case. I'm not giving it up." She blinks away sudden, angry tears, feels as childish as if she's fighting a bigger kid for her toy at the playground. She tightens her hold on Cal. "Just because we had a baby together doesn't give you the right to control my life."

"Okay, okay." Nic's eyes are on Cal. "Look, no one is saying this is easy." He reaches across the table to put his hand on her upper arm and shakes it gently to relax her grip. "We'll make some adjustments, give you more of a break. You can ask your mom to help out—"

Abby snorts. "My mom lives on the other side of town. With traffic here, it basically means we are in a long-distance relationship. And she works even more than me. She thinks she's helping out when she shows up to take Cal for a walk on the weekends." Roz Rosenberg, the principal of one of the city's biggest public high schools, was many things, but natural grandma was not one of them.

"A nanny—"

"We can't afford it, Nicky. You know that, and he's too young for day care."

Nic pulls his hand back. "What are you suggesting?"

Cal disengages from her breast with the satisfying pop of a cork releasing from a wine bottle and looks up at her expectantly. Abby carefully wipes the edges of his mouth with her thumb and shifts him to the other side. When he has latched on again and is back at work, she forces herself to look at Nic. "That you stay home instead."

Nic looks as shocked as if she's just slapped him. "What are you talking about? I don't get paternity leave. I'm not—" he gestures at her "—it's not my body that's keeping him alive. Yes, I mean, in three months, sure, I can take my vacation, but now, when he needs to eat every three hours? When he needs his mother? That's crazy."

"You can take your vacation days now. You can bottle-feed him. And you can take him to see me at work once a day. Or I can come home, we don't live that far."

"You want me to stay home and bottle-feed him?" Nic says the words slowly, like he is talking to someone very stupid.

"Yes. I can pump." She pauses. "Actually, I bought a breast pump yesterday and already started to get a supply going."

Nic stares at her. "How have you done that and managed to keep breastfeeding?"

"I'm supplementing with formula."

"You made that decision without telling me? Did you even consider the health consequences for him?"

"Plenty of babies get only formula. It's not like I'm starving him."

"But the nurses said that breast milk was the best—"

"Fuck the nurses," she says harshly. "My brother and I

were bottle-fed because my mom couldn't make enough milk to feed twins. We turned out perfectly fine."

"You can't just make these decisions on your own and not talk to me about it."

"Why not? It's my body, as you just pointed out. God, I am sick and tired of being told that if I don't do *x*, *y*, or *z* thing I'm a bad mother."

"I never said—"

"No, you don't say it, Nicky. You just *look* it. Like when you come home and the house is a mess and Cal is asleep on the sofa—"

"Where he could roll off and crack his skull on the wood floor—"

"Or when you get after me because I like to nurse him in the bath."

"When I walked in on you, you were falling asleep. Do you have any idea how dangerous that is?"

"That's my favorite time with him," she whispers. "And yeah, that one time, I got tired."

"All it takes is one time, Abby. He could have drowned."

"Fine," she says, struggling to keep her voice low and not disturb Cal. "I'm selfish. I'm negligent. I suck at this. So let me go back to work."

Nic sits back in his chair and folds his arms across his chest. "This is wrong. This is really, really wrong."

She keeps going, talking over him. "There's already a few bottles of breast milk in the freezer. And I talked to Jonathan. His caseload is slow right now and he's happy to—he wants to come by in the afternoons and help."

"You already got a supply going? You already talked to Jonathan? Behind my back? Our son was born six weeks ago. He's a baby. You're his mother. Doesn't that even mean anything to you?"

"Of course, it means something to me," she snaps. "I love him." She looks down at Cal's downy head and tears come into her eyes again. She blinks them back furiously. How could she possibly explain this to Nic? That she loved Cal beyond all reason and at the same time his existence felt entirely unreal to her. That every minute she was with her baby she was also sitting in the audience watching a play that had been terribly miscast. That when she wasn't too tired to have thoughts, her only thoughts were of work. That she fantasized, not about blissful lazy days adoring this beautiful creature she and Nic had made, but of going back to court and picking Luz's jury.

"I can't do this all day every day until February. It's not who I am. I told you, when we were deciding about whether to—" She stops. "It was a big decision for me. After we found out. Barely having dated for three months—and that was—" she swallows, remembering their first drunken hookup "—a casual thing."

"Not for me."

She flushes, keeps going. "Then everything with Rayshon, the investigation, me thinking I might get disbarred. It was—it was crazy. When we talked about it, about what to do, I told you I was going back to work."

"After your maternity leave. Not five minutes after the fucking epidural wore off."

"Nicky, you know me—"

"Do I? Jesus Christ, Abby. This is not normal. Maybe you need to see someone. A professional."

"Because I want to do my job? Having a baby hasn't changed me, Nicky. I am still the same person. None of this should come as a surprise. You knew, you have always known, what you were getting into with me."

Nic puts his fingers to his temples, starts massaging the

skin around his eyes. "Your life is different now, Abby. We are a family. You can't—you can't expect things to go back to the way they were before. You're a mother now."

"Do you understand that when you say that," she says fiercely, "I feel like I am being erased? Like you are erasing me?"

Nic reaches across the table again but Abby sits back, abruptly moving out of his reach. "Look. I love you. I've been in love with you since the first day I saw you. You know that."

"Since the first day you saw me in court. That's who I am."

"There are other parts of who you are and they are just as important. You've gotten to experience them. With him. With me. It's been good for you. Healthier. You were—"

"Drinking, I know."

"Drinking so much. You don't want to end up like—"

"Don't." She puts up her hand. "I know why my father is dead."

They sit in silence for a minute. Abby says, "This is how you show me you love me. I don't want a diamond ring or a white dress. I don't want happily-ever-after. I want to try this case. I want you to make that possible for me."

"Don't do this, Abby. There are half a dozen people in your office who would do a great job, including, no doubt, this JAG guy. It doesn't have to be you."

She shakes her head. "I've tried to tell myself that, too. But I actually think the opposite. I think I can try this case in a way no one else can."

"Why?" Nic's voice is cold.

Abby looks down at Cal, passes her fingers lightly over his soft downy head. *I love you, darling boy.* She wonders if he can hear the unspoken thought, if he knows that the love she feels is deep and desperate and yet driving her away.

"Because I'm a brand-new mother, too. The way Luz was, those few times that I met her—I feel that now. She killed her husband in this horrible, violent way, but she did it to save her baby."

Nic shakes his head. "You have no idea why she killed her husband."

"I know that's the story the jury needs to believe. Before I had Cal, I understood that story as a legal theory. Now I understand it in my bones."

Monday, December 11, 2006
10:25 a.m.
Office of the Federal Public Defender
Los Angeles, California

Will raises his hand to knock on the closed door, hears arguing, and lowers it. A woman's voice, raised and angry. Paul, answering her, in his distinct West Indies accent; measured, but testy. Will strains to hear while keeping a respectable distance from the door. A few words come through. Her: "My case," "you can't," "fucking ridiculous."

Paul: "careful consideration," "client's best interests," "already decided."

Will waits another minute, then two. The voices continue. He considers leaving, but Paul does not like people to be late for meetings and Will's excuse—that he delayed after eavesdropping—is not a good one.

He knocks.

A pause and then, "Come in, Will."

When he opens the door, Will sees an elfin woman standing over Paul's desk, her dark hair pulled back into a ponytail, her heart-shaped face pale and devoid of makeup. She's wearing a flowy long-sleeved tunic top that catches on her small belly, her stick-figure arms and legs made even more stick-figure-like by contrast. Her head swivels in his direction, the gaze warning and accusatory.

Will gives her his warmest wide-open smile before turning smartly to face Paul. "Sir, I've just come from Mrs. Rivera Hollis's arraignment."

Paul, too, has been standing, but now he sits, gesturing for Will to take one of the two empty chairs opposite. Will sees the flash of gold cuff links, the expensive watch. Paul is neither vain nor materialistic, but everything he owns is of exceptionally fine quality.

"Yes, thanks. We'll get to that in a minute. Will, this is Abby. Abby Rosenberg."

Will blinks. This is Abby Rosenberg? Never in a million years had he thought that she would look like some pissed-off chick who thought you'd jumped the line at Starbucks. And her maternity leave had just started. What was she doing here?

"Pleasure to meet you, ma'am." He steps forward, extending his hand. "And congratulations to you and to Mr. Rosenberg—" Too late, he looks at Paul, who shakes his head slightly. Will stops, looks at her bare hands, and remembers. "I mean, congratulations to you and your—the—to the both of you on the birth of your—" he pauses, decides to guess "—daughter."

"Son." She still looks genuinely angry, but also the tiniest bit pleased that he is stepping in it so royally and repeatedly.

Will looks at Paul, but there is no help coming his way. "Well, that's really, I mean, that's really terrific."

"Yeah," she says flatly, "it's just great."

Paul coughs. "Abby's partner, Nic Mulvaney, is a US marshal. Former military, like you. I bet you'd have a lot in common."

Abby's glare is so withering, Will is amazed that Paul isn't feeling the physical impact. But Paul, as ever, seems unperturbed. "I was just bringing Abby up to date about your work on the case now that you've taken it over because of her maternity leave."

"Which is over. I'm returning next Monday."

Will tries not to react visibly to this announcement. One of the few perks of working at the federal public defender's office was that having a baby meant all those months of paid time off. For the dads, too, although he wasn't sure if any of them actually took it.

Paul smiles, but it looks effortful. "So far ahead of schedule. It's been—what—six weeks?"

"Forty-six days."

"Well, we're delighted to have you back, of course, if that's what you've decided is best for you and your family."

Abby keeps up the death stare, and Will shrinks back slightly, relieved not to be the target. Paul coughs again. "And, needless to say, there's no one-size-fits-all with these things."

"Yes, sir," Will says cheerfully, though no one is actually soliciting his opinion.

Paul tilts his head at Will, says to Abby, "I've been trying to get him to call me Paul, but the first name thing isn't easy when you've spent your whole life on military bases, like Will has. His dad was a naval officer and he's lived all over the US and in Japan, Holland, Korea. When he was in JAG, Will was based at Altus Air Force Base and then Maxwell, where he became an instructor."

"How many trials have you had?" It's the first time Abby

has asked him a question directly and Will decides to try out another smile. No dice.

"Thirteen, ma'am."

"That's quite a lot," Paul points out. "More than you."

"In military court." Abby looks disdainful. "It's different."

"We're all here to learn from each other," Paul says, and a look passes between Paul and Abby that Will can't parse. "Initially, I thought I would second-chair the trial, but—and actually I was about to tell you this, Abby, when Will walked in—I've been promoted. No official announcement until next week, but I'm going to the tenth floor to be the deputy in chief."

Will knew this already, as did most everyone else in the office through the ever-churning rumor mill, but he tries to look as surprised as Abby. "George is out?" she says.

"His wife has been sick for a while. And he's eligible for early retirement."

"Who's taking your place?"

"Roger."

"So I'm in his group now?"

"No." Paul pauses. "You stay with me." This, too, Will had known. Roger Morrison wouldn't take Abby and neither would any of the other five supervising attorneys. The DIC was not supposed to supervise because of the administrative workload, but in the end, Paul had had no choice.

Paul and Abby are looking at each other, another unspoken communication passing between them, and then Paul sits back in his chair and closes his eyes. Will and Abby wait, Will looking at the gold-framed picture of Paul, his wife, and their twins on the desk. Paul and Angie—who met when they started the same year at the public defender's office—are a head-turning couple: she's blonde and voluble, born and raised in Alabama; he's deliberative and mild-mannered, born and raised in Haiti. Even Angie, outrageous as she was, still had enough sense to stay home after she'd given birth. She was back now, but only after taking a full year off.

Paul opens his eyes. "Given that this is a somewhat unorthodox arrangement, I'm going to switch things up a bit and have you two try this case as a team. Equal responsibility across the board." Paul makes a leveling motion with his hand, like he's sliding onion slices into a frying pan before they can make him cry.

"Paul—"

"That's the decision, Abby."

Will swallows. Abby Rosenberg is a brilliant lawyer. People were still talking about her closing argument in the Rayshon Marbury case, the way the words poured out of her like she was giving up her heart, righteously indignant, but deeply moving at the same time.

But there was a seamier side of things, or so he'd been told. Of course, people talked smack, he knew that, particularly to the new guy. In some ways, the federal public defender's office was no different than the military bases where he'd grown up; everyone perennially in everyone else's business. The office hookup culture— some of which resulted in marriages like Paul and Angie's and some of which ended less happily—was rampant. Even so, a woman like Abby—young, pretty, gifted—made for a juicy target. The envy was understandable. A week after Marbury was freed, the *LA Times* ran a profile of her called *Joan of Arc Storms the Public Defender's Office*. He's seen the framed picture in her office—the only one actually on the wall and not stacked in a corner—a courtroom sketch of Abby with the client, foreheads touching, his fist on top of hers. *Celebrating exoneration.*

Abby Rosenberg was the closest thing their status-less, grimy job had to a celebrity. Until, spectacularly, she was not. Marbury had gotten himself murdered, proving true the grim public defender axiom that every victory is a Pyrrhic one. There was also the lingering, still-unresolved question of exactly how Abby had come by the evidence she used to free him.

Then there was her drinking—she tried to hide it but everyone knew it was a problem—and making, well, other poor choices, often because of it. A few months after the trial she had gotten knocked up by Rayshon Marbury's marshal. *Slut* wasn't the right word for Abby Rosenberg, Will knew that wasn't the right word to describe *anyone* anymore, but just the circumstances of her situation, not to mention that she was basically abandoning her own baby after six weeks. Who would do that? *Forty-six days.* Counting down like it was some kind of jail sentence.

*That case made her,* one of his colleagues had told Will, *but it fucked her, too.*

Yes, people talked smack out of spite, but in Will's experience, that didn't make the smack they talked any less true. He could only imagine what Meredith would say when he told her tonight at dinner. At least she'd have no reason to be jealous herself. The woman standing in front of him bore no resemblance to the image he'd carried in his head of a light-filled avenging angel who spoke in a lilting poet's voice.

Will startles, realizing too late that it's his turn to say something. "Well," he offers, "that's great, sir. And I—" he forces himself to look at Abby "—really look forward to working with you, ma'am—Mrs.—" He takes a deep breath. "Abigail."

Paul claps his hands together. "Terrific. Let's schedule a time to sit down next week, after Abby's had a chance to go over the discovery."

"Yes, sir. And also about the arraignment?"

"Right, of course. How was it?"

"Fine, everything went fine. The trial date is March 19." "The government asked for the extra time to get the witnesses from overseas."

"Who's the judge?" Abby asks.

"He's one of the new Bush II appointees. Got a funny name." Will grins. "Dars Ducey."

The ensuing silence feels explosive. He looks at Paul, then at Abby, but they are locked on each other again. It's like Will has disappeared from the room, at which point the realization dawns. Newly appointed. Funny name. Dars Ducey had been the prosecutor in Rayshon Marbury's case.

"He'll recuse himself," Abby says to Paul. "He has to."

Paul negates this assertion with one firm shake of the head. "Dars is a federal judge now. He can do any damn thing he wants."

# 2005

From: sexxygirljax@yahoo.com
To: travman@hotmail.com

Travis,
I never thought it would be like this with us again.
i'm on the verge just thinkin about it, you on me, you in me,
over and over. i know its messed up with you being back
home only cuz your dad died, but no one knows you and
your fam better than me. i'm thinking its god's will bringing us back together.

yeah, so u made a dumb ass mistake & got married. yeah,
im w/ Lance but not for realz. not like us. im gonna end it.
☺ i know its me you love not her, its just a matter of you
figuring that out.

sent some sexy pix.
J

**Wednesday, October 12, 2005**
**3:54 a.m.**
**Ramstein Air Base**
**Ramstein-Miesenbach, Germany**

From: travman@hotmail.com
To: sexxygirljax@yahoo.com

Jaxx-eeee!!!

i needed u and u were there 4 me. ur the best thing that could've come out of all this. My dad gone just like that. still grieving, not believing, can't sleep thinking about it all. Being with u. nothing here for me except same shit patrols day after day waiting to get sent back to hell. i am goin to figure my way out of this.

pix is amazin. keep sending.
T

**Saturday, December 24, 2005,**
**6:45 a.m.**
**Willowick, Ohio**

From: sexxygirljax@yahoo.com
To: travman@hotmail.com

merry xmas, t. Got a special present 4u. i missed last month and missed again this month so last week i took the pee stick test and guess what???!!! i'm thinking it's a boy he'll look just like u.

luv you like krazzzeee
jax

**Sunday, December 25, 2005,**
**10:29 p.m.**
**Willowick, Ohio**

From: sexxygirljax@yahoo.com
To: travman@hotmail.com

t—wassup? waiting for you to answer me needing to hear
from you.

**2007**

Jorge Estrada's law office is in a strip mall so nondescript that Will had passed it on the first two tries. Not much to look at from the inside, either, just a small entry area with an empty receptionist's desk and this larger backroom office. Estrada's practice was, according to his website, "generalist" in nature. *I take all comers and handle all matters: personal injury, medical malpractice, DUIs, criminal cases, family law, wills, trusts, and estate planning.*

"Mr. Estrada?"

The older man stands up from behind his desk, which is piled high with paper. A nice-looking guy, probably closing in on sixty, but still hustling. No personal touches in the room except a picture on the credenza behind him of a teenage girl with long dark hair and a wide smile, set against one of those blue-sky photo-studio backgrounds that suggests an occasion—high school graduation, probably. She must be his daughter. No wedding ring, though.

"You found me." He extends a hand.

"Will Ellet."

They shake, and Estrada gestures at the single chair opposite him. "Sit down."

Will obliges, trying at the same time to make out the name of the law school featured on the framed diploma on the wall. There was something called the California Western School of Law? He makes a mental note to check to see if it's even accredited. "Thank you, sir, for making the time."

Estrada smiles. He's got a decent crop of silvery hair and eyebrows to match. "Military guy, are you? Or just brought up real polite?"

"Both, sir."

"Well, it's nice to meet you, Will. And I appreciate your coming out all this way."

"Not a problem." It had, in fact, been something of a journey even by LA standards. The freeway had been backed up to West Covina, an accident involving an 18-wheeler. The hour-plus-change drive to Riverside had stretched to two, then two and a half. The air-conditioning in Will's Hyundai had broken down yet again, the internal temperature reading in the car exceeded 100 degrees at various points. Will's shirt is lacquered to his back, a fact he hopes to mask by not removing his jacket. He leans forward, hands on his knees, trying and failing to break the seal of sweat.

"So what can I do for you?"

"Well, sir, as I explained on the phone, I represent Mrs. Rivera Hollis."

Estrada nods.

"It's quite a serious matter. First-degree murder, like I said."

"Yes," Estrada agreed, "you did say. And I've read about it in the papers. Getting a lot of coverage, especially in the local news being that she's from out here and all."

"Right. Well, I— It's my understanding that in the months leading up to her husband's death, she consulted with you about—" Will stopped. He did not know what Luz had consulted Estrada about. All he had was a copy of Estrada's bill, with the government's blue pagination numbers stamped in the lower right-hand corner. It had been seized, along with many other documents, during the search of the Hollis residence in Germany. The bill had ten entries dating from early December 2005 to the final call late in the evening on October 10, 2006, less than four days before Travis died. All of the billing entries were identical. A long distance phone number accompanied by the words *Tel. conv. w/ client*. The last call was ninety-seven minutes.

Estrada sits still, waiting, so Will plows ahead. "About a legal matter," he finishes lamely. "So, of course, I'm hoping to discuss that matter with you and get the file today, if possible."

Estrada rocks back slightly in his chair. "I assume you have written consent."

Will tries not to look startled. "From Mrs. Rivera Hollis? We—I—didn't think we had to." In fact, it had never occurred to him. Yet another foundering assumption. Will imagines how pissed off Abby will be when he comes back empty-handed on this technical foul and slips on his easy, open-faced grin. "Maybe there's been some kind of misunderstanding. I'm her defense attorney. We're all on the same team here."

Estrada nods. "We're all on the same team, no doubt about that."

"So then—" Will wants to say, *what's the friggin' problem, man?* Instead he tries "—maybe I can shoot you the consent by fax as soon as I get back to the office."

Estrada leans forward, plucks a paper clip from a tray on his desk and taps it against his teeth. "Will, can I ask you something?"

Will leans back, spreads his hands. "Sure, anything."

"Does Luz know you're here?"

"That I'm here right now?" Will is stalling for time, trying to figure out how his play has gone so far south. He can hear the air conditioner, practically feel it turning his sweat to ice.

Estrada watches him, waiting.

"Not—not specifically, no."

"Does she know that you've contacted me? Did you tell her you were coming to get her file?"

In fact, no. "Look, Mrs. Rivera Hollis has the documents the government turned over after they searched the house, including your invoice. It's not exactly a—a state secret." Irritation is giving way to confusion. *What the hell is going on?*

Estrada nods, as if expecting this answer. "But what Luz called me about and what she told me, those matters are a state secret."

Clever. Will tries out his grin again. "Yes, exactly, the attorney-client privilege, work product, of course."

"Privileges and protections which she would have to waive in writing even for you." Estrada pulls the inside of the paper clip out in the opposite direction, so that it's twice as long now, laid flat.

"She doesn't need to be protected from me." No way

this guy's law school was accredited. He'd bet $100 on it. "Like I said, I'm her lawyer."

Estrada returns the inside of the paper clip to its old position, but it looks misshapen now, bumpy. "A little bit of knowledge can be a dangerous thing, son."

Will blinks. "Sir?"

Estrada balances the reconstructed paper clip between his two index fingers. "Sometimes, a little knowledge can affect the way you see things. Sometimes, in my experience, it's better not to know. Can throw you off your game."

"I'm pretty tough, sir. Hard to throw."

Estrada doesn't look up from his paper clip. "You might want to ask yourself whether you need to see that file, son. And ask your client if she wants you to."

Will stands, straightening his jacket as best he can in an attempt to retain some sense of dignity. "I can be back tomorrow with a signed consent form if that's what you're insisting on."

Estrada looks up then, gives a slight nod. "You could," he says, "but you won't."

"The judge denied the motion to recuse. Ruled right from the bench."

Abby stares out her office window, then back at the speakerphone, impatiently waiting, but now Will is talking to Paul. She hears, "Yes, sir," and, "See you tomorrow," and something muffled from Paul before Will is back on the line.

"Sorry about that."

"What did he say, exactly?" Abby makes a hurry-up gesture toward the phone, as if that would help.

"Paul?"

"No. Dars. The *judge*, Will."

"Right. I should be back in the office in about five minutes. I'll come up to your office."

Abby adjusts the cone-shaped cups built into the elastic band around her middle to make sure they are firmly suctioned to her breasts. She turns the dial on the machine. Immediately, the whirring starts and with it, dots of milk appear, gathering, then sliding down the clear plastic tubes that connect the cone-cups to the waiting bottles on her desk.

"What's that sound?"

"Nothing. Just stop somewhere quiet and read me your notes."

"Why? I said—"

"Because I'm topless with plastic cones suctioned to my nipples, okay?"

"I— Okay, I didn't know that."

Abby allows herself a small smile as she watches the milk collecting in the bottles. She is a champion pumper, but to keep up with Cal's insatiable appetite and avoid the embarrassment of leaking through the front of her blouse, she has to do it every three hours—four if she's lucky.

Over the speakerphone she hears a door open, the swell of voices, and then another door opening and shutting. Silence.

"Where are you?" she asks.

"In the Starbucks bathroom. Too loud out there. Good lord, it smells." She hears the crinkle of unfolding paper, then Will's voice, reading aloud.

"Judge Ducey thanked both sides for their excellent briefing. Reminded us of the legal standard. The issue isn't whether he would be unfair but only whether a reasonable person looking at the situation from the outside would think that he might be."

Abby stares at the phone, mouths *blah blah blah*. The standard sounds good in theory, but is meaningless in reality. It gives Dars a fig leaf, but it's a skimpy one. To recuse himself, he would have to admit the reality of how he is perceived by others, which, in a way, is even worse than privately acknowledging his own bias. And the bigger problem, as she had known all along, is that Dars would not be able to pass up the chance to dig into her.

"He said the recusal motion had given him occasion to revisit the past and think carefully about Rayshon Marbury's case. Said that, yes, he had used harsh words about you—Ms. Rosenberg—but that it was in the heat of the moment. Says you handed him his hat, outlawyered him. It was a hard loss to accept, particularly since he wasn't used to losing. But the facts were the facts. In the case of Rayshon Marcus Marbury, misconduct by one rogue police officer who tampered with evidence meant that Judge Alvarez—now his esteemed colleague—had to dismiss the charges. Says he believes the ruling was correct, a belief evidenced by the fact that the government did not appeal. Says regardless of what he thinks about Mr. Marbury's guilt or innocence, the case is over and, in any event, Mr. Marbury is dead."

*Not any event*. One event. An event that no law enforcement agency had done much to investigate, probably because they were all too busy celebrating. "What about Dars's decision to refer me to the state bar to ask that they take away my law license?"

Abby hears a banging in the background and Will calls out, "One second," and then to Abby, "so I argued that point and Judge Ducey said, yes, he asked that your conduct be investigated, but that was a decision warranted by the inexplicable circumstances by which you had come into possession of exculpatory evidence. 'So-called exculpatory evidence' was actually what he called it. Said the investigation had apparently concluded with no findings against you. Based on everything he knows, having opposed you in court and by your general reputation, he is of the opinion that, while your methods may be somewhat unorthodox, there is no proof that they are unethical. Says you are a brilliant lawyer, that Mrs. Rivera Hollis could not hope for better representation, that he looks forward to the truth coming out through the adversarial process over which he has been assigned to preside and will preside with fairness to all involved."

Abby had been expecting as much, though it's hard not to be impressed with the way that Dars had so elegantly dressed his lies. He must have really been enjoying himself. Abby hears another knocking sound, louder this time, and Will says, somewhat exasperated, "Okay, I'm coming out."

Abby stares at the whirring machine, the white liquid zipping along now. Time for plan B. "We'll file a motion for reconsideration."

"On what grounds?" She can hear Will trying, unsuccessfully, to control the frustration in his voice. "The record he made is ironclad. For crissakes, Abby, the man went out of his way to say how much he admires and respects you."

"We'll come up with something."

A pause and then Will's voice, resigned, "I can go back and put in an order for the transcript."

"No. There's no time for that. We'll get something on file tomorrow."

"What? What exactly are we going to file tomorrow?"

She almost says, "It doesn't matter," and catches herself. "Just something quick and dirty." That is an accurate way to describe it—not the motion, but what she has planned to do all along, knowing they would lose. "Look, Dars may change his mind and he needs a legal out. We just need to give him one."

A deep sigh on the other end of the phone. "He's not

going to change his mind. You weren't there, you don't know. It's hopeless. Paul thinks so, too. Look, I think—" Will breaks off, calls out one more time that he is coming, really he is coming out this time, then says, "I think we have to at least consider the possibility of you playing a less prominent role in this case or maybe—"

"Just get out of the bathroom and file the motion, Will."

Ten minutes later, when Jonathan knocks on her door, Abby is dressed again and screwing the lid on the second bottle of milk.

"Heard the news about your motion," he says, sliding into a chair across from her desk.

Abby looks at her best friend, who is wearing a wool-blend Armani suit that would eat half her paycheck. Jonathan's boyfriend, Quinn, is a wildly successful Hollywood screenwriter, and Jonathan, with his boyish good looks and impeccable taste, is hands down the most stylish lawyer Abby has ever seen not on TV.

"Word travels fast," she says dryly.

Jonathan apparently has been checking her out, too. "You look great, by the way."

Abby looks down at her Ann Taylor Loft sheath, which she bought several years ago and has probably worn fifty times. "Really? I mean, thank you."

"Yeah, you really do. You look—" Jonathan scrunches up his face, trying to summon the words "—I don't know. Hot. Filled out. Great color, your skin is glowing."

"Jonathan, stop. This is weird." She's blushing furiously.

"I am just saying what the straight guys are thinking," he says saucily.

Abby rolls her eyes.

"Anyway, back to the point of my visit."

"Which is what?"

"Asking if you are going to get off the case." Jonathan takes off his tortoiseshell glasses, makes a show of cleaning them with his pocket handkerchief.

"No."

"You should. It might be the best thing for everybody."

"Et tu Brute?"

Jonathan holds up his hands. "Look, Abby, you know I support you—I am helping take care of your kid, for God's sake. But this situation with Dars is untenable."

"It's not over," she says.

"Right, your loser motion for reconsideration." They make eye contact and Jonathan opens his mouth, then closes it as the realization sets in. "Holy fuck," he says, "you think you can convince him. Why? What do you have on him?"

"Nothing," she says truthfully.

"But you're going to go see him, aren't you? Alone. To bluff?" He nods, answering his own question. "Oh, God, no. That's a horrible idea."

Abby busies herself putting away the bottles and zipping up the case that holds her breast pump. In the silence she hears Jonathan take a sharp breath. "Don't do this, Abby."

"I never said I was."

"Please. I'm amazed you're still here. But you are waiting for later, aren't you? After everyone's gone home." He looks at her and she looks away, not answering him.

"No, Abby. No." Jonathan gets out of his chair and stands over her, his hands on her desk. "Do you realize how close you were to losing your license the last time you tangled with Dars? If he goes to the state bar again, you are going to be in a world of pain. And this time, he'll be in a position to testify against you. You know that going to see the judge outside the presence of the prosecutor to talk about an ongoing case is flat-out unethical."

"Dars isn't going to report me," she says quietly.

"Don't make me go to Paul."

"You can't go to Paul," she says. "You're my lawyer, remember? The very able lawyer who extricated me from the nasty clutches of the state bar the last time around. You know that going to see Paul to tell him what I tell you is flat-out unethical."

Jonathan rolls his eyes at her reference to his role as Ethics Counsel within the public defender's office. It is a thankless job that rotates every two years, with no extra pay and that no one wants. Last year it happened to be Jonathan's turn, which is how he ended up representing Abby.

"And anyway," she continues, "I never said I was going to see Dars. That's just—" she shrugs "—uninformed speculation."

"It is informed by years of knowing you. Look, even if Dars doesn't turn you in the word is going to get out. It always does. And you cannot afford more rumors of—of impropriety, especially now. You just had a baby, you met a nice guy, you stopped drinking and doing the—the other stuff." Jonathan's eyes search hers. "You have a chance to turn the page on the last eighteen months and prove that you are a different person."

"I'm not a different person. Jesus, Jonathan, what is that even supposed to mean? That I am supposed to forget everything that happened? That none of it mattered? That I should just walk away from this client, so Dars gets to have her, too?" Abby rubs furiously at her eyes, which are stinging.

"Dars didn't get to have Rayshon. You won last time, remember?"

"What a victory," she says bitterly.

"That case is over. That part of your life is over."

The firmness of Jonathan's tone, its sanctimony, infuriates Abby, and she lashes out at him. "You sound like Nic. Expecting me to have some magical motherhood transformation. That's never going to happen."

"Walk away, Abby. Walk away."

"If I wanted your advice, counselor," she says coldly, "I would have asked for it."

"Abigail." Dars does not get up from behind the enormous desk. He's in shirtsleeves, monogrammed cuffs rolled up, his black robe hanging on a coatrack behind him. His dark hair is slicked back in its usual pompadour, his small eyes trained on her like he's hunting. He's jowlier than she remembered.

The room is cavernous. Red-veined marble walls, twenty-foot ceilings, old mahogany furniture—in addition to the massive desk, there is a long conference table to her left, ringed by eight upholstered chairs. The carpeting is so thick Abby's heels are sinking. Directly over her head a giant iron multipronged light fixture hangs like a malevolent spider. If it fell it would crush her, but the light it casts is dim and gloomy.

Dars has not invited her to sit, but Abby picks one of the upholstered chairs opposite the desk and deposits herself in it anyway. Her calves ache from wearing heels all day after weeks of padding around the house in Nic's gym socks.

She can feel Dars eyeing her silently as she removes her purse from her arm and sets it on the empty chair beside her. She makes sure to take her time, smoothing her skirt and crossing her legs.

"Thank you for seeing me on such short notice, Dars."

"That's Judge Ducey to you."

"Not in here."

"Ah, Abigail. How I've missed our banter." *Heh-heh-heh*. She'd forgotten about that laugh. How much she hates it. "Odd, though, that childbearing doesn't seem to have softened you any. My wife on the other hand—she never could lose that last ten pounds after our third one. Got some saddlebags on her now."

Abby tries not to let her revulsion show on her face.

"Then again—" Dars is still musing on this theme "—you look a bit, how shall I say this? Inflamed. Then again, at least you didn't get fat in the face. That happens to a lot of women." He puffs out his cheeks to demonstrate. "Not you, though. Those last few months, you looked like a garden snake that had swallowed a basketball." Another *heh-heh-heh*.

She continues to look at him, saying nothing.

"Which marshal was it again?"

"Why?" She nods toward his private bathroom. "Are you thinking of giving him extra work scrubbing the skid marks off your judicial toilet bowl?"

Dars waves a hand. "Being linked to you for the rest of his life is punishment enough. You didn't marry him, though, did you? Or was he the one that didn't marry you? Which is really saying something, given his station in life." He shakes his head. "Well, either way, Abigail, single-parent households are not good. Not good at all. But of course, I don't have to tell *you* that, do I? Sad situation for the poor kid, especially if it's a boy. And you had a boy, didn't you?"

"Yes."

"What's his name?"

"Cal."

"Calvin?"

"Macallan."

Dars shakes his head. "After the scotch?"

"The place."

"In Texas?"

"Scotland."

A long pause. Dars rubs his chin, then gives. "So, to what do I owe this most unexpected of visits? And without Mr. Ellet? Never mind the prosecutor. Quite unusual, this sort of ex parte contact. Not very kosher, but then, it doesn't exactly surprise me coming from you."

Abby leans forward. "You need to recuse yourself. My client has a constitutional right to a fair and impartial judge. That's not you, Dars."

Another head shake, more vigorous this time. "I'm sure Mr. Ellet has advised you of my ruling."

"So un-rule. It happens all the time. Upon careful reconsideration, you have reached a different conclusion."

"The fact that I bear an abiding personal dislike for you has nothing to do with my ability to be fair to your client."

"An abiding personal dislike," Abby repeats slowly. "Yes. Though you said it a bit less elegantly over a year ago when we met in the executive suite of the US Attorney's Office to discuss Rayshon's case. Back then I believe your exact words were, 'I wouldn't fuck you if you were the last cunt on earth.'"

Dars smiles. "Your memory may be a bit faulty on that

one, Abigail. That's common in women who have recently given birth. Yet another reason, perhaps, to reconsider the length of your maternity leave."

She nods. "Except it's not actually my memory I'm working from. I have it recorded on my cell phone."

A shadow passes across his face but it's only for a second. "Bullshit."

"Not bullshit. True shit."

A finger point. "There was no reason for you to record that meeting. It was about a favorable plea offer that we were extending to your wholly undeserving client."

Abby settles back in her chair. "Yes, of course, but I didn't know that at the time. I was walking in blind. Blind and alone. And you sounded so, well, how *shall* I say this, so frantic on the phone the night before. It made me wonder, Dars. It really did. I just had no idea what was going to come out of your mouth. And I was nervous, too. My first meeting on the fifteenth floor with the big shots. I wanted to make sure I remembered every minute of it."

The finger point is now a stabbing motion. "No. It's a felony to record someone without their permission and you know it. I could have you indicted."

"You could," she says agreeably, "but at what cost?"

"Give me your phone."

"I've upgraded since then. But not to worry, there are plenty of copies. One safely stowed with my lawyer, Jonathan. You know Jonathan, right?"

"Play it for me."

"No."

He sits back now, too, relaxing. "I knew it. There is no recording. It's reckless beyond even what you are capable of."

"Oh, but I am capable of it, Dars. You tried to prove there

was something wrong with the way I got the ballistics report that exonerated Rayshon Marbury. Unfortunately, the dirty cop's wife who gave it to me wouldn't cooperate with the state bar investigators you sicced on me." Abby lifts her shoulders and gives him a wide fake smile. "Too bad. But now that all of that unpleasantness is in the rearview mirror, I can give you the details. Unless, of course, you'd rather not hear about it."

"Do go on," Dars says, "you know how much I love your stories."

"Late in the trial, after I realized that Rayshon was probably going to get convicted, I got desperate and showed up at the wife's house late one night uninvited. She had gotten a restraining order against the dirty cop at that point and I thought, maybe she has something on him."

"After she complained to my office that you were harassing her and the judge told you to stay away from her."

Abby nods. "But that's not the half of it, Dars. I watched while she drank herself into incoherence. I told her she would lose custody of her children if she didn't help me take down her husband, legal advice that was unsolicited and almost certainly wrong. I interfered with and polluted the relationship she already had with her own lawyer. A lawyer who, unlike me, was acting in her best interests."

Dars shakes his head. "You're lying."

"About what I did to win the case?"

"About your cell phone." He motions with one hand. "What you did to let that murderer walk free is entirely in keeping with your character. But he didn't get far, did he?"

Abby feels her throat close. She had sat between Nic and Paul at the memorial service. Rayshon's little boy had cried and cried. At the time, it had literally been noise to her. Remembering it now makes her want to cry herself, not that she would ever give Dars the satisfaction. Being a mother, she's come to realize, is a terrible vulnerability.

"Give me your bag."

She hands it over and he dumps the entire contents out on the desktop: baby wipes, nipple guards, a spare diaper, two pacifiers—both covered in lint—crumpled tissues, lip gloss, dental floss, Tic Tacs, her cell phone, her date book. He inspects every item, leaving the phone for last.

"What's the password?"

"I told you it's not on—"

"What's the password?"

She gives it to him and waits while Dars scrolls through the various screens, checks her list of callers, her voice mails, and her photographs. Once it would have been mortifying: the drunken texts and other evidence of her numerous hookups. Now there is absolutely nothing of interest. Messages from Nic, Jonathan, Will, Paul. Her mother. And the pictures, the endless shots of Cal: cooing, sleeping, screaming. Lying on his side, staring wide-eyed at nothing she can see.

Dars is still scrolling, his mouth twisted. "Ah, Jonathan. I do recall him now. Your coworker, personal lawyer, and little gay bestie. Sure is interested in this baby of yours. Make sure to text him back as soon as you leave, sounds like he and Quinn—" Dars's voice goes up an offensive octave "—are hanging out with your baby daddy at your house and wondering if you'll be home in time for dinner."

Abby takes a slow, quiet breath, before pasting on an inviting smile. "You should check out the video of the birth. Kind of gory, though. I needed twelve stitches."

Dars drops the phone into her purse and shovels in the rest of the contents like he's sweeping up garbage. "Come over to my side of the desk."

"Why?"

"I'm going to pat you down."

"You think I'm wearing a wire?" This she had not expected and her heart starts beating fast. He's taking the bait.

Dars snaps his fingers. "Let's go."

The thought of his hands on her body feeling her up and down is so awful Abby can't suppress a shudder. "I'm not going to let you touch me, Dars."

"Well, then, we have a problem, don't we?"

The solution that pops into Abby's head at that moment is so crazy she can barely believe she's even considering it. Jonathan's warning flashes through her mind—*word is going to get out*—even as she hears him saying, "Hot. Filled Out. Great color, your skin is glowing." On her best days, she is pretty; never hot. Too pale and sharp-edged with her little girl's body. The fact that the idea is inspired by Jonathan's stray comment before he started scolding her makes it delicious. If he's right, he's just handed her a new tool.

Now she says to Dars with a dead calm that surprises even her, "We don't have a problem and I'll prove it. I am going to take off my clothes."

Dars snorts.

"Don't believe me? Watch." Abby stands up, removes her suit jacket and lets it drop to the floor. She unzips her skirt and leaves it on top of the jacket. She pulls off her shoes, slowly peels off her pantyhose, and drops the lot onto the growing pile. Standing in her white cotton underwear, she unbuttons her blouse and opens it. She feels both intensely present in her body and outside of it at the same time, as if the real Abby—the nice-looking but not hot one—is watching her from somewhere high above alternatively screaming at her to stop and cheering her on.

Dars is staring at her, eyes wide open.

"Do you want me to stop?"

Dars moves his head a fraction to the left and back again. If she'd blinked, she would have missed it. Or maybe she had imagined it. But he wasn't saying a word.

Abby gives him a big smile as she removes the blouse, then twists her arms behind her back to undo the row of hooks that hold up her nursing bra. In ten seconds, she is standing, one hand on her bare hip, fully exposed. She smiles, and it is genuine this time. It's intoxicating, the power she is exerting over him. "Underwear?" she asks politely.

His nod is almost imperceptible, and Abby looks down on her white cotton Hanes Her Way bottoms as if considering it. Too bad she hadn't planned this out in advance, she'd have gone out and bought something sexy. Something Hot Abby would have worn. She snaps the elastic band. "No, I don't think so. You wouldn't really be checking for a wire at that point, would you? But your interest is much appreciated." She smiles again. "Especially after, well, that hurtful comment you made that day on the fifteenth floor. It still stings, Dars. Every time I replay it."

Beads of sweat have formed on Dars's hairline.

"Want to see some more?" Abby walks around to his side of the desk so that she is standing directly in front of him but well out of reach, her arms at her sides. She raises them so he can see she isn't concealing anything, then puts her hand back on her hip, shimmying as she does a slow 360-degree turn. Jesus fucking Christ this is empowering. Jonathan is right: this is quite possibly the best she will ever look. Suddenly conscious of the size and hardness of her breasts, she has to force her baby from her mind. No leaking.

Now she's facing him again, she sees that Dars has swiveled slightly in his chair. He's still staring at her, breathing heavily through his nose. They remain like that for a full minute.

"Just say the three magic words, Dars. 'I recuse myself.'" She drops her voice to a breathy whisper. "I recuse myself. So simple. Just say the words and then presto!" She snaps her fingers. "Next week, there'll be some other poor defendant lined up for you to fuck over."

Then Dars starts to smile his awful smile. And then comes the *heh-heh-heh*, a low thrum from the back of his throat, and now there is a sinking feeling in her stomach.

"Thank you for the show." Dars's smile widens to show his teeth. "I thoroughly enjoyed it. Your little tale, well, that was less compelling." He stops smiling. "Now get dressed and get out. I'll see you, as they say, in court."

# 2005

**Monday, December 26, 2005**
**3:47 a.m.**
**Willowick, Ohio**

From: sexxygirljax@yahoo.com
To: travman@hotmail.com

wtf travis, i'm having your baby. rite back.

**Tuesday, December 27, 2005**
**4:05 p.m.**
**Ramstein Air Base**
**Ramstein-Miesenbach, Germany**

From: travman@hotmail.com
To: sexxygirljax@yahoo.com

Jaxx,
of course im happy its a beautiful thing if we made a baby
together. don't get mad but how do u know its not lance's
anyway? u wuz with him 2.

**Tuesday, December 27, 2005**
**4:11 p.m.**
**Willowick, Ohio**

From: sexxygirljax@yahoo.com
To: travman@hotmail.com

cuz i used protection w/ lance and not w/ u. want a paternity test? Cuz I went all monica on you and kept sum jizz u left on my sheets. gotchu coming and going no pun intended!

ur pissing me off travis. yeah, and I made a new FB friend today you'll never guess who.
happy new year motherfucker

**Tuesday, December 27, 2005**
**4:19 p.m.**
**Ramstein Air Base**
**Ramstein-Miesenbach, Germany**

From: travman@hotmail.com
To: sexxygirljax@yahoo.com

things here is complexxx. i will work it out, but u got to have faith and not go all crazy on me. u telling is not the way. knock off that FB shit with her.

# 2007

"Thank you," Will says, as he takes his place beside Abby on the couch. "We appreciate your taking the time, Dr. Cartwright." Will and Abby are here about Luz, of course, but sitting on a shrink's couch with the shrink herself staring them down, it is hard not to feel as if he and Abby are the ones under evaluation: a mismatched couple mired in mutual misery.

Tabitha Cartwright is a forensic psychologist. After her PhD is yet another jumble of letters, the piled degrees indicating a vast store of knowledge about human behavior derived from decades of rigorous training. She is small and impossibly slender, perched on the edge of her armchair with her head cocked, gray hair in a short, cap-like cut, round tawny owl eyes unblinking. Not an ounce of meat on those bones; Will imagines that picking her up would entail no more effort than lifting a child. First Luz, then

Abby, and now the doctor. Will feels surrounded by petite women with outsize demands on his time and mental energy. He longs suddenly for Meredith—her just-right height and weight, her easily satisfied needs: take out the garbage, pick up his socks, sit beside her on the coach to watch the *Bachelorette* Season Whatever.

One thing is for sure, he and Meredith would never be sitting beside each other on a therapist's coach. Misery beyond anything they've ever contemplated must come through Cartwright's door on a near constant basis. Perhaps to offset this reality, the doctor's office is big and airy, with a wall of floor-to-ceiling windows that look west, toward the UCLA campus and the Santa Monica mountains. The decor is tasteful, decidedly therapist-neutral. The paintings on the wall are modern but in no way disquieting, mostly neutral colors thickly applied in broad swaths. The furniture, too, is modern, but comfortable, the beige couch they are sitting on adorned with two small patterned decorative pillows at each end. Kleenex boxes have been placed discreetly on small glass tables on either side.

Dr. Cartwright says, "I thought it was best to discuss the evaluation of Mrs. Rivera Hollis in person, and then you can let me know if you want me to memorialize it."

Will and Abby exchange a glance, then nod their heads at the same time. They all know the game here. Any written report may have to be turned over to the government even if they decide not to use it, so best not to have one in the first place unless they are sure.

A favorable written report will carry great weight. Dr. Cartwright's *curriculum vitae*—her words—had made Will's eyes glaze over. Scholarly papers and published studies about the many experiments she had conducted over four decades, gathering data so granular and scrupulously validated as to make her conclusions seem unassailable. One of the foremost experts on battered women's syndrome in California. That reputation had buttressed and finally won Abby's argument to Paul that she was worth the money: $2,000 just to conduct the initial evaluation of Luz, which is what they are here to discuss, another $4,000 for her written report, and $350 an hour for her testimony. All of those fees at a highly discounted rate, as Dr. Cartwright had reminded them more than once.

Dr. Cartwright picks up a notebook from the side table at her left and puts on her reading glasses, which are hanging from a thin chain around her neck. "You asked me to interview and evaluate Mrs. Rivera Hollis in order to form an opinion as to whether she was suffering from battered woman's syndrome such that it affected her state of mind when she killed her husband, Travis Hollis. In addition to a two-hour clinical interview, I also administered a number of psychological tests, including the MMPI-2, the MCMI-III, the Rorschach Psycho-diagnostic Inventory, and the Structured Interview of Reported Symptoms. Additionally, I used the Spousal Assault Violent Acts Scale to determine the severity of the abuse Mrs. Rivera Hollis reported experiencing during the marriage."

Will nods again, trying to look interested. *Come on, lady.*

But instead of continuing, Dr. Cartwright pauses for a moment. "I should start by saying that your client was reticent to an unusual degree. Bordering at times on uncooperative."

Even though he knows it's inappropriate, Will feels a smile spreading across his face. He is heartened, almost happy, to learn that Luz is no different with a renowned psychologist than she is with him. "Yes," he says eagerly, "yes, she is. I—" he looks at Abby "—I mean, we have been trying to get her to talk to us for weeks now and it's just been—" he looks at Abby, hoping for confirmation "—well, difficult."

Abby gives him a dirty look, like he's talking out of school, and Will stops abruptly.

"We started with the basics, questions about her family and growing up," Dr. Cartwright continues, filling the awkward pause. "That seemed to help her open up a bit. As did my asking her pointed, direct questions. Even then, she tended to give short answers and never elaborated on anything I asked her."

"Why should she?" Abby says. "Talk to any of us, I mean? To her we are a bunch of white people in positions of authority who think we know better."

Dr. Cartwright nods. "I think it is fair to say that she hasn't had great experiences with, as you say, the patri-archy."

Will considers pointing out that Abby had said no such thing: she was talking about race, not gender. But Abby is nodding her head in agreement. "There is so much mis-trust," she says to Dr. Cartwright, "and rightly so."

Dr. Cartwright returns to her notebook. "Mrs. Rivera Hollis told me that she is an only child, brought up by her grandmother, Maria Elena Rivera, with whom she cur-rently resides. The family is originally from a rural part of Mexico called Guerrero. Maria Elena and her husband, Felipe, now deceased, came to southern California to work in the strawberry fields sometime in the late 1960s. They were granted amnesty through a bill signed by President Reagan in 1986.

"Mrs. Rivera Hollis's own parents never married. Her fa-ther, a construction worker, left the household shortly after she was born. Mrs. Rivera Hollis has not seen him since that time; apparently, he resides in Modesto, with what she calls his 'new family.' After her father left, Mrs. Rivera Hollis's mother, Marisela, became severely depressed. They moved in with Maria Elena when Mrs. Rivera Hollis was two; when she was six, Marisela committed suicide."

Abby and Will exchange glances. Luz had told them none of this.

Dr. Crawford turns a page of her notebook. "Mrs. Rivera Hollis told me, 'I was angry with my mother because she left me. When you have a child, you make a promise to raise that child. My mother broke that promise. I would never do to Cristina what my mother did to me. Because if I did, my daughter would always know that she wasn't enough to make me want to live.'"

Dr. Cartwright peers at them over her reading glasses. "I can't emphasize enough the importance not only of the suicide, but the fact that Mrs. Rivera Hollis was abandoned by both of her parents. These are a child's primary attachment relationships, the template for every other relationship the child will have. The absence—the willed, deliberate absence—of both mother and father has been shown to result in a lifelong distrust of other people. Abandoned children fear forming intimate relationships because they disbelieve in the willingness and ability of other people to stick around, especially when life circumstances become difficult."

Will tries and fails to think of how any of this information plays into whether Luz was a battered woman. The Luz that Dr. Cartwright is describing just sounds angry, justifiably so, but still. Anger is not good for them. He cracks his knuckles and Abby shoots him another look.

"Mrs. Rivera Hollis describes her relationship with

Maria Elena as 'pretty good,' but there was a fair amount of friction, particularly over Mrs. Rivera Hollis's mediocre grades and the amount of time she spent talking to schoolmates—generally boys—on the telephone. Mrs. Rivera Hollis says that her grandmother made a number of demands, including that she do much of the cooking and cleaning around the house, and that she finally told her, 'I am not your maid.' She left high school at seventeen and moved to Barstow, where she worked as a waitress at a bar near the Fort Irwin military base. She lied about her age and got a fake ID."

As if reading Will's thoughts, Dr. Cartwright says, "I doubt it was very convincing, but it also doesn't sound as if this particular establishment cared much. They wanted pretty girls who could sell drinks."

*Men have told me my whole life that I'm beautiful.* Will is reminded of that conversation and his discomfort. Then he thinks about what Abby and Dr. Cartwright have just said. Who was he to judge her?

"That's where Luz met Travis," Abby says, "in 2004, after he came back from his deployment to Iraq?"

Dr. Cartwright nods. "He was her first real boyfriend. There were plenty of boys interested in her before, but those relationships never lasted long. She liked the attention, describing a particular time when she was out with a boy and pointed to a pair of turquoise-and-silver earrings that she wanted. They were expensive, but the next time she saw him, he gave them to her as a present. Mrs. Rivera Hollis describes that episode as 'like a test, to see if he liked me as much as he said he did, and he passed the test.' Eventually, though, she would want something the boy couldn't give her, and she would move on.

"Mrs. Rivera Hollis told me, 'I get bored. It's hard to

keep my attention, and anyway, I don't trust people much. I don't trust people at all, actually. People have let me down my whole life and it's like, why would I want to keep setting myself up for that? At least, that was my mindset before I met Travis.'"

Will leans forward in anticipation of what must be coming next. "Were any of these boys abusive toward her? Even verbally?"

Dr. Cartwright shakes her head. "There is no history or pattern of abuse in these prior relationships, if that's what you would call them. I'm not sure she would. They were sexual relationships, of course, but Mrs. Rivera Hollis does not equate sex with closeness."

Will tries not to look insulted on Luz's behalf. Of course she sought sex for closeness. The girl had been frigging abandoned as a child. In the face of this new, tragic information, he is putting aside his own doubts and the fact that there is something about Luz—the abrupt shifts to coldness and vacancy, the steadfast refusal to answer crucial questions—he finds deeply unsettling. "Okay, but there's the jealousy, the need by some of these guys to assert control over her. A pattern, right?" He can hear the twitch in his voice, feel his irritation at their expert wandering far afield.

Dr. Cartwright gives him a thin smile, possibly the best she can do in any situation. "Mrs. Rivera Hollis has no patience for jealousy. When she started working at the bar in Barstow, some of the guys she was casually dating did get angry over the way she interacted with the male customers." Cartwright ran her index finger down the page. "I asked her about that specifically, and she said, 'I told them to fuck off, get over yourself. It's my job to flirt and play nice. That's how I get my tips.'"

"But there was abuse, with Travis, over being jealous.

He was abusive toward her, there's no doubt about that."
Will hears himself getting louder; beside him, Abby clears
her throat. "He had come back from that tour in Iraq, having been in combat, was having issues with it. We have his
medical records: fights on the base, excessive drinking."

"As do I," Dr. Cartwright intones coldly, but Will isn't
finished.

"Wouldn't he take his—" he reaches for a therapy-sound-
ing word "—trauma out on her?"

Dr. Cartwright looks at him like he's a kindergartner
who has interrupted story hour to make a wrong guess
about the ending. "The relationship was a tumultuous one,
but it was not violent in the beginning. Once he returned
to Fort Irwin from his deployment, Sergeant Hollis was a
regular presence at the bar and a big drinker. He would stay
late and talk to her, sometimes about his problems with his
girlfriend back home in Ohio."

"Jackie Stedman," Will says.

"Yes. A long-distance relationship that had started back
when Travis and Jackie were both in high school. They were
having difficulties. Ms. Stedman wanted to get married
and move across the country to California. Sergeant Hollis
was feeling pressured by her and starting to have doubts."

Will shifts uncomfortably, suddenly reminded of a similar feeling of pressure from Meredith, and the seeding of
his own doubts. Resolved in her favor, of course.

Dr. Cartwright was reading from her notebook again.
"Mrs. Rivera Hollis said she enjoyed Sergeant Hollis's com-
pany. She told me, 'I was surprised when I didn't get sick
of him. Maybe it was because he was just talking about his
feelings and not asking for anything. And I felt like I could
talk to him about some stuff, too. With Travis, it felt okay.'

"Eventually, Sergeant Hollis broke it off with Ms. Stedman and started dating Mrs. Rivera Hollis. She describes the first few months to me as, 'good, he was sweet and romantic, but dealing with Jackie sucked because she was always trying to stir up drama.'"

Dr. Cartwright turns another page in her notebook. "I asked Mrs. Rivera Hollis if she felt threatened by Jackie and she laughed. 'Why would I feel threatened by her? From Day One, it was obvious that Travis wanted to be with me, not her.'"

Will looks at Abby, as if to say, *your turn*. But Abby isn't looking at him, and she isn't looking at Dr. Cartwright, either. She's staring fixedly out the large plate glass windows and fiddling with the locket on her necklace. The expression on her face, Will has come to learn, means she's tuning everyone else out while she works through the problem on her own.

"When did Travis propose?" Will prompts.

"In March of 2005, shortly after he received his orders that he would be deployed to Germany, in preparation for a possible second tour in Iraq. They were married in April. The Hollis family flew out. Mrs. Rivera Hollis says she felt his parents, particularly Mrs. Hollis, were not happy about the marriage, both because she was of Mexican origin and because they had a close relationship with Ms. Stedman and had always assumed that Travis would marry her."

Again, Will shifts uncomfortably, remembering his mother's pleased expression and his father's hearty slap on the back when he had made precisely the opposite decision. Will and Meredith had told them after church. They were sitting in the dining room, just finishing up his mother's traditional Sunday lunch: pork roast, mashed potatoes, green peas, and plenty of sweet tea. Will had stood up to make the announcement, Meredith shyly joining him at his insistence. He hadn't had the money to buy a ring at that point, had had to ask his father to lend him $900 while he paid off the rest in installments.

Dr. Cartwright is reading from her notes again. "Mrs. Rivera Hollis and Sergeant Hollis arrived in Germany in May 2005. It was a difficult adjustment. Mrs. Rivera Hollis reports feeling isolated. The other wives, she said, were unfriendly toward her. Many of them had young children. She was bored. When Sergeant Hollis was working nights patrolling the base, she would go out and have a few drinks, shoot pool with some of the enlisted guys, go out dancing. Sergeant Hollis didn't like that, he got jealous, she said. They began fighting, yelling, name-calling, slamming doors, things like that."

"Was the end result that she stopped going out as much?" Will can hear his voice go from irritated to pleading.

Dr. Cartwright shakes her head. "Most battered women eventually cut off their socializing completely, particularly if it involves other men. The abuser exerts tremendous psychological pressure on the woman he batters. He alienates those closest to her. He cuts off avenues of escape. Mrs. Rivera Hollis says she remained quite defiant and continued to engage in her social activities even though she knew it made Sergeant Hollis angry."

Will shakes his head. "Why would she bring that on herself? There was that incident in August 2005 at the bar where Travis broke some dude's nose in a barroom brawl after the guy made a comment about her—" He reddens.

"Juicy Latina ass," Dr. Cartwright supplies. "Yes, she mentioned that incident, and also that Sergeant Hollis was written up for it and referred, I think, to some kind of anger management. It was at that point that the fighting between them began to escalate, often when he had been drinking heavily. Sergeant Hollis began to slap her, using his open palm so that it wouldn't leave a mark. He would push her to the ground and get on top of her."

"That's a lot of weight," Will says. "Travis was at least 260, and she's not much bigger than—than you two." He gestures awkwardly.

Dr. Cartwright waits a beat, then says, "Mrs. Rivera Hollis also said he would try to choke her, sometimes when he was on top of her and sometimes after he would push her up against a wall. Every time, she said, she would scratch him, rake her nails down his back and arms, pull his hair, spit at him, and he would get off her."

For the first time that morning, Will is starting to feel better. "So he was abusive," he says, trying and failing to stifle the note of triumph. He looks pointedly at Abby, who has returned her gaze to Dr. Cartwright and is still refusing to look at him.

Dr. Cartwright takes off her glasses, polishes them, and puts them back on. "Even if I were to take every report of domestic violence by Mrs. Rivera Hollis as the absolute truth, none of it comes close to the level of severity experienced by battered women who kill their abusers. We are talking about chronic, horrific abuse in which the woman's life is threatened and she experiences intense fear and helplessness, usually on a daily basis. I would advise you to look at the metrics used by Dr. Barbara Bowen in her 2004 study."

Will interrupts, "We understand, but things got worse over time."

"Yes, and then again, no." Dr. Cartwright makes a weighing motion with her small hands, lifting them up and down, then level with each other. "Mrs. Rivera Hollis reports that the relationship deteriorated further after

Sergeant Hollis's father died unexpectedly and he returned to the States for the funeral. Apparently, they were so estranged that Mrs. Rivera Hollis elected not to go."

Will considers pointing out that Travis took that opportunity to impregnate Jackie, but takes another look at Dr. Cartwright and decides to stay quiet.

Dr. Cartwright pauses. "It is also worth pointing out that nearly all of these fights were resolved through sex, which often occurred immediately afterward. Mrs. Rivera Hollis describes the sex as rough and at times violent but is adamant it was not rape."

Will feels his face reddening again both in embarrassment and anger. God, this woman was so obtuse. "Of course Luz doesn't call it rape. She can't even admit it to herself because what he did to her was so degrading…" He trails off as both Dr. Cartwright and Abby fix him with hard stares. A silence falls.

"It may be," Dr. Cartwright says finally, "that your views about sexual relationships between married couples hew to a more traditional view. But let me assure you, there are many, many people who engage in this kind of sexual activity because they find it genuinely pleasurable."

Will opens his mouth and shuts it again.

Abby says, "It seems like they were at a low point when he went back to the US for his father's funeral and had the affair with Jackie."

Dr. Cartwright nods. "That was in early October of 2005. There was serious contemplation of divorce on both sides during that time."

"Which changed in the beginning of December when Luz told Travis she was pregnant with Cristina, right?"

Dr. Cartwright nods approvingly at Abby, and Will has to suppress the urge to roll his eyes. "That's right. And in the meantime, and we are talking about a period of weeks here, the level of violence when they fought remained virtually the same. Mrs. Rivera Hollis was always clear with me that she believed the situation could be brought quickly under control. She wasn't afraid to confront her husband when he did something to make her angry, like criticize one of her outfits as too suggestive or when he didn't pick up after himself. She didn't hesitate to express anger toward him. Again, this is atypical. Battered women walk on eggshells, blaming themselves for the tiniest mistake, so inhibited they no longer are aware they have feelings to express, other than shame and fear."

"Was he abusive during the pregnancy?" Will asks.

"She says no. It was not an easy pregnancy, extreme morning sickness in the first trimester. At first, she says, he was excited, very supportive, and their relationship improved, but after a couple of weeks he was often distracted, would drift off in the middle of a conversation. Around Christmas, he started having nightmares and yelling in his sleep. It got bad enough that she asked him to sleep on the living room couch."

"When he got the news that Jackie was also pregnant," Abby says.

Dr. Cartwright nods, goes back to her notes. "Which Ms. Stedman told her by email the night of the murder."

"Which the prosecution is going to argue is her motive for killing him. Not fear, revenge," Abby rubs her temples. "There's a four-hour window between Jackie's email and Travis coming home drunk from the party. Four hours of Luz stewing in the news that her husband not only had an affair with his ex-girlfriend, but fathered a child with her, and at least for a while, was even giving her the idea that he would—"

"Leave Luz for a new family," Will interrupts, thinking aloud. "Just like her dad."

"As you might expect," Dr. Cartwright says, "I asked Mrs. Rivera Hollis a number of questions about how she felt when she found out. And about the way she found out, which must have been rather shocking and humiliating. And, yes, infuriating. She said, 'I was angry at myself more than anything. I made a bad choice. I thought he was a strong person, but he was a weak person.'"

"Did she think Travis was going to leave her for Jackie?" Will asks.

"Interestingly, no. She did not seem worried about that possibility at all. I think she might actually have been alright if Travis had come clean and taken responsibility even if that meant making child support payments. What angered Mrs. Rivera Hollis was the continuing contact, her husband's inability to end the affair. She told me, 'It showed me that me and Cristina weren't enough for him. And that, you know, that was really disappointing.'"

But Abby is still fixed on the point that Will had stopped her from making. "Four hours is an eternity. Two hundred and forty minutes to go from boiling to ice-cold. To think. To plan." She looks pointedly at Dr. Cartwright. "That email plus four hours is why she's getting convicted of first-degree murder unless we can offer up a more compelling story."

Dr. Cartwright's expression—really a study in non-expression—remains unchanged. They are all quiet for a moment, Dr. Cartwright continuing to look at Will and Abby with her sharp, unblinking owl's eyes. She is waiting, accustomed, no doubt, to long silences. Will fidgets, picking lint off the sleeve of his suit jacket.

Beside him, Abby takes a deep breath. "She's not a battered woman. That's what you've been saying ever since we sat down. We can't make that argument."

Will looks at Abby, annoyed. "Hold on—"

But Dr. Cartwright interrupts him, "Based on my clinical observations, she's not. And there is no data to support a diagnosis of battered woman's syndrome. Her levels were not elevated on the MMPI-2, or the MCMI-III, and her Rorschach is outside even the margins. She scores at the bottom range on the Spousal Assault Violent Acts Scale. If called to testify, I would say that her state of mind at the time of the offense was not impacted by that kind of trauma."

Dr. Cartwright pauses. "And there's something else. The tests I administered have controls in place to assess malingering—that is, making up, masking, or exaggerating symptoms."

"Masking." Will jumps on the word like a life raft. "Right. She could be in complete denial." He is beyond caring what Abby or Dr. Cartwright thinks, about his outdated ideas about sex, about his white male privilege. He drives on. "I'm sure that's common."

"She is in denial," Dr. Cartwright agrees. "But not about the abuse. The tests show malingering in only one respect—the description of anger. It isn't inward, as she described. It's outward, in the way she speaks and describes Sergeant Hollis, particularly when it comes to the infidelity. And it isn't a burning fury, either. Based on observing her and reviewing these test results, I think it is more probable than not that what she felt toward him, more than anything, was a high level of contempt."

In the car ride back to the office, Abby and Will tear into each other just like the unhappy couple Will had imagined them to be when they were sitting on Dr. Cartwright's couch.

"Fuck fuck fuck." Abby is trying unsuccessfully to back the car out of a tight space in the parking garage.

"Watch it," he yells. "You just friggin' sideswiped that BMW." He opens his door, looks at the other car, and starts to get out.

"What are you doing?"

"Leaving a note on the guy's dashboard. There's a huge scratch on the driver's-side door."

She revs the engine.

"What are *you* doing?"

"Leaving."

"No." He shuts his door and turns to her but her eyes are firmly on the rearview mirror. She finishes backing up and heads down the twisting ramp, the parking ticket on the dashboard.

"You can't leave the scene of an accident, Abby. That's a crime."

She continues to speed toward the exit.

Will tries speaking calmly, like he's addressing a tantrumming child. "Just stop the car when we get to the next level so I can get out, leave a note, and then I'll take over driving. You're too excitable right now to think clearly."

She brakes hard, mid-descent, and Will jerks forward in his seat, the tight belt across his chest the only thing keeping his head from hitting the windshield.

"Excitable? What is wrong with you? It's like you're some kind of relic, transplanted from the 1850s. And yes, I am sure you are all too happy to take over, Mr. JAG-thirteen-trials-Captain America. You've been trying to fucking take over from the beginning. Guess what? That is not going to happen."

"Trying to take over—are you kidding me? You think I would ask for this? To have to—" He stops himself, trying again to be matter-of-fact, but firmer. "The only reason I am on this case is because Paul asked me. You were on maternity leave, remember?"

"Which you still think I should be."

The car behind them is now honking continuously. Abby finishes descending, then speeds toward the ticket machine, lowering her window. They are several feet away from the machine and she can't reach the slot to insert the ticket. "Jesus." She motions at the driver to back up, reverses, and tries again. And again. Finally the ticket is jabbed into the slot, then Abby's credit card, and the safety bar releases, allowing them to exit.

"Third time's the charm."

Abby ignores him, making a series of turns until they pick up the freeway on Robertson and join a line of cars backed up as far as the eye can see.

Will slides down in his seat, rests his cheek against the glass. "You should have taken Beverly Boulevard instead of the 10. Even I know that and I've lived in LA for five minutes."

"Fuck off."

Will stares at her, speechless, then turns to look out the passenger-side window. In addition to being a bitch, Abby is a terrible driver. She has no judgment, no sense of direction, and no sense of space between her car and other cars. Or objects. Even objects that aren't moving. But responding, he knows, will only make an unsafe situation worse.

Abby's phone rings and she reaches into the back seat to pick up her purse, rooting through it unsuccessfully with one hand. The car swerves into the other lane.

Will grabs the purse, locates her phone, and holds up

the screen so she can read it, then, gratuitously, reads it himself. It's from Nic. A missed call followed by a text. When are you coming home? They crawl forward, stop, crawl forward again. The minutes on the dashboard tick by.

Abby keeps her eyes on the road. "We need to have a sit-down with Luz. A real come-to-Jesus moment. We are going to have to lay out the stakes and make her answer for herself."

"What about all the race and patriarchy talk back in Cartwright's office? Are you going to take some kind of sensitivity class on white privilege before we do this?"

"No. Marinating in it isn't going to get us anywhere. The fact that Luz may feel that way doesn't change the fact that if she doesn't talk to us she is going down."

Will feels his heart beating fast. Abby is going to run over Luz like a train. She is going to ruin her. The grilling, the lack of empathy, the demand for a legally satisfying explanation from a traumatized girl. He thinks again of the *French Lieutenant's Woman*, which he had picked back up the other night and started to reread. Charles, the protagonist, had made it his mission to understand the perpetually misunderstood Sarah. He had ignored the judgments— whore, witch, evildoer—heaped upon her by a society that could not understand why a woman would behave as she had. And the answer, that Sarah was truly broken through no fault of her own, was something that Charles was ultimately able to draw out of her. It was Charles who freed Sarah to show that truth, and her remarkable resilience, to others. Luz was the same. Like a good stone in a cheap ring she could be removed, reset, restored.

Will shakes his head as his certainty crystalizes. "You don't know how to connect with her. It would be better if it were me."

Abby snorts.

"The two of you are so far apart," Will says, "especially when it comes to being mothers."

"What is that supposed to mean?" Abruptly, Abby's tone changes and she is practically hissing at him.

Will feels his own anger surge. "Just look at her choices compared to yours. Her baby is her whole life, you heard Dr. Cartwright. She would do anything to be with Cristina. Anything to protect her."

"And I wouldn't?" Abby nearly rear-ends the car in front of them and slams on the brakes. For a second time, Will feels the press of his seat belt as he is thrown forward.

"How dare you judge me?"

"Because what you're doing is wrong. You are so selfish. Luz thinks so, too." In fact, Luz has never said anything of the sort, but as soon as he says the words Will believes in their powerful toxicity, almost as if they had appeared like graffiti on his garage door.

Abby turns pale but says nothing.

"For crissakes," Will continues, "you should have exited stage left as soon as you found out who the trial judge was. What do you think is going to happen in that courtroom after everything that went down in Rayshon Marbury's case between you two? It is going to be a bloodbath and it's going to be at her expense."

"To the contrary," she says coldly. "Dars said on the record that he would be fair. You told me so yourself."

Will laughs bitterly. "You're always betting, aren't you? Betting Dars will fear the optics too much to work us over. Betting you won't get caught for your reckless behavior, like that little hit-and-run back in the parking garage, or whatever unholy thing you did to win Rayshon Marbury's case. Maybe you'll get lucky again, maybe not. I don't really care one way or the other. But I'm no fool, so don't think for a second about pulling any of that with me. Or dragging me down with you."

A silence falls, lasting for several slowly driven miles.

"And what is it," she says icily, "that you think you can do to reach Luz?"

The question catches Will up short because he hasn't thought it through fully. His focus was on getting Abby away from Luz, not what he would do if he succeeded. "I would—" he stops to gather his thoughts "—develop a relationship with her based on sympathy and trust. I've already started to do that, in our earlier meetings. We have a strong connection." As he says these words he almost believes them. "I can help her tell the story of the worst night of her life in a way that will make the women on the jury feel an instant connection to her and will make the men on the jury feel outrage on her behalf."

"How will you do that?" Abby's tone is still cold but she also sounds genuinely curious.

"I am going to keep working with her, every day, to break down the barriers that are preventing her from talking to us—to overcome the fear and anxiety and the sense that no one understands her. I think," he says, and pauses, "I think I do understand her." The time in Dr. Cartwright's office was not a waste. She has given Will a window. A way in.

"Okay."

Will looks over at Abby but her face is expressionless. "Okay, what?"

Abby signals, shifts two lanes to the right, and takes the downtown exit. She pulls over to the side of the road next to a no parking sign, turns on her hazard lights, and shuts off the engine. The expression on her face is the same as when she was staring out the window in Dr. Cartwright's office—she's gone somewhere else, isn't seeing Will at all.

"I'm thinking about Luz on the witness stand," she says finally. "We can dirty up Travis. We can hammer away at the government's witnesses. But Luz *is* our case. At the end of the day, nothing else matters if the jury doesn't believe her. If the jury can see what she was up against—if you can embody that because you're a man and I can't because I'm not, or because Luz has contempt for me, for my choices—" She breaks off.

Will waits, understanding that he might actually get what he wants.

Abby is nodding now, more to herself than him. "We have to get this right. This decision, more than all the others, is the one we have to get right." Will watches as Abby reaches for her locket, moving it back and forth on the gold chain. He waits, and just when he has gotten impatient, is about to say something to prod her, she looks directly at him. "Okay. Go for it."

Will nods back, doing his best not to look triumphant, and settles back in his seat, able to relax at last. But almost immediately, Abby jerks him toward her, cupping his chin and turning his face forcibly toward her own. Her fingers are cold, her grip unexpectedly strong.

"You need to understand something, though." Their faces are inches apart, her eyes fixed on his. The sudden intensity of her gaze takes him aback and he has to fight the urge to pull away.

"Listen to me," she says quietly. "Luz is a liar."

He looks at her in disbelief.

"Luz is a liar," Abby repeats. "And if you don't remember that, it'll be her that takes you down."

**2006**

**Wednesday, January 18, 2006**
**1:13 p.m.**
**Willowick, Ohio**


From: sexxygirljax@yahoo.com
To: travman@hotmail.com

Wassup cutie im starting to show. wearing a big T shirt for
now but pretty soon everyone iz gonna know. Lance thinks
its his and gonna take responsibility even tho i dumped
his ass. don't worry my lips are sealed as long as you treat
me right. dont prove me wrong or u will be fucking sorry.


**Friday, January 20, 2006**
**10:31 p.m.**
**Ramstein Air Base**
**Ramstein-Miesenbach, Germany**


From: travman@hotmail.com
To: sexxygirljax@yahoo.com

How do I know its mine???

**2007**

Antoine Jones's legs extend in opposite directions far beyond the confines of the table, which, like most tables at restaurants in Little Tokyo, seems child-sized. Will wonders if this is a Japanese thing or just a calculated decision to cram as many people as possible into an already cramped space. TOT isn't crowded today; they've missed the lunch rush hour, luckily for the patrons who would have to navigate around Antoine. The guy is nearly seven feet tall and was apparently a big shot basketball player in college, then in Europe somewhere, before switching his focus to a different kind of court.

Abby is there already, on Antoine's side of the table, her pale face and his dark one staring intently at the screen of his laptop. They both look up and Will smiles, extending his hand.

"Hey, man." Antoine's voice is deep and smooth, like a

DJ on a jazz station. According to Abby, he's the best investigator in their office. They had been assigned to someone else, a younger woman named Kim. But Abby had not stood for that, despite Paul saying that he didn't want to meddle, and, in any event, that all of the investigators in the federal public defender's office were very good. "Actually, most of them suck and you know it," Abby had told him. "I want Antoine."

Rayshon Marbury was the unspoken name in the room; Antoine had been on that case, too. And so Abby had gotten her way, generating a solid dose of ill will in the process. No unit likes to be told what to do when it comes to its own people. But generating ill will did not seem to be a concern for Abby, and Will supposed it would be up to him to make nice later. *Let's hope you're worth it*, he thinks, staring at Antoine's smooth, impassive face, taking in the black tracksuit, the large blue signet ring on his left hand.

The waitress comes to take their order and Antoine closes the laptop. Antoine and Abby order the chicken teriyaki bowls; Will, who has not even picked up the menu, says he'll have the same.

"Shauna sent over the juvenile file," Abby says to Will.

Will tries not to look irritated that she's obviously shared this fact with Antoine before telling him. "What's in there?"

"It was a fight at school," Antoine says. "Luz and another girl. She pulled a knife."

"The other girl?"

"Luz."

"Over what?" Will feels like he's waiting for a diagnosis from a maddeningly terse doctor.

"Confrontation in the bathroom," Antoine says. "The other girl said that Luz was sleeping with her boyfriend. She was real mad about it. Slapped Luz, pulled her hair, and tried to scratch her face. Luz pulled a knife out of her purse, slashed the girl's arm."

"Self-defense?"

"That's what she told the police officer. But he didn't buy it and neither did the DA. *Not justified by the threat posed* is what they said."

"It probably didn't help that the victim needed sixteen stitches," Abby adds.

Antoine shrugs. "Another problem was that she had a knife in her purse to begin with."

Will says, "Our situation is different."

"I know," Abby says, "but the ultimate question is the same. Travis Hollis might have been drunk and overbearing, even threatened her life, but was he such an immediate overwhelming danger that she had no choice but to slice him open?"

The question hangs there a moment and then Will says to Antoine, "Did she go to trial for the school fight?"

"No. Original charge was assault with a deadly weapon. Pled down to simple assault. She got probation, had to pick up some trash on the freeway, did community service at her church. Great result, considering. She must've had a good attorney."

"It was Jorge Estrada, wasn't it?"

Antoine looks surprised. "That's right."

Will looks at Abby. They had discussed Will's visit and agreed not to probe further. "He's not going to talk to us, and anyway, we may be better off in the dark," Abby had pointed out. "Because let's say we do find out from Estrada that Luz plotted to murder her husband? Then we aren't going to be able to tell the jury that she didn't." Will thought it was unlikely—what lawyer would participate in that kind of plot? But taking the chance seemed too risky and so he had reluctantly agreed. It makes him uneasy, that Estrada had not volunteered this additional information—that his relationship with Luz went back not months, but years.

"She was a minor," Will says. "Her juvenile case is sealed."

"I'm sure Shauna will make a motion to try to convince Dars to admit it," Abby says. "But she'll lose, the law is clear. The government can't use juvie records at trial." She pauses. "Unless Luz somehow opens the door by bringing it up herself, directly or indirectly."

"That's not going to happen," Will says.

"No," Abby says, "because you're not going to let it happen, are you?"

This question, too, hangs in the air. Will stares back at her frostily.

Antoine clears his throat. "We were talking about the hard drive from Travis's computer. We got a copy today from the government. I was telling Abby I think we should do our own analysis."

Will keeps his eyes on Abby. "To find out what? We know Luz got Jackie's email about Travis. We know what time she opened it."

"The government analyzed Luz's emails," Antoine says. "They didn't look at Travis's. There might be something."

"What? Another woman?" Will tries to think how a second affair could be helpful and concludes it would not. "And anyway, even if we do find something good in Travis's emails, why would the judge let it in? A dead man can't testify that he was the one who wrote it. There's no foundation, no way to authenticate it."

"I'm thinking we might have a shot with Dars. Maybe he'll go out of his way to be fair because I'm there." Abby smiles sweetly at Will before turning to Antoine. "Will doesn't think so, though. He and I had a spirited discussion the other day about how Dars's and my relationship will play out at trial."

Antoine smiles. "My money's on you, Abby. My money is always on you."

"Quit it with the flattery." But Will can tell by the way that Abby is looking at Antoine that she's pleased. It's obvious that Antoine's opinion matters to her. Will wishes his did.

Will says to Antoine, "That kind of forensic analysis is not going to be cheap."

"Got a friend. Used to be in military intelligence, now he has his own business. He'll do it for a couple thousand."

"We can use the money we saved on Dr. Cartwright," Abby says. "Paul already allocated it."

Not for a fishing expedition with a completely different expert on a completely different topic, Will thinks. Like Abby dissing the investigator staff, it is just another head ache he'll have to deal with when the trial is over.

Antoine says, "No harm in having the information. Not like we have to turn it over to the prosecutor if we don't like it."

Will shakes his head. Antoine is right—they would be committing malpractice if they gave Shauna damaging information on Luz. Still. He doesn't know why he is resisting so strongly, but his gut is telling him this is a bad idea. But it's obvious that the decision has been made and his opinion is irrelevant.

Antoine says, breaking an awkward silence, "Would be good if we could get Mike Ravel to talk to us."

Ravel was Travis's best friend in the military and the government is almost certain to call him. It's Ravel's signature as the witness on the life insurance policy—the one that removed Travis's parents as the beneficiaries and re-placed them with Luz several weeks before he died.

"It would," Abby says. "What have you found out about him?"

"Dishonorably discharged a couple of months back. He's in a sober living facility outside Tucson. Some kind of di-version program run by the state court after he was caught breaking into a pharmacy to steal oxy."

"Drugs got him kicked out of the military?" Will asks.

"Yeah. First it was legally prescribed. He was wounded in Iraq, same tour as Travis. Back injury. But then he got addicted, started stealing."

Will considers these facts, how they might play. If Ravel is hostile to Luz, and there is reason to think he might be, they can use his addiction and theft to undermine his cred-ibility. Still, being an addict and a thief doesn't necessarily make him a liar, especially not if his problems are combat-induced and likely to stir the jury's sympathy. "What do you think he can tell us?"

Antoine shrugs. "Don't know till we ask."

The waitress arrives with their bowls. Antoine and Abby slide their chopsticks out of the paper wrapper and break them apart. Will calls the waitress back, and asks sheep-ishly for a knife and fork.

They eat in silence for a while, Abby ravenously, drain-ing her water glass repeatedly and asking for refills.

Antoine says to Abby, "How's Nic? He cool with you doing this trial?"

Will stops sawing at his chicken with the plastic utensils. Abby is looking steadily at Antoine. "No," she says, "he's not cool with it. But my doing this trial isn't up to him."

Antoine shakes his head. "Bumped into him the other

day when he came by with the baby. Didn't know the marshals got paternity leave."

Abby reddens slightly. "He's using his vacation time and sick leave." When Antoine's eyebrows go up, she adds quickly, "It's just until after the trial and then I'll be the one taking care of Cal."

Antoine grins. "Sure you will."

Abby drains her water glass. "If I were a man, we wouldn't even be having this conversation. It's 2007, and you would think—" she looks pointedly at Will "—that I'm committing some kind of child abuse. I'm just doing my job. A job, by the way, that pays more than Nic's. Having a baby is a partnership. Both parents have to sacrifice."

"Well, Happy Valentine's Day to you and your sacrificing partner." Antoine is still grinning.

Will starts. "Damn, I forgot about that."

"Can't forget Valentine's Day, man. Buy the lady some flowers on your way home."

Abby rolls her eyes. "Don't tell me you actually celebrate that fake buy-me-an-overpriced-dinner-and-I'll-give-you-a-blow-job bullshit."

Every Valentine's Day, Meredith makes Will his favorite dinner: lasagna with lamb meat instead of regular hamburger. He buys her a bottle of wine that costs more than $6 and a dozen roses. It's been a tradition for going on ten years. Will returns his attention to his chicken.

As Abby signals the waitress for the check, Antoine says, "First-degree murder seems like a stretch to me. Always has. The kind of women that get a verdict like that, they hire a hit man. Or they get a young kid to do it and they're fucking him, like in that movie about the news anchor lady. But Luz, she's basically still a kid herself, and you can argue she was protecting her baby."

"My worry is that the jury will want to compromise," Will says. "Not let her go, but not convict on the most extreme charge, either."

"What then, second-degree murder?"

"Second-degree is almost as bad as first. Twenty years, give or take."

"It's not life," Abby says. "Dars might have mercy, and even if he doesn't, Luz could still get out before she's forty."

"It's Cristina's life," Will says pointedly, and sees Abby flinch, then look past him, signaling to the waitress. "I worry," he says, raising his voice slightly to regain her attention, "that the jury will compromise on manslaughter, the plea Shauna offered."

Antoine nods. "She killed him in the heat of passion. Fits a stereotype—hot-blooded little Latina stabs her lying, cheating man in a fit of jealous rage. Through the heart no less."

Abby looks at Antoine, the corners of her mouth tilting upward. "Could have been worse. She could have done it on Valentine's Day."

Antoine smiles. "Always best to focus on the positive."

How could they possibly joke about something so effing serious? Gallows humor, Will understood, was a staple of their office—of any public defender's office—but he finds it difficult to stomach and in particularly poor taste here. A manslaughter conviction, in Will's mind, is what they have to fear the most. Shauna wouldn't traffic in racist stereotypes—no doubt she's been on the receiving end of plenty herself—but the jurors will take one look at Luz, then at the pictures of Travis's ravaged body, and come to their own conclusions.

Antoine stirs the remaining rice around in his bowl. "We've got to show self-defense, meaning Luz stabbed him through the heart believing she was about to die with no way out of a situation that was not her fault."

Abby nods.

"Tall order. She's got motive, she's got time, and she's got no real injuries." Antoine looks at Will. "So that's your job. With her."

"That is my job with her." Will stares back hard at both of them.

The waitress returns, clears their plates, mops at the table top, and reaches into the pocket of her uniform to hand Will the check. Abby takes it from him and does the math. "Eleven dollars each."

As they dig through their wallets, Antoine says, almost as an aside, "Luz is gonna need to change her look for the trial. And her attitude."

"Yes," Abby says. "I'm sure Will's on top of that."

Will nods, trying to look as if this were true instead of wishful thinking. He needs to bring back Lady Madonna, the doe-eyed young mother he saw that first and only time under the wooden cross in her grandmother's living room.

"Alright, well, we were talking," Antoine says, nodding to Abby, "about how maybe you might want to use some of this 3D technology." He opens his laptop and turns it toward Will. "I've been looking into software that can draw up the crime scene and create the two people, you know, her and him, so the jury can see the way it was on-screen. On the stand, Luz would describe an action and you would use the computer to demonstrate to the jury what it actually looked like."

"Or a good simulation of what it looked like," Abby says.

"Check it out," Antoine says.

Will stares at the laptop screen, clicks on the arrow and sees the hallway of the apartment in Ramstein. There are two bodies: one short, one tall, looming. In short, jerky bursts, the tall figure strikes out at the shorter one, who backtracks, arms outstretched to block her face. He keeps clicking, watching a chase, a collision, a run to another room. Will hits the stop button, looks up.

"What do you think?" Abby asks, leaning forward, elbows on the table. "It's kind of like what I was saying in the car the other day—about making it physical."

Will closes the laptop. "It's too removed," he says. "Too clinical." The realization hits him suddenly. "We need to use real bodies."

"Whose bodies?" Antoine says.

"Luz's," Will says. "And mine." He looks at Abby.

"I love that idea." She is actually smiling at him—the first real smile she's ever turned in his direction and it's like a thousand flashbulbs going off in his face. He hadn't realized until that moment that his dislike of Abby lives side by side with a craving for her approval.

2006

**Friday, January 20, 2006**
**11:13 p.m.**
**Willowick, Ohio**


From: sexxygirljax@yahoo.com
To: travman@hotmail.com

oh so its like that now. yeah, ill get the test. u want the results mailed to the base???


**Tuesday, January 24, 2006**
**8:14 a.m.**
**Willowick, Ohio**


From: sexxygirljax@yahoo.com
To: travman@hotmail.com

Haven't heard back from u. should i mail the results to the base, c/o the Mrs.?

T, i need u to take responsibility if u don't i will act.

### Tuesday, January 24, 2006
### 5:28 p.m.
### Ramstein Air Base
### Ramstein-Miesenbach, Germany

From: travman@hotmail.com
To: sexxygirljax@yahoo.com

Jaxx do not do anything krazee im doing what i can on my end but for now im stuck here in this situation of my making i know but i have to figure a way out you gotta trust me.

    V day is cuming up, so send me some more pix, puleeze!!! betchu look hot all knocked up...

### Tuesday, February 14, 2006
### 10:05 a.m.
### Willowick, Ohio

From: sexxygirljax@yahoo.com
To: travman@hotmail.com

hey there sexxxy valentine! ☺ ☺ ☺ did you get the cards and the pix?

so good to hear yr voice on the phone last week wish it wasn't so $$$ so we could phone fuck every week. not sure if its this pregnancy thing but im hella horny. did u look at the sonogram? gonna be gorgeous like his daddy. Waitin for u to tell The Mrs. like you promised. did u???!!!

**Tuesday, February 28, 2006**
**8:03 p.m.**
**Ramstein Air Base**
**Ramstein-Miesenbach, Germany**

From: travman@hotmail.com
To: sexxygirljax@yahoo.com

Jaxx,
Thx for the v day presents came late damn mail but they were well-received that i can tell u.

there's been some issues here and i can't move fast the way you want. i'll explain later but u gonna have 2B patient.
T

**2007**

"You have to do it harder."

Will steps back, releases his grip. There are red marks where his fingertips have pressed into Luz's neck just below her jawbone. She stays where she is with her back up against the wall, where he has cornered her. They are both breathing heavily, Will stripped down to his undershirt. "I don't want to hurt you."

She looks at him, hair disheveled, eyes dark and unreadable. "You have to. Just like I have to hurt you. It won't work if it isn't real."

This is the fifth, or maybe the sixth time—he's losing count—that they have reenacted those last fatal moments in the hallway where Travis died. Each time, Luz had pushed him: to yell, to shove, to hit, to strangle harder. Each time, Will had gone a step further and so had she: screaming, kicking, scratching him. His face burns where she's slapped him and there is a line of blood scabbing on his cheek where she's raked the skin with her fingernails. Each time, Will had reacted instinctively: pushing, shoving, and choking her more forcibly, then instantly pulling back, horrified and disgusted at what he was doing to someone half his size and little more than half his age. To a girl.

Will imagines one of his colleagues walking in, thankful they are here on a Sunday night. His brilliant idea is starting to seem foolish, even dangerous. He had been so excited about the chance to execute his plan that he had spent most of the afternoon rearranging the furniture, pushing the conference table and chairs to the side wall so that the long, rectangular space was wide open. Then, as best he could, he had reconstructed the layout of the Germany apartment with blue tape, referring repeatedly to the bird's-eye floor plan and measurements provided by the government as part of their reconstruction of the crime scene. Will had gotten so absorbed that he had forgotten to be irritated when Luz had arrived late, yet again, wearing a sundress rather than the sweatpants and tee shirt like he'd told her, to mimic the clothes she was wearing that night.

"This isn't who I am," he says, a note of desperation in his voice.

"It's who he was," she says.

Now that they've broken out of role, Will is having a hard time looking at her directly. She is too close to him. He smells her perfume and beneath it, sweat. He takes another step back. "Let's take a five-minute break. Get some air." He points to the sliding glass doors that lead to the concrete terrace outside the conference room.

She shakes her head, crosses her arms over her chest. He averts his eyes from her cleavage.

"You said everything rides on my testimony. You said it was the—" she reaches for his word "—centerpiece of the case." Her eyes search his. "That's right, isn't it?"

"Yes," he says reluctantly.

"If the jury doesn't believe that I thought I was going to die when this was happening," she says, and motions with her hand back and forth between them, "then I'm convicted."

Will presses his fingers to his cheek. They come away bloody. "Yes," he says again.

That, in essence, was about all he had been able to get across. At the beginning, Will had tried to talk it through with Luz: to get her to tell the story of that night, to share her feelings with him about what had happened. But Luz had not been interested in talking and sharing. She had shut him down, saying, *You'll only understand if I show you.* And Will had backed off. He wasn't one for long talks and feelings-sharing, either. It wasn't what Meredith would have called his strong suit. But it was necessary, he thought, to establish control over the situation—control over her. The lack of information feeds his unease. He had pictured a movie where he was the director and she was his star. She followed his instructions to carry out his vision. She let him save her. It wasn't working out that way.

"If they don't believe that story, I'll go away." Luz's voice catches and she shakes her head. Tears form, then run down her face, black with mascara. "I will not be separated from Cristina. I will die first."

To Will's horror, his eyes start to fill. He can't remember the last time that happened—it's been years. Crying, Will's father liked to say, was for funerals. He braces his forearms against the wall, his head between them, and shuts his eyes.

But the tears come anyway. "I understand," he says trying to get his voice under control, "these are high stakes, I know—"

"No, you don't." Beside him, he hears her let out a long, ragged breath. "You have no idea. What's it like to be a mother and have your baby taken away from you."

"You're right," he says, holding his hot, wet face against the cool, dry surface of the wall. "I have no idea. But I am going to do everything I can to stop that from happening."

When she doesn't answer, he looks over at her in profile beside him: her wild hair, the dark lines on her cheeks, the smear of lipstick at the corner of her mouth. Her hoop earring has twisted sideways and he reaches over to fix it. She takes his hand and raises it to her mouth. He tries to jerk away and she tightens her grip.

"What are you doing?" he whispers.

She turns to look at him, her face inches away. She opens her mouth, slides his index and middle finger inside.

"Don't," he says, hearing the panic in his voice as his body responds. "No."

With her other hand, she reaches for his belt and pulls him closer until he is right up against her, hard. Then she takes his free hand and guides it under her dress.

Feeling the heat between her legs, and the smooth, perfect curve of her ass under the silky material of her underwear makes him groan. "No," he says again, but he doesn't move his hand away. She sucks each of his fingers in turn, runs them down the line of her throat. Will stands frozen, the tears drying on his face, his heart hammering in his chest.

"This is how it ended," she says softly, putting her cheek against his so that her lips are against his ear. "Except for that night, this is how it always ended. This is how I made it stop. It's the part that's missing. We need to do this part or we won't get the rest of it right."

"No," he repeats, but the refusal, even to his own ears, is tinny and unconvincing.

She bites down on his earlobe hard. "I want to go again," she says. "Throw me up against the wall."

"I can't," he says. And then he does.

Dars Ducey's perpetually harried clerk calls Luz's case last, at which point it is nearly 4:30 p.m. The courtroom, emptied out except for the reporters, is deadly quiet. The only other person in the gallery is Jorge Estrada.

As Abby and Will walk with Luz over to the counsel table, Abby notices that Luz looks pale. Luz had spoken with Estrada during one of the breaks in the endless afternoon cattle call, off to the side in the hallway. From what Abby could see, it appeared that Estrada had done most of the talking. She whispers to Luz, "This is a crazy move by the prosecution and it's not going to work, so don't worry." She turns to Will, trying not to look irritated. "Could you please—"

Will steps forward robotically and pulls out Luz's chair, his face tight and drawn, a long scratch on his right cheek livid under the fluorescent lights.

Dars makes a show of welcoming them all, then settles

back in his chair. "I understand the government has a motion," he says, and nods at Shauna.

She stands. "Your Honor, the defendant consulted with an attorney, Jorge Estrada, in the months and days leading up to the murder. The government believes that Mr. Estrada will be a key witness at trial, which is scheduled to begin next week. We've subpoenaed him here today because he has rebuffed our attempts to speak with him, claiming that his conversations with the defendant are protected by the attorney-client privilege."

Dars passes his hand over his pompadour, slick as sealskin. "Well, aren't they? That's what I learned in my first year of law school anyway. But maybe we do things differently at Harvard." He smiles at Abby. "Ms. Rosenberg, isn't that what you recall learning when you were there?"

Abby feels her smile freeze in a rictus on her face.

Dars turns to Shauna. "I'm a bit older than your worthy opponent, so we didn't overlap. But as I recall, an attorney has a sacred obligation to keep the contents of his communications with his client a secret. What's that case when Bill Clinton was in office, the White House Counsel who killed himself?" Dars looks up and snaps his fingers. "Vince Foster. The Supreme Court said even when Foster was buried six feet underground, they still couldn't make his lawyer talk." Dars smiles his ghastly smile again. "So why should I make that extraordinary demand of Mr. Estrada?"

Shauna says evenly, "Your Honor, there is a crime-fraud exception to the attorney-client privilege. If the communication was for the purpose of aiding the defendant in committing a crime—"

Dars raises his eyebrows. "Indeed, there is. But what evidence do you have that that's the case?"

"The dates on Mr. Estrada's invoice. The defendant

spoke with him the day before the victim requested to change his life insurance policy. And that's not all. Before, the proceeds were equally divided between Sergeant Hollis's mother and father. The new policy names the defendant as the sole beneficiary. Weeks later, she murdered him."

Dars turns to Abby. "Have you spoken with Mr. Estrada?"

Abby looks briefly at Will before getting to her feet. "Not as to the contents of his conversations with our client, no. We don't believe it would be appropriate, for the reasons Your Honor stated."

"Really?" Dars tilts his head at her, steeples his fingers under his chin. "That explanation, coming from a lawyer so thorough and dogged as yourself, seems a bit thin to me. Maybe, just maybe, what you don't believe is that talking to Mr. Estrada would be helpful to your case."

Abby feels her stomach start to turn, like the first sign she's eaten a bad oyster. "If the court will indulge me," she begins.

"Always, Ms. Rosenberg. As you know, I am always happy to indulge you."

Abby tries her best to keep smiling. Dealing with Dars when he was the prosecutor in Rayshon's case—his casual misogyny, his calculated race-baiting, his arrogance—had been a trial in itself, but at least back then they had been equals. Now that he's wearing a black robe and high up on a dais, she's had to accept the hard truth: Dars's determination to dig his thumb into every bruise was something to be endured rather than combated.

"Ms. Gooden is taking a perfectly ordinary situation and trying to recast it as an evil plot. Every soldier is provided a life insurance policy by the government. It's called Servicemembers' Group Life Insurance and it automatically provides a death benefit of $400,000. Sergeant Hollis needed to change the policy. His father, one of the original beneficiaries, had died. And he had a wife and a baby on the way. The baby, Cristina Rivera Hollis, is the contingent beneficiary on the policy. He could not leave the money to Cristina directly because she is a minor. This arrangement—leaving the money to Mrs. Rivera Hollis to use for the care of the child in the event of an unexpected tragedy—was the most practical thing to do."

"Practical," Dars repeats softly. "Yes, I suppose that's one word for it."

"People with young children who have preexisting policies naming other family members do it all the time," Abby continues stolidly. "There's nothing nefarious about it." She pauses. "In fact, my son's father, who is a veteran, just did the same thing himself."

"Did he now? Well, that's heartwarming to know." Dars smiles cheerfully. "And did you stab him afterward?"

Over Luz's audible gasp, Shauna clears her throat. "Your Honor, if I might, Sergeant Hollis made no changes to the policy prior to this point. To paraphrase Ms. Rosenberg, it is common practice for people to change the beneficiary on their life insurance policy when they get married, to make sure their spouse is taken care of. That did not happen. It did not happen for months after he knew he was going to be a father. It happened less than three weeks before his wife—the newly named sole beneficiary—killed him. Without that policy, the defendant was never going to inherit anything other than the $244 in their joint checking account. They had no home, no car, no investments. The policy was the victim's only real asset and until the defendant spoke with Mr. Estrada, that policy named his parents."

Abby tries again, "The deceased never consulted with Mr. Estrada at all. There is no evidence linking Sergeant Hollis's decision to change his life insurance policy to my client's decision to talk to a lawyer. And Ms. Gooden's insinuations undermine her own theory, which is that my client killed her husband hours after finding out about his infidelity because his girlfriend, Jackie Stedman, emailed her to disclose it and to disclose the fact that he had a child with her."

"What about it, Madame Prosecutor?"

Shauna shakes her head. "With all due respect to Ms. Rosenberg, the defense is in no position to be telling this court what the government's theory is. And anyway, the government is entitled to investigate its case and alter its theory when new information comes to light."

Seeing Dars start to nod, Abby interjects, "There are multiple calls between my client and Mr. Estrada starting back in December of 2005. Sergeant Hollis died in October of 2006. Mr. Estrada has a general practice. My client could have talked with him about any number of matters."

"Well, that's what we are going to find out." Dars claps his hands together. "Ladies, ladies, I thank you for this excellent oral argument. Truly. It is amazing to me that we once prohibited you from practicing law." He gives each of them an avuncular nod of approval, and Abby, whose stomach is now roiling, takes her seat. Dars turns back to Shauna. "Ms. Gooden, you are excused."

Shauna looks up, startled. "Your Honor—"

Dars jerks his thumb toward the door. "Move along. You can't be here, not unless and until there's a reason to believe Mr. Estrada can break the privilege." He looks at the rows of reporters. "You people, too. Out." There is the sound of murmuring as the disgruntled reporters gather their possessions. "Mr. Estrada, have a seat in the witness box. The clerk will swear you in."

Beside her, Abby hears Luz gasp again. "Look down,"

Abby whispers, "look down at the ground and do not say a word."

The courtroom doors swing shut behind Shauna and press gaggle as Estrada comes forward, his back straight, eyes looking neither right nor left. He is wearing a gray suit and a white shirt, well-pressed. Will had told Abby that Estrada was an older guy, and he is, but not in the hoary, done-in way she expected of strip mall storefront lawyer. He looks good for his age, handsome with his carefully combed silver hair and wire-rimmed glasses.

Estrada sits down and raises his hand as the clerk haltingly administers the oath.

Dars swivels to face him. "This is a closed proceeding and the transcript will be sealed. You can speak freely, so go ahead and give me a summary of what you and the defendant talked about when you spoke on the phone. Ten, twenty minutes, you're off the stand, I make my ruling, and everyone goes home. How does that sound?"

Estrada looks at Dars for a moment. "No."

Dars's eyebrows lift. "Excuse me?"

"As I told Mr. Ellet, my conversations with Mrs. Rivera Hollis are protected by the attorney-client privilege."

"Mr. who—" Dars turns, looks at Will, then turns back to Estrada. "Do I look like Mr. Ellet to you, sir? Or like Ms. Rosenberg, or Ms. Gooden? I am a federal judge. Appointed by the President, confirmed by the United States Senate. This is my courtroom. It isn't a request, it's an order."

"I'm sorry, but I won't be able to comply with it."

Dars's face and neck have turned an unhealthy scarlet and Abby, despite the gravity of the situation, cannot help but take momentary pleasure in the fact that his mask is so badly askew. If Rayshon were here, he would have fist-bumped her under the table.

"You will comply," Dars says, his voice raised, "or you will be held in contempt."

Estrada shakes his head. "Mrs. Rivera Hollis did not seek my advice for criminal purposes and there has been no fraud perpetrated on this court."

Dars points a shaking finger at Estrada. "Are you challenging my authority?"

Estrada pauses for a moment, then says, "Yes, I suppose I am."

Dars leans in, as if to put physical force behind the words. "I am not a potted plant," he says in a low whisper, and the sound, amplified by the microphone, is so unnerving that Abby wishes he had just yelled instead. "You don't get to decide what I can and can't know. You tell me what your client told you, or you go to jail. Do you understand me?"

Abby feels Luz flinch, puts a restraining hand on her arm. She looks over at Will, who appears to have finally woken up from his stupor. He looks back at her in alarm, then trains his eyes on Estrada.

Estrada looks several shades paler than he did a moment ago, but his voice is low and even. "My answer is still no. Your order is a violation of my ethical obligations to my client, and I don't believe it is enforceable."

Dars stares at him for another moment, as if waiting for Estrada to correct himself, then slowly shakes his head. "You don't think my order is enforceable?" He raises his gavel and slams it down. "This witness, Mr. Jorge Estrada, is hereby found in criminal contempt of court and sentenced to fifteen months imprisonment."

Luz makes a strangled noise in her throat and Abby is on her feet. "Your Honor, we object—"

"You don't have grounds to object." Dars is yelling now,

his finger pointed at her. "You are not his lawyer. Now sit down."

"He needs one, Your Honor. I request that the court adjourn so we can find counsel to represent—"

"Honey, did you hear what I said? Sit down, goddammit, or you are going with him."

For a moment, the courtroom is utterly silent. Then Abby hears Will scramble to reach around Luz's back, feels him grab her by the arm and pull her down into her seat. Dars points to the marshal seated behind them, and Abby turns around. Jared again, looking just as gobsmacked as he did at the bail hearing, albeit for a completely different reason. "You." Dars makes a lifting motion with one hand. "Take the witness into custody. And you." He points at Jared's partner, seated beside him. "Bring Ms. Gooden back in here."

As Estrada slowly makes his way down from the witness stand, Jared beckons him over to the back of the courtroom. Shauna, walking inside, does a double take as she sees Estrada surrender his shoes and belt before turning around to have his hands shackled behind his back.

Dars waits until Jared and his partner have left with Estrada, then says to Shauna, "The witness has been less than forthcoming, and so I've decided to give him a little time-out to think things over."

Shauna starts, "Your Honor—"

"Not to worry, Ms. Gooden. It's all to your benefit." Dars's face has returned to its normal color and his smile is back in place. "Mr. Estrada will remain in jail until he decides to divulge the contents of his communications with Mrs. Rivera Hollis. I have no doubt by the time trial starts next week that he'll be singing like a nightingale. Now, do we have any other business to take up?"

Abby and Shauna look at each other, say no at the same time.

"Well, then," Dars says, as he picks up his gavel and bangs it down again. "This court is adjourned."

Abby's thoughts form and instantly break apart. She looks at Will, who is staring straight ahead of him as he watches Dars walk through the door to his chambers, then at Luz. Her hands are clasped, her eyes closed, her lips moving. When Abby leans toward her, she hears whispered incantations in Spanish.

Luz is praying.

Abby looks up, sees Shauna leaving the courtroom, and says to Will, "I'm going to try to catch her. Let's meet back at the office."

"Shauna." Abby's voice is too loud, echoing off the walls of the hallway. The reporters, who are milling around the elevator bank, now turn to look. A few of them call out to Abby and Shauna, asking for a word on the off chance either of them will make the stupid decision to break the gag order rule. She ignores them. "Can we?" Abby inclines her head toward the women's bathroom. Shauna pauses for a moment, then walks toward her.

Once inside, Abby makes sure to lock the door. They stand on opposite sides of the sink outside the single stall, after Abby checks to make sure it is empty. Shauna looks at her steadily. "Well?"

Abby crosses her arms over her chest. "You can't let Mr. Estrada go to jail. You know it's wrong. Just    just withdraw your request for his testimony—"

"That's what you brought me in here to say. Really?"

"Do you think," Abby says fiercely, "that Dars would do what he just did to Jorge Estrada if he were a white man? And the way he treats both of us—" she draws her hand back and forth between them "—it's outrageous. He is a racist, sexist, odious—"

Shauna holds up her hand. "Do not," she says quietly, but with barely controlled rage, "compare yourself to me."

"That's not—"

Shauna shakes her head for Abby to be quiet. "When I worked with Dars back when he was in the US Attorney's Office, he told me that the decision to hire me made him re-think his opposition to affirmative action. Because you know, I'm so competent and articulate." She smiles mirthlessly. "Oh, and I went to Harvard, too, just so you know. Interesting, though, that Dars makes that connection only with you."

"Do you think I enjoy that?" Abby can feel her voice rise in outrage. "That he attempts to imply that we are similar in any way? It makes me sick."

"You are. You're both white."

"Jesus, Shauna. Come on." When Shauna says nothing, just continues to stare back at her, Abby feels her face getting red. "Okay, look. I wasn't comparing myself to you. I was just saying if we present a united front in the face of—"

"We are not a united front. We are exactly the opposite of that, in fact. And it is in my interest—the government's interest—for Mr. Estrada to tell the court what he knows."

Abby feels her stomach sink at the depth of her miscalculation, throws a Hail Mary. "You don't think what is happening is wrong? You don't think you have an obligation here?"

"I think a lot of things are wrong. Including your attempt to enlist me in this—" she pauses "—*righteous* cause of yours." Shauna shakes her head. "I like you, Abby. I do. But we are adversaries. Not sisters."

Wednesday, March 14, 2007
11:48 p.m.
Apartment 4F
Culver City, California


Will is careful closing the front door, and he takes off his shoes before stepping onto the parquet floor in the hallway.

But Meredith has waited up for him. He hears the television in the living room, then, "Hon, is that you?"

His heart falls, dread descending. His legs are still shaking and he stands against the wall for a moment, tensing the muscles in his calves and thighs until they are rigid.

When he walks into the living room, his wife hits the mute button on the remote and Jay Leno's braying goes quiet. She pats the space beside her on the couch for him to sit, but he can't bear to, dropping into the leather recliner opposite her. He sees her look of hurt confusion and quickly looks away, to his socked feet.

"You went to the gym again?" she asks.

Will runs a hand through his wet hair, nods, tries to smile, and stops when he feels the fresh scratch on the back of his neck. Not a lie, he has gone to the gym. He has been going to the gym every night for the past three weeks. But just to shower.

"That's good," she says encouragingly. "It's supposed to help with the stress, right?"

That's what he had told her in the beginning, although it had never been part of his routine when preparing for any of his other trials. He feels his mouth drying at the thought of adding to the growing pile of lies. "I'm sorry, babe," he says, "about these last few weeks, I—"

To his horror, his voice cracks. The room momentarily blurs and he squeezes his eyes shut. Christ, what is happening to him?

Instantly, Meredith is by his side, kneeling, her face upturned, her hazel eyes fixed steadily on his. She puts her hand on his arm, rubbing it gently, and it takes every ounce of self-control he has not to flinch. "Will, honey, what is it? I know there's something terribly wrong."

Up close, Will can see her smattering of freckles, the incompletely removed bits of mascara sticking to the corners of her eyelashes, her fine, pale hair flattened slightly on one side from resting her head on the couch. This is his wife of five years, his girlfriend of ten, the not-so-distant future mother of his children. The person he has promised to love and cherish forever. Who loves and cherishes him, always has, always will.

He longs for an answer that is not his fault, an answer that makes him the victim. *I was hit by a car. I was robbed at gunpoint. I have an inoperable brain tumor.*

The truth is unspeakable. *I spend every night shoving and slapping my client. I call her horrible names, and then we fuck.* Luz's word. *Fuck me.* Her nipples dark and swollen in his mouth, as he kneads her perfectly round ass, firm in his hands. *Fuck me.* Her eyes fixed on his, her cheeks burning red where he'd hit her, her panties pushed to one side, her legs wrapped tightly around him, pushing him deeper inside as he holds her down on the conference table.

Now she no longer wears panties. Just knowing that she comes to meet him wet and ready under her skirt makes him hard. Often and in the most inappropriate moments he stiffens: waiting to meet with one of his other clients at the jail, listening when Abby updates him on some new development, taking—sweet Jesus—the quiz at the end of the mandatory online sexual harassment training for new employees. His mind turns up images of her with the relentless precision of a Vegas dealer flipping cards. A small blessing that, at least right at this moment, his feelings of guilt and the terror of being found out are enough to make his dick shrivel.

"Will?"

He blinks. Now it's Meredith's eyes that are brimming.

"Mer," he says weakly. He should hold her, he knows. He should press her tightly against him and finish his sentence: that the trial was less than a week away, that it would all be over soon, that afterward, everything would go back to normal. But he can't bring himself to say the words, and the idea of touching his wife fills him with panic. She will want to make love—her word—not out of raw desire but out of a desperate need to reclaim him and feel close again.

He does a mental inventory of his body: the other places where he has been scratched, bitten, kicked. Meredith knows that he and Luz have been practicing—that was the word he had used excitedly when he'd told her of his idea, too excited by his own brilliance, he realized now, to appreciate that she was apprehensive, as any sane spouse would be. So most of it was explicable, though maybe not the rake lines across his lower back, the purple welt near his collarbone where he saw, in the locker room mirror, the imprint of small, even teeth.

But these problems, real as they are, are not the only reason he won't make love to his wife. He doesn't even know if he could get through the series of rituals that are as familiar as the way he brushes his teeth (back to front) or washes himself in the shower (top to bottom). Worse, he doesn't want to.

"I'm sorry," he says again. But his voice is tired and flat, and he knows the words sound empty. "I'm not myself," he says, and realizes how deeply true it is. He has become depraved, taken over by a craving for Luz that consumes everything else, even the basic instinct for self-preservation. The craving subsides only right after he comes, still deep inside of her, and for the rest of that night, when he sleeps like a dead man. But in the morning, the craving is back, screaming like a kettle that won't go off. Again he thinks of Charles and his obsession with Sarah, the French lieutenant's woman. Never has he identified so closely with someone who—he keeps having to remind himself—is a fictional character.

A million times in the last three weeks he has told himself to stop. That he has to stop. What he is doing isn't just a crime against his marriage, it's a crime against his profession. If anyone found out, he would be dismissed, disbarred, disgraced. Every morning, alone in the small apartment after Meredith has left for school, he stares at his reflection in the mirror, holds the razor up to his face before it begins the first slide through the white foam.

*She's nineteen.*

*She's your client.*

*The last person she fucked, she killed.*

It's all true, and yet somehow beside the point. The craving isn't just a heat, it's a voice, too. This is bigger than him, bigger than his marriage. This is about saving a woman's life and the life of her child. These are mortal stakes. Abby, Antoine—even Paul—had approved of Will's strategy, albeit in PG-13 form. They had understood that he and Luz are making a piece of art with the power to change the outcome of the case. And what Will understands in his more lucid moments is that his perfidy adds a kind of demented integrity to the performance—because what he is saying and doing when he acts out the death of Sergeant Travis Hollis has become a kind of absolute truth.

Now, Will forces himself to keep looking at Meredith. "This is going to be over soon," he says. He says this because it is true, and because it is meant to offer relief, to his wife, but to himself, as well. It will end; the case, and he prays, his craving, too, breaking like a fever, leaving Will and Meredith to go back to the way things were. But the words offer him no relief; like Charles in the aftermath of Sarah's abrupt departure, he can think of Luz's absence from his life only as an incomprehensible loss.

# 2006

**Tuesday, May 2, 2006**
**12:36 p.m.**
**Willowick, Ohio**


From: sexxygirljax@yahoo.com
To: travman@hotmail.com

u motherfucker. she's pregnant and I found out cuz she posts a pic w/ u grinning like an ape on Facebook? all this time I've been sending sonograms and belly pix and titty pix to ur lying ass. You done me dirty, t, real dirty, and u are gonna pay.

**Thursday, May 4, 2006**
**5:28 p.m.**
**Ramstein Air Base**
**Ramstein-Miesenbach, Germany**


From: travman@hotmail.com
To: sexxygirljax@yahoo.com

do u think i planned this??? do u think I want this??? my life is hell u just dont know im praying to get re-deployed 2 get out and maybe end everything for good by getting blown the fuck up.

　　and yea, jaxx, i know all about ur little FB friendship cuz she told me you been posting pix all about ur dr. appts w/ happy baby daddy lance and flashing around sum bling he got u and im the liar??? Or who knows maybe that is the truth after all and u been playin me.

**2007**

Monday, March 19, 2007
8:30 a.m.
United States District Court
for the Central District of California

Standing at the lectern and pretending to organize the notes she won't be using, Abby sneaks a sidelong glance at the jurors as they settle into their seats. Eight men, four women. The oldest, a retired Black nurse with a tight bun of gray hair and an oversize purse, is seventy-two; the youngest, a Latino computer programmer with several days of stubble and a nose ring, is twenty-four. Everyone else—a real estate agent, a screenwriter, a web designer, an accountant, a community college student, a dentist, a gym teacher, two stay-at-home moms, and one stay-at-home dad—is white.

Abby does not know what to make of Luz's chances with these twelve people. But in the end, she'd had little choice in who sat in the box. Even with the gag order, the massive amount of pretrial publicity left many with firm ideas about Luz—in the main, that she was guilty—and most of the people who hadn't watched the coverage on the news or read about it had their own reasons for wanting out. All day yesterday they had sat while Dars had asked the long list of questions Abby and Shauna had submitted. "Have you ever been a victim of domestic violence or known someone who has been?"

"What are your feelings about the war in Iraq?"

"This is a murder case. You are going to see pictures of the victim's body that you may find gruesome. Will that affect your ability to be impartial?"

One after the other, the potential jurors had timidly raised their hands and asked to go to sidebar, where they whispered their secrets as the lawyers huddled around the court reporter. *I was raped in college. My son died when his Humvee hit an IED. I'm afraid of knives. I'm afraid of blood. I can't look at a dead body.*

Watching Dars's fatherly demeanor, listening to his sympathetic murmurs as he excused one after the other and politely instructed the clerk to call out a new round of names, Abby could almost doubt she'd heard correctly his earlier announcement, delivered when it was just the lawyers in the courtroom. "Mr. Estrada has decided to remain silent and in custody," he informed them, his index finger stabbing in Luz's direction as if to formally assign her direct responsibility for this travesty. Luz, no longer needing to be told, stared down, her face expressionless as Abby and Will exchanged a quick, relieved glance over her head. Within twenty-four hours of Dars's decision to jail Estrada, they had contacted an attorney who had filed an emergency appeal, denied the same day in an unsigned order. Every day since, they had waited for Estrada to break.

Over the course of the morning, the pool of jurors shrank to a puddle, with only a few people remaining in the benches when it was time to break for lunch. At 1:30 p.m.

a whole new group was brought in and Dars had given up the act. Midafternoon, after yet another hushed conversation at sidebar that resulted in the dismissal of a teary-eyed juror, Dars had snapped, "This courtroom is turning into a confessional. I should have ignored the both of you ladies and your ridiculous ideas—" he'd waggled a forefinger at Abby and Shauna "—and just asked the regular questions: name, address, phone number, can you be fair, the end." Abby had glanced pointedly at Shauna, then watched as the court reporter raised her hands to the stenographer's machine and replaced them primly in her lap without typing anything at all. They were all the same: editing out the worst of all of the judge's outbursts. The transcript Abby received of the proceeding with Estrada had been curiously free of epithets—or the word *honey.*

Now Dars is nodding curtly in Abby's direction. Showtime.

In her mind, Abby has gone over her opening statement countless times. In the dead of night, she practiced aloud sitting in the bathtub while Cal nursed. The sound of rushing water calmed him, the rising steam calmed her. They fell into a rhythm; Cal, seemingly on the brink of sleep, eyelids fluttering, Abby laying out her case in a soft low voice—a lullaby about a killing. Once in a while she would stop mid-sentence, feeling him release her breast and looking down to find him staring up at her, entranced. Holding tight to his little body, now grown plump and sturdy, gave her an unexpected surge of strength. The source of her terrible ambivalence, Cal is also her greatest achievement, the tiny person who holds all of her heart-smashed love.

*I made this beautiful boy. I can do anything.*

Now she is feeling less sure. Shauna had gone first, and she had been strong. There had been a slideshow: Travis as a baby, Travis as a soldier, Travis as a stabbed man, his blood-soaked body curled in the fetal position. And finally, Travis as a cadaver, broken open on the medical examiner's table. At the last picture, which Shauna left projected on the screen for several minutes, Luz had made a sound that Abby did not recognize, canting forward before Will reached out to grab her wrist. Shauna told the jury, "There is no dispute about how Sergeant Hollis died and who killed him. Ask yourself, how did the defendant summon the strength to shove this knife through layers of skin and muscle, through bone? That's not fear, ladies and gentlemen. That is cold, hard anger. Hours earlier, the defendant had settled on her target and when the time came, she drove toward that target with malice and deliberation and deadly accuracy."

Abby looks at the jurors. With the fingers of her left hand, she worries at the gold locket hanging from a chain around her neck, pressing it deeply into the base of her throat.

She begins, "There is a saying about marriage—we all have our opinions, but no one knows what goes on behind closed doors." Abby leaves the lectern and walks over to the jurors. She is wearing a muted navy dress and matching jacket, has taken care with her hair and makeup, going for polished and minimal. Just a bit of foundation to hide the circles under her eyes, a dusting of blush to give her some color; no lipstick, no mascara, no nail polish. Standing before these jurors—her jurors—Abby hopes to signal the unsexed version of Luz that she and Will are hoping to sell: slight, sweet, utterly unthreatening.

"In this trial, we are going to take you behind the closed doors of the marriage between my client, Luz Rivera Hollis, and her husband, Sergeant Travis Hollis. You will hear what they said to each other, you will see how they treated each other. Not in public, not how the government's witnesses will describe it, but when they were alone together.

"You will bear witness to the most intimate moments of their lives. You will know about the kind of sex they had, about the birth of the child they conceived, about Sergeant Hollis's infidelity, and about the tremendous stress brought on by his deployment to Iraq. Most of all, you will learn what it was like for my nineteen-year-old client to live with this man. A man who was more than a foot taller and outweighed her by a hundred and fifty pounds. A man with a drinking problem that turned him jealous, angry, and violent.

"Ms. Gooden would have you believe that Sergeant Hollis was planning to leave my client for another woman. But the facts will show otherwise. Sergeant Hollis was never going to let go of his wife, a person he was determined to possess—to own. Like all young love, the love that Sergeant Hollis felt for Luz Rivera was romantic, urgent, and overwhelming. But because of who he was and what he had been through, that love became a darkness. It became a sickness that consumed his body and his mind. When Sergeant Hollis felt hopeless and out of control—and that was increasingly often in the months leading up to his death—he drank. Not modest amounts. The amount of alcohol he consumed in a single night would kill any one of you. And when he drank, he became abusive to his wife, his most treasured possession, not just verbally, but physically."

Abby puts both hands on the railing and leans forward. Her voice has been rising, the words coming faster, and she knows she has to soften her tone, that she has to slow down. She thinks of Cal looking up at her in the bathtub like he's hanging on her every word and takes a breath, letting her gaze travel across the back row and then the front, making eye contact with each juror.

"The pictures that the prosecutor showed you just now are powerful, powerful images. Sergeant Hollis was handsome. Sergeant Hollis was brave. Sergeant Hollis died a horrible death. No one is disputing any of that.

"But what you will come to find out," she continues, "is that, behind closed doors, Sergeant Hollis was also a nasty, belligerent drunk. When he was drunk, Sergeant Hollis forced himself on his wife. He hit her. He choked her. He called her terrible names. And she tried to handle it, as best as she could. Behind closed doors. Because that's what a marriage was to my client, a nineteen-year-old devout Catholic girl with a new baby. Marriage is between two people, and it was her job to manage it, to find a way to survive."

Abby steps back from the railing, lets her hands fall to her sides. "In the early morning hours of October 14, 2006, it was no longer possible to manage Sergeant Travis Hollis. He had a blood alcohol level of .26. He was coming at his wife, all six foot four and 260 pounds of him. He was beating her, and he was going to kill her. And while this is happening, their baby was aslccp just a few feet away.

"Only one of them was going to walk out alive from behind those closed doors. When Luz Rivera Hollis grabbed that knife and stabbed her husband, she did not commit a crime. She did not even make a choice. Because it isn't a crime to save your own life and there is no choice when the alternative is death. There is only survival."

Abby watches the jurors react and feels the familiar surge of adrenaline course through her. Dars can say all he likes that it's his courtroom, but when she's in front of the jury, she owns every inch of it. The power she has right now, to hold the jurors' attention with the story she is telling, is a high she is always chasing. She loves these moments the way that some people love drugs or sex or money. There is nothing else in the world that exhilarates her like performing for an audience in trial.

"Thank you for listening so carefully," she says, and she means it.

Monday, March 19, 2007
6:30 p.m.
1710 Vestal Street
Los Angeles

Will makes the mistake of parking on Echo Park Avenue, figuring the walk up to Vestal Street would be insignificant. In fact, the small, Spanish-style bungalow Abby shares with Nic is nearly at the top of the hill and the longer-than-expected climb is unforgivingly steep.

Vestal Street is pretty. Leafy trees rise from sidewalk planters and Will can hear crickets in the quiet dark. There's little hint that ten years ago the neighborhood was torn apart by shootings from rival Latino gangs. Gentrification has made its way steadily east to Echo Park, pushing out the working-class families who had lived there for generations with rising rents. Replacing them are people like Abby: young, overwhelmingly white professionals with low six-figure incomes willing to bargain for spectacular views, ready access to upmarket restaurants, and convenience to downtown jobs by tolerating occasional outbreaks of the

old violence and more common low-level street crime—
graffiti, vandalism, littering.

Not Will. When apartment-hunting last summer with
Meredith, he had immediately written off Echo Park as
grimy and unsafe. Now—as it seems with so many aspects
of his life—he finds himself taking a closer look and having second thoughts. Up here, high in the hills, any danger
seems remote and the view is indeed spectacular. Pausing
to catch his breath, Will looks out at the ugly city, trans-
formed at nightfall into a galaxy of lights twinkling along
the serpentine freeways that coil and cross as they make
their separate paths to the horizon. He thinks about his and
Meredith's bland apartment in the outskirts of the Mid-
Wilshire district and its single notable attraction: proxim-
ity to The Grove, a Disney-fied outdoor shopping mall that
teems with tourists buying tee shirts emblazoned with the
Hollywood sign and lining up to see the latest superhero
movie. There is no need to join a gym in Echo Park, either;
just a few sharply graded streets away there is Elysian Park
with its miles of rocky trails. Abby has mentioned in passing that Nic often goes mountain biking there, and that they
have walked to games at Dodger Stadium.

The idea of Abby and Nic doing something as normal
as going to a baseball game together is hard for Will to
imagine. Nic himself is hard to imagine. The domestic
situation Will has pieced together from Abby's occasional
references and the office rumor mill seems like something
only a spineless sap would tolerate.

And so it is with some surprise when the door opens
and Will confronts the Nic who looks every bit his biography: federal cop and ex-marine—a type well-known to
Will from his years in the military. He's wearing a gray tee
shirt tucked into faded camouflage pants, his brown hair

cut close. Nic is well over six feet, and while not big, not skinny, either. When he reaches out to shake Will's hand, his grip is firm, the arm sinewy with muscle. His blue eyes bore a hole into Will's skull, either because they are so blue or because the gaze is so direct, Will isn't sure.

They are standing in a living room, decently sized, with smooth hardwood floors and a wall of windows that open out onto a back garden. But baby things have been allowed to accumulate, shrinking and crowding the space. The chairs and coffee table have been pushed aside to make way for a playpen and a bouncy chair, there are piles of blankets on the sofa, and toys are strewn everywhere. Boxes of infant diapers are stacked on top of the bookshelves.

Abby appears from what Will assumes is the bedroom. A blue pouch is fastened to her body by straps that wind around her waist and shoulders. The pouch has a bulge in the center, and Will can just make out a few wisps of blond hair over the top. Even with the mommy apparatus, Abby still manages to look distinctly unmaternal: she's wearing jeans and a hoodie. Her professional look, he realizes, is a kind of costume. Bare of makeup with her peaked, unlined face and dark shadowed eyes, she could almost pass for a teenager; defiant and hard-edged.

"Cal just went to sleep," she says, nodding toward the pouch, "so we should keep our voices down."

"You should put him down in his crib," Nic says. "He'll sleep better lying flat somewhere quiet."

"He's fine here. Anyway, he might wake up if we try to move him and I don't want to deal with that again today."

Will watches, increasingly uncomfortable, as Abby and Nic stare each other down. Finally, Abby says, "Just go, Nicky. It's your night out and Jared's waiting for you at the Short Stop. If Cal starts screaming, it's my problem."

Nic rubs his jaw for a moment. "It's your problem," he says finally. There is no inflection in his tone, but his eyes are hard. "Alrighty then." He opens the door, turning back once to look at Will. "Good to meet you."

"Likewise," Will manages. The door shuts.

The ensuing silence is noisy with unsaid words. Will looks back to Abby. Her eyelids, he now notices, are swollen, from crying or lack of sleep he can't tell, and her hair looks like it could use a good brushing. Will, who has spent the past month racked with guilt and shame, feels something akin to happiness that Abby's personal life has also taken a hit as the result of desires she has indulged in at the expense of her family. But then his brain freezes on the word *desires* and its wildly different application to his own situation, and the schadenfreude evaporates.

Abby stands there for a moment, staring at the closed door and worrying at her locket, sliding it back and forth on its gold chain. Then she looks at Will and says, "Let's talk in the kitchen. I have the case file there."

Will follows her obediently through an open doorway into a small L-shaped room. Appliances line up along the longer wall, and at the shorter end, there is a table with a massive accordion file on it and two chairs by a window. He moves to pull out one of the chairs for her but she shakes her head. "Cal likes motion." She pauses. "At least with me he does." She looks pointedly in the direction of the door that Nic has just walked through, then goes to the refrigerator and opens it. "What can I get you? Jonathan made meat loaf the other day and we still have some leftovers."

"Just a beer if you have one," he says. Will has found eating a difficult task lately, more of an ordeal. No matter how hungry he gets, he can't seem to finish a meal, the food sitting in his stomach like a lead ball. The other night, working late, he'd tried to force down a hamburger at his desk and choked midway through, then thrown it up in the men's bathroom, thankful there was no one still around to hear him retch.

Seeming to sense what he's thinking, Abby says sympathetically, "I have trouble eating when I'm in trial, too. And about to be in trial. It didn't used to be as big of a problem because I wasn't responsible for feeding someone else." She reappears from behind the refrigerator door, holding a bottle of Sam Adams. "Now I'm supposed to be consuming, like, 3,000 calories a day." She roots around in the silverware drawer for a bottle opener, pops the top, and hands the beer to Will.

"How do you manage that?" Will asks. "They can't be from—" He hesitates.

"Calories from alcohol?" Abby smiles. "None of them can be, I know."

Will flushes. "I just meant, it must be hard to eat that much."

Abby picks up a tin can from the counter and holds it up. "Protein shakes." She smiles thinly. "Nic buys me cartons of Ensure. Kind of like a chalky milkshake. This one's vanilla, I think." She tips the can toward her mouth. "The more real food I eat the less of them I have to drink, so that's some incentive. Also, being on a liquid diet makes me feel like an old person."

"Or a baby," Will says without thinking.

"Or a baby," Abby agrees. She puts the can down, wipes her mouth with the back of her hoodie sleeve. "Well, thanks for trekking out here. I wouldn't have asked, but I haven't been home much—"

"It's fine." Will doesn't add that he has no desire to be at home himself. He sits down, pushes the case file aside, and takes a sip of his beer. It is silk-smooth in his mouth, crisp and delicious going down.

Abby pushes her hair off her face, raising her arms to twist it into a knot at the back of her head. The shorter pieces come loose and she shakes them back impatiently. "Shauna starts putting on her case tomorrow, so we should take stock."

"What's the status with Travis's best buddy Mike Ravel?" he says. Ravel had walked out of an Arizona rehab facility earlier that week, and after spending a few days on the streets had voluntarily checked himself back in.

"I think we have to assume he'll be testifying." Abby takes another swig of Ensure and rocks the bundle in the pouch slightly back and forth.

They are silent a moment, considering this. Ravel is not a good witness for them.

"There is an obvious bias," Abby says. "Back when Antoine went to see him in Arizona last month, remember he told us that Ravel came off like someone holding a grudge?"

Will shrugs. "Of course. He loved Travis like a brother and he's angry about what happened to him. I completely understand that."

"But his thinking is so distorted."

Will shakes his head. Military relationships are like a brotherhood, but someone like Abby would never understand. He doubts Nic has ever tried to explain it to her. In Will's experience it's a bad idea to try. *I can't even imagine*, the response always begins, before going on to imagine with clumsy analogies that make Will cringe. *Then don't. Don't imagine*, he always thinks as he nods politely.

"Ravel minimizes Travis's drinking," Abby continues, "and says Luz is to blame for the jealousy. That she caused it by flirting with other guys. That she asked for it."

"Asked for Travis to abuse her, you mean?"

Abby looks at Will. "Do you think that's what it was, abuse?"

"What would you call it?" Will wishes he'd kept the edge out of his voice. For once, he and Abby had actually been getting along.

Abby, her fingertips grazing the baby's hair, does not answer. She says, "We know that Ravel is going to say that Luz put pressure on Travis to change his will. That it was her idea after talking to Estrada and she badgered Travis until he did it."

"Estrada to Luz to Travis out of the mouth of Ravel? That's double—no, that's triple hearsay. Dars won't let it in."

"I disagree. Estrada is unavailable because he's made himself unavailable."

"Even so, we are talking about an attorney-client communication."

"Which is not protected if Luz shared it with Travis."

"Who is not available to testify."

"Because Luz made him unavailable by killing him," Abby points out. "Shauna will argue that what Travis told Ravel comes into evidence under the exception of forfeiture by wrongdoing. And as a last resort, she can say she isn't offering any of it for the truth, only to show Travis's state of mind."

Will says, tightly, "Travis's state of mind isn't what's relevant here. He's not on trial."

"We've made it relevant by raising self-defense. Was Travis Hollis a violent person who dominated and abused his wife or was he a troubled, patriotic soldier with a drinking problem who was manipulated by his conniving wife?" Will starts to say something and Abby holds up her hand.

"I know, it's a stretch to say that Ravel should be allowed to talk about what was going through Travis's mind weeks before the killing. But I know Dars. It's coming in." She brushes back a lock of hair that has fallen across her cheek.

"You know Dars," he repeats flatly.

She turns. "What is that supposed to mean?"

Will takes another pull from the bottle. "One thought that's been running through my mind since last week's debacle is how Luz is supposed to get a fair trial, with you, as you say, knowing this judge like you do."

"I'm relieved to hear there is a thought running through your mind," Abby says sweetly. "For days now you've been like a dead man walking. One thought that's been running through my mind is how Luz is going to get a fair trial with you sitting there like a zombie."

Will rises in his chair as he considers dumping the rest of his beer down the sink and following Nic out the door. Maybe Will can locate Nic at the Short Stop and commiserate with him. They'd certainly have plenty to talk about.

Abby waves him down. "We can't afford to fight. This is about Luz, not us, so let's just focus, use the time we have." She is back to rocking Cal, her eyes half-shut in concentration. "Ravel's testimony is going to be damaging, the only question is how damaging. We need to be prepared. And we need to be on the same page."

That she's right only adds to Will's frustration. He has to put aside the way he feels, they both do. He reseats himself, then says in what he hopes is a conciliatory tone, "With the right questions, we may be able to show that Ravel had his own feelings for Luz. According to her, he did."

"What man can resist her?" Abby's tone is light, but Will doesn't like the way she's looking at him. He changes the subject.

"Have we heard back from Antoine's expert about Travis's emails?"

"No," she says. "Some kind of software issue, something about the hard drive, I don't know. We had to request another copy of it. Antoine thinks we may not get it until in the middle of the trial."

"At which point we're supposed to do what with it? We already have admissibility issues and Shauna will say we're sandbagging her."

"It's not sandbagging if it's newly discovered evidence," Abby says. "Let's just deal with it when we get the report." Her voice has risen, and now there is a stirring from the pouch. Will sees the shape of an elbow jutting against the fabric. Abby resumes her back-and-forth rocking and Will resumes drinking, getting up to set the empty bottle down by the sink. "There's more in the fridge," Abby says, in what Will guesses is her best attempt at a mollifying tone. He nods, not needing to be told twice.

"So," she says, when Will is once again seated at the table, beer in hand. "I was thinking Tuesday for Luz's mock cross-examination. In the conference room like you've been practicing so she's in a familiar space. You'll go through the direct, then I'll cross her. Jonathan has agreed to play Shauna's part in raising objections, Paul can be Dars, and I've invited a few other people from the office to observe and give us their feedback. I think it's just as important to have other people weigh in on your direct as it is to have her practice getting cross-examined."

The panic Will feels is scorched with rage. "You did this without asking me?" He fights to keep his voice in check, his expression in check, but his throat feels constricted and he's starting to sweat.

Abby stares at him. "Without asking you? I thought you'd be happy that I dealt with the logistics of setting it up."

"No," he says, and it is an effort to unlock his jaw. "I'm not happy."

"Clearly." Another long stare and Will looks away.

"This is what our office does," Abby says. "We put our witnesses through the meat grinder. Especially the clients who testify. Maybe it was different in JAG, I don't know, but this is our procedure. We know we did our job when our clients say that dealing with us was worse than facing the actual prosecutor." Abby's voice has gone up again, and there is another shifting in the pouch, accompanied by an ominous mewl.

"What happens with Luz is my responsibility," he says tightly. "You do not interfere."

"This isn't interference. Like I said, it's our office's procedure."

"It's not our procedure," he says. "Hers and mine."

Abby's look is one of amazement, and Will can see that she is starting to feel a panic of her own. "You—you want to put her up there, a nineteen-year-old girl, without letting anyone have a crack at cross-examining her? Without letting anyone—not even me—watch the direct examination before you actually do it in court?"

The mewling from the pouch has become louder, more sustained, and Abby is back to rocking, furiously now. Will stares out of the kitchen window to his right, drinking steadily. Eventually, Cal stops making noise and there is silence, deep and prolonged; Will can hear the clock on the far wall ticking.

"We made a deal," he says, "that day in the car. I expect you to stand by your end of the bargain."

"No," she says fiercely, "we agreed that when it comes

to her testimony you would have the primary relationship with her, not own her. We're a team, Will."

"You are a piece of work, you know that?" Will tries to laugh—both at the truth of this statement and the homely expression, which might as well have come from a ventriloquist dummy on his father's lap—but the sound strangles in his closing throat and he has to stop to drink some more beer. "You don't even know what the word *team* means." He leans across the table and zips his index finger across her face as he raises his voice to imitate her. "That's my problem to figure out. Just file something, I'll deal with it afterward in my own fucked-up secretive way." He fixes her with a hard stare, then settles back in his seat. "You have never wanted me, you have never trusted me, and you have never told me the truth. Not from the beginning and not now. Well, guess what, darlin'? It works both ways." His throat is bone-dry, and he lifts the bottle to his lips again, drinking deeply.

There is silence then, the ticking of the clock so loud Will feels its emanating like a metronome placed next to his eardrum. All the while, Abby continues to rock Cal, who had started up the mewling noises when Will had raised his voice, but has quieted. Finally, she says, almost casually, "Meredith called me last night, looking for you."

"What?" Beads of sweat are sliding down his back now and his throat closes up again.

"You were more than an hour late coming home. She called to see if I knew where you were."

Will trains his eyes on the windowpanes. There are six of them, three on top, three on the bottom, the edges bordered by a coppery-looking metal. The beer that had pooled in his stomach is roiling, and he is afraid he will be sick.

"What did you tell her?"

"That Luz had been late to your meeting. That you were on your way home and she had nothing to worry about."

He feels his body go limp with relief and straightens up, careful to keep his eyes on the window. "That's the right answer."

"Is it?"

There is a scraping sound; startled, Will turns to look at Abby, who is attempting, gingerly, to set herself and the bundle down in the chair across from him. The pouch opens slightly and he can see inside: a halo of corn-silk hair, violet eyelids opening and closing on two startlingly blue eyes. The baby regards him seriously with his father's probing expression.

"Do I have anything to worry about, Will?"

Will finishes off his beer and stands so that he is towering over her; it feels important right now, that he be the one in the higher position to drive home his point. "You want to worry about something, Abby? Why don't you focus on your own relationship. People in glass houses."

"This isn't about me and you know it," she says, and the quiet in her voice unnerves him, though he does his best to pretend it does not.

"No?"

"Listen to me, Will. If we do this right, we can win. We can walk Luz right out of that courtroom."

Will blinks, the realization setting in. That's what she wants more than anything. A walk, which in federal court, is nearly impossible. Some lawyers go their entire careers without a single acquittal. Abby has had her big win, but it has only made her hungrier. He looks at her glassy eyes and realizes he's looking at an addict. How has it taken him so long to see it—and to understand that it's the surest way to get what he wants: to have Luz to himself.

He takes care to keep his voice neutral. "You do your part, I'll do mine." He sets his beer down. "I'll deliver, okay? She and I will deliver. But we need more time. She's fragile. Raking her over the coals is going to ruin all the hard work we've done up to this point."

As he says the words, Will can almost believe they are true. In fact, Will is the fragile one, the tiny cracks spreading wider and deeper every day. It is Will who wouldn't survive five minutes of coal raking.

Cal has started crying. Abby stands up, tries rocking him again, but the mewls are screams now, and she soon gives up and begins unfastening an endless series of straps. Will crosses to the kitchen sink and sets the second empty bottle beside the first. Abby has Cal under one arm now, still tangled up in the harness.

"I'm leaving," he says in the second of quiet that comes with one of Cal's freighted inhales.

"No," Abby says. As she struggles to unwind herself, Cal lets out a series of staccato wails, the sound stabbing Will someplace deep behind his eyes. "Wait," she yells, "let me just feed him and we can finish talking."

"We are finished talking," Will says as the baby pauses to suck in another breath. When he shuts the door behind him, Cal is screaming again.

In full dress uniform, Captain James Aronson walks to the witness stand with his shoulders straight back, standing at attention as the clerk administers the oath. He looks younger than his fifty-one years, his skin unlined except around the eyes and mouth, his small toothbrush mustache and close-cropped hair with just a few glints of silver.

Abby listens as Shauna spends the first ten minutes establishing Aronson's not-insignificant biography and credentials. He enlisted in the air force in 1989, was honorably discharged in 1994, graduated college, and was a happily married civilian father of three managing a Walmart store in St. Louis when 9/11 happened. He joined up again immediately afterward, this time as an officer. After taking a series of exams and obtaining a series of promotions, he was deployed to Germany in 2003. Two tours in Iraq and one Purple Heart later, he became the first African American soldier to be named security forces flight commander at Ramstein Air Base, in charge of hundreds of military personnel and their families.

"As Sergeant Hollis's supervising officer, have you had the opportunity to review his personnel file?" Shauna asks.

"Yes, ma'am."

"Based on your review of that file, can you tell the jury about Sergeant Hollis's military career?"

"Before Sergeant Hollis's deployment to Germany in 2005, he served on an air force base, Fort Irwin, in Barstow, California, as a member of the tactical security fire team. I brought the file with me. May I—"

Shauna smiles, gives an encouraging nod. Aronson takes out a manila folder and removes several stapled sheets of paper.

"The job was to find and neutralize security breaches along the perimeter of the base and to provide—let's see here—brief postings to leadership and distinguished visitors." Aronson looks up, sees that Shauna is waiting, and continues, "After serving in that position for approximately nine months, he was recommended for promotion to MP."

"MP, meaning military police?"

"Correct."

"Can you tell the jury the basis for that promotion?"

"'Sergeant Hollis has demonstrated razor-sharp tactical skill as an assault force member during annual unit force-on-force exercise.'" Aronson is reading directly from someone else's report, double hearsay from a document not in evidence. But Abby isn't saying anything. Popping up with technical objections will annoy the jury and serve no useful purpose; Aronson will just use his own words to repeat what he's already said. None of which is good for them. "'He is committed to career advancement and expeditiously completed security forces career development courses. An articulate, gregarious young airman whose devotion to duty makes him an asset to the air force—promote now.'"

Shauna nods, looking pleased. She asks, "Did you know Staff Sergeant Travis Hollis personally?"

"Yes, ma'am. I've supervised him going on two years."

"In that two-year period, did you come to know him well enough to form an opinion about his character?"

"Yes, ma'am."

"What was that opinion?"

"He was strong, tough, never complained. Followed orders. Did a twelve-month tour in Iraq in 2003, where he served with distinction. Big and burly, but a gentle giant."

Abby writes down the last two words as Shauna shifts gears. "I want to turn your attention to the night of—well, the early morning hours of October 14, 2006. Do you recall receiving a phone call from a woman who identified herself as Mrs. Rivera Hollis, the defendant?"

Aronson inclines his head slightly. "Yes."

"You received the call at 02:46 hours, correct?"

"Correct."

"Why was the defendant calling you?"

"She said that her husband, Staff Sergeant Hollis, was drunk and being loud and waking up their baby. She said something to the effect of 'he can't stay here,' and she was asking that I remove him from the house."

"Did she sound upset?"

"No. She was talking in a normal tone of voice, not yelling. She sounded maybe a little tense."

"Angry?"

"Maybe a little, yes."

Shauna turns to face the jury. "Did she say she was

afraid? That her husband was threatening her or that she was in danger?"

"No, ma'am."

"Did she say the baby was in danger?"

"No, ma'am."

Abby's eyes are on the jurors. They are fixed on Aronson, who answers the questions in an even tone while looking slightly uneasy. A decent man balking at airing someone else's dirty laundry. Far better if he was puffed up with self-importance, enjoying himself at Luz's expense.

Satisfied, Shauna walks back to the podium. "After the defendant told you that the victim—"

Abby objects and Dars overrules her. "When it's your turn, you can use a different word."

"After the defendant told you that the victim was being too loud to stay in the house, what did you say?"

"I said, 'Well, what is he doing exactly?' Because I was trying to find out, you know, what the situation was."

"What did the defendant say?"

"She didn't say anything. There was silence, and then some kind of thumping and I could hear kind of a muffled sound, like maybe she had put her hand over the receiver. And I—I didn't know what to think at that point. I was— well, I was getting concerned, and I said, 'Put Hollis on the line. Put him on the line now.'"

"Did Sergeant Hollis get on the line?"

"Not to speak to me directly. I heard a sound, though, like heavy breathing."

"What did it sound like?"

Aronson leans forward, puckering his lips and blowing slowly into the microphone. Shauna makes a continuing motion and Aronson does it a second time, then a third before resuming his default upright position.

"Then what?"

"I said, 'Hollis? Hollis? This is Captain Aronson. What is going on there?'"

"Did the victim respond?" Shauna asks.

"Not to me directly, but yes, he spoke." Aronson hesitates. "He used a profanity."

Dars leans in, caterpillar eyebrows drawn together, an unmistakable gleam in his eye. "What profanity did he use, exactly?"

Now Aronson looks distinctly uncomfortable. "Your Honor, I'm not sure it is appropriate—"

Dars shakes his head firmly. "This is a murder trial, not ladies' social tea, Captain Aronson. Answer my question."

"He said—" Aronson looks once more at Dars, then apologetically back at Shauna "—'you stupid cunt.'"

The gym teacher puts a hand to her mouth and one of the stay-at-home mom's eyes go wide.

Shauna does an excellent job of looking unfazed. "Did the phone call continue?"

"No. It was cut off. There was a smashing sound—and then nothing. Not even a dial tone."

"Did you try calling back?"

"Yes, several times, but there was nothing. I got out of bed, pulled on a pair of pants and a tee shirt. A sweatshirt, too. It was fall at that point, turning cold. I grabbed my car keys off the table and my wife, she's been up long enough to hear some of my side of the conversation and she asks, 'Where are you going?' and I say, 'To Sergeant Hollis's house to see about a possible domestic situation.' Then I got in my vehicle and I drove over there."

"How long did it take you to get in your car and drive from your house to the Hollises'?"

"I was in my vehicle approximately ninety seconds after

the call was over. From there, it was about a six-minute drive."

"So that would get you there at approximately 2:53–2:54 a.m.?"

"Approximately."

"Okay, tell us what you saw and heard when you pulled up to the house."

"The lights were on in the foyer area. I could hear a baby crying inside and a woman screaming. There were a lot of sounds. I pulled out my phone and called to dispatch law enforcement patrols. I advised my commanding officer and all police patrols that we had a domestic incident in progress, possible injuries, dispatch immediately. And as I—as I am doing that, I'm running up to the house. The door was slightly open but there was a weight against it when I pushed on it and I just barely got inside."

"What did you see?"

"Mrs. Rivera Hollis. She was sitting down, her back was up against the door and she was holding Sergeant Hollis's head in her lap and she was screaming."

"What was she screaming?"

"I don't think it was words."

"Was she attempting to render first aid or help the victim in any way?"

"No."

"Then what?"

"I felt this squishing where my feet were. I looked down and I was standing in a pool of blood."

"How big was it?"

"Maybe twelve inches across and twice that length and about half an inch deep." Aronson gestures with his hands. "The blood was coming out of Sergeant Hollis's chest—pumping out onto the floor and spreading out. It was very dark blood and it was starting to get thick, kind of like a gel."

"Did you see any weapons?"

"Next to the body, in the pool of blood, there was a steak knife."

"What did you do?"

"I kicked it away with my foot."

"Away from whom?"

"Mrs. Rivera Hollis."

"With the court's permission, at this time the government would ask that Exhibit 1 be marked and placed before the witness." Dars inclines his head and Shauna withdraws a black-handled kitchen knife, wrapped several times in plastic and tagged. She walks solemnly to the witness box and hands the knife to Aronson, blade down.

"Captain Aronson, can you describe the object you are holding."

"It's a steak knife, with a five-inch blade."

"What is on the knife?"

"Blood. All over the blade and on part of the black handle."

"Is this the knife you found in a pool of the victim's blood that you kicked with your foot so that Mrs. Rivera Hollis could not grab it?"

"Objection."

"Overruled."

Aronson puts down the knife. "Yes."

"Okay. After you removed the weapon from the defendant's reach, what did you do?"

"I turned so I was facing her, facing him. It was obvious just by looking that Sergeant Hollis was severely injured, possibly dying, but there was also Mrs. Rivera Hollis and the baby I had to think about. The baby was still crying but I didn't know where the baby was. There was so much blood, Mrs. Rivera Hollis's shirt and lap were soaked in it, and I asked her, 'Are you hurt, is the baby hurt?' She shook her head to indicate no. She was still screaming, though, not moving, so I half picked her up and kind of pushed her over to one side so I could get to Hollis. I pulled out my cell phone to call 911 and she shook her head again, like for me to put it away, and then I could actually hear the ambulance, right then, so I knew they were coming—that she must have called them already. And a few seconds after that, I could hear the police sirens and I knew my officers were almost there, as well. I figured I had maybe one minute, two minutes to do what I could."

"What did you do?"

"I turned Sergeant Hollis over on his side so he didn't choke on his own blood. I felt for his pulse. There was one, but it was faint. I kept my fingers on his wrist and I checked his airway. It was hard for me to hear over the screaming and I told Mrs. Rivera Hollis that she had to—I said something to the effect of 'You have to stop screaming.' When she didn't, I yelled, 'Luz,' real loud, and she looked at me and went quiet. She tried to get up, and I said, 'Stay there,' also in a very loud voice."

Abby feels something brush against her sleeve. A note from Will. She scans it. *How did he know her first name?*

Abby looks up quickly as Aronson continues his answer. "To my mind, this was a crime scene and she, quite possibly, had committed a crime. I didn't want her doing anything that might compromise the crime scene. I didn't want her to destroy evidence. I was pretty sure by that point the baby was okay, just crying, and anyway I didn't want her picking up the baby covered in blood."

Abby reads the note a second time.

Shauna is nodding approvingly at Aronson, her arms crossed over her chest. "You were saying that you turned your attention to the victim?"

"Yes, but you have to understand, this is all happening in seconds. Every action is very, very fast. At this point I had been in the house maybe under a minute. I bent my ear to Sergeant Hollis's mouth and I could hear him breathing but it was very slow, labored. And as I am listening, the breathing changes into a—almost like a snoring sound. I say to Mrs. Rivera Hollis, 'How many times was he stabbed?' and she just kind of stares at me, so I yell her name again, 'Luz,' real loud, and I repeat my question."

Shauna nods, turns a page in her binder.

Abby looks at Aronson. A commander in charge of hundreds of MPs and their families. *How did he know her first name?* She turns the note over, scribbles a few sentences and hands the paper to Luz, who reads it, then slowly begins to write out her response.

"What happened after you repeated your question to Mrs. Rivera Hollis asking how many times she had stabbed her husband?" Shauna asks.

"She tells me, 'In the chest, one time,' and so I find the wound and I start applying pressure to stop the bleeding."

"Were you able to stop the bleeding?"

"No. And while that's happening, I lose his pulse. I can't feel it anymore. I keep pressing down thinking maybe I'm wrong, but still nothing. And then, he makes a rattling sound. At that point, I grabbed hold of his hand and I held it."

"Why did you do that?"

"I wanted Sergeant Hollis to know, to the extent that he could know anything, that he wasn't alone. And I knew— from my experience, I knew it was very important that I be able to say to his mother that someone was holding his hand when he took his last breath."

There is a sudden silence in the courtroom, like they have all momentarily stopped breathing. Luz has dropped the pen. Her face is white, her small shoulders turned inward, her dark eyes wide and unfocused. Abby looks at the jury. Several of them—men included— are moist-eyed. Even Abby, who has grown to despise Travis Hollis the more she learns about him, feels a pang. She hears sobbing behind her, turns and sees Travis's mother and sisters, holding each others' hands. What if it were Cal? She would murder Luz herself, with her bare hands, make what Luz did to Travis look surgical by comparison.

Shauna turns another page in her binder with a smart snap, and the moment evaporates, the regular back-and-forth of question-and-answer reestablished, and Abby can almost hear her own thoughts click immediately back into place as she returns to the notes she has jotted down on her legal pad. "You said that the police and the emergency medical technicians were en route?" Shauna asks.

"Yes. Basically, right after Sergeant Hollis stopped breathing, two EMTs came in followed by about ten military police. It was chaos, all these people packed into a narrow hallway, so I needed to take control of the situation."

"What did you do?"

"I briefed the EMTs on the victim's condition and sent the female one to the baby's room. She came out very fast, handed off the baby to one of the MPs. The EMTs had a gurney with them and I directed two of my men to help lift Sergeant Hollis onto the gurney. They had him out of the house in less than a minute with the sirens going.

"While that was happening, I told two of my guys to

check Mrs. Rivera Hollis for injuries, then take her to the hospital for a full exam. I did see that a lamp had been broken and there was glass on the floor and I didn't know if she had gotten cut or maybe hurt some other way."

"Did the defendant comply with your officers?"

"It wasn't that she was resisting, it was just that she was so hysterical it was hard to get her to listen to anyone." Now, Abby thinks, would be the time for Aronson to look at Luz, to make it clear to the jury that the bowed, silent wraith seated at the defense table is the same blood-drenched banshee he just described, but he doesn't. He has not once looked at Luz during his testimony.

"What did you do then?"

"I went over to her—she was standing up at that point, but in more or less the same place that I'd moved her to—and I used her name again, real loud. Once she was focused on me and quieter, I explained what was going to happen. That she was going to the hospital to be checked. She didn't want to go, she wanted to stay with the baby. So I explained, you know, that she couldn't do that right now."

Shauna says, "You couldn't let her clean up, because her clothing and anything on her skin was evidence?"

"That's correct. So I asked her, 'Is there anyone, a female friend, another army wife on the base that I can call to take care of the baby while you are gone?' And she said, 'No, there's no one.'"

"The defendant did not have one friend on the base that you could call?"

Luz hands the note back to Abby. Line after line of girlish cursive. Abby starts reading, half listening as Aronson answers, "That's what she told me. I told her, 'Okay, Sergeant Ruiz will take care of your baby.' That was the female MP that was holding her. And I asked was there formula or something in the house that we could use and she said there was formula in the kitchen cabinet to the left of the sink. She explained the measurements, and I sent Ruiz in there to mix up a bottle." He shakes his head. "I— Never mind."

Shauna nods encouragingly. "Go ahead."

"It's just, I remember thinking how strange it was that all of a sudden, Luz was so calm and precise, down to the teaspoon, it had to be exactly right." Aronson is still shaking his head as if this discordant fact is only now seeping into his consciousness.

"What did you do next?"

"I checked Mrs. Rivera Hollis for injuries. I didn't find any."

Shauna raised an eyebrow. "Any injuries at all? Bruising? Swelling? Lacerations?"

"Not that I could see. I relayed the information about her condition to the officers and directed two of them to take her to the hospital. After they left, I called OSI."

"What is OSI?"

"It's the Office of Special Investigations, kind of like the FBI for the military. I was put through to an agent and she advised me to secure the crime scene, that she would be there immediately."

"Was that the end of your dealings with Mrs. Rivera Hollis?"

"Yes. I turned my attention to the hallway, to supervise the collection of the evidence by the men under my command."

"What was collected?"

"May I consult my evidence report?"

Dars nods to allow Shauna to approach with it, and Aronson flips through a few pages. "The knife, first of all. The glass shards of a vase that had been broken. There were cardboard moving boxes full of clothes at one end of the hallway. Three of them. A search of the house was conducted, and other items were removed from the baby's room, including a phone that had been smashed." Shauna stops after each object is named to hold it up for Aronson to identify, then moves it into evidence. Even the ordinary items have a sinister cast: some of the jagged pieces of the broken vase are gummed together by what looks like red gelatin, and the knife, now unpackaged and on full display, is like something out of a horror movie, caked to the handle in rust-colored blood.

"What about your clothes, Captain Aronson?"

"They were burned."

Tuesday, March 20, 2007
11:15 a.m.
United States District Court
for the Central District of California

Twenty minutes. It is all Abby is allowed. And it's a gift
from Dars, who had called a recess to take what he made
clear was an important judicial phone call.

Twenty minutes to try to get to the bottom of something she should have known months ago. Abby could have
killed Luz, but now the person she wants to kill is Will. As
soon as he shuts the door to the witness room, before either Abby or Luz has a chance to sit down, the words are
out of his mouth.

"Did you sleep with him? Did you?" He is staring at Luz,
his face drained of color. Luz, who is putting her phone
back in her purse after texting Maria Elena to bring over
Cristina, looks up, startled.

As if that were the most important fact—or even a helpful one. Thank God the room—windowless and big enough
only for a table and a few chairs—is soundproof. Abby

wants to slap Will across the face. "You need to leave," she says, as calmly as she can manage. "Right now."

He starts to say something, and she holds up her breast pump. "I have to do this."

"No, you don't."

Abby ignores him and focuses on getting set up. She places the machine on the table, plugs the electrical cord into an outlet, and connects the tubes to the suction cups. She turns to face him as she removes her jacket. "I am going to take off my shirt and bra," she says. Some men in Abby's office would have told her to turn around and face the wall—no fucking way were they going anywhere. But not Will. Whatever it is he has done, he remains Will: too modest, prudish even, to fathom staying in a room where his cocounsel's breasts would be exposed. He turns and walks out without a word, leaving Abby and Luz alone.

Abby undresses from the waist up and hooks up the breast pump. Almost immediately, there's a knock on the door behind her and Abby motions to Luz to get it. Behind her, she hears a few muffled words in Spanish, inhales the baby shampoo smell of Cristina. It makes her long for Cal. If only she'd known about this break, she could have asked Nic to bring him. She wishes she was holding him right now. Because she loves that time with him and because she has come to believe that Cal is like her secret weapon. The power that comes with the knowledge that she could create and sustain his life pulses through her when she is with him. It makes her feel invincible. Which is not at all the way she feels now.

Instead, Abby is in a baby-feeding face-off with her client—the Good Mom/Bad Mom tableau so bizarre and grotesque she wants to laugh hysterically, but it's not funny. Instead, Abby forces herself to wait until Cristina latches on, then says to Luz, "I thought I told you never to lie to me again."

Luz has her eyes on Cristina. "You never asked me anything about him."

Abby takes a deep breath, but ends up yelling anyway as she slams her hand down on the table. "Do you think this is a fucking game of twenty questions? How the fuck were we supposed to know to ask you if you had an intimate—" Cristina begins crying and Abby breaks off abruptly, trying to gain some control over her language and lower her voice. "How were we supposed to know to ask you if you were—were—close to Captain Aronson?"

Luz resettles Cristina, then looks up, meeting her gaze. "What is it that you want? For me to answer his question?" She lifts her chin slightly in the direction of the door Will had exited.

Abby stops, caught up short. Stalling, she says, "What I need to know is exactly how many times you talked to Captain Aronson about what was going on between you and Travis. As specific as you can remember."

"I wrote that down," Luz says, "on the paper."

"Everything?"

"Do you want me to answer his question?" Luz repeats. "Because you didn't ask me that."

Rapidly, Abby tries to calculate. It had to be true, because there is no other reason why Aronson would have hidden these communications from the government. Extramarital affairs are a criminal offense under the Uniform Code of Military Justice; Aronson wouldn't just be out on his ass, he might be charged—never mind the effect on his wife and three kids.

What's true, though, isn't necessarily helpful. From the beginning, Abby and Will have made it their mission to portray Luz as a victim. Victims are pure. Victims are innocent. Women who entice married men to cheat, women who cheat themselves, those women are whores, and whores are guilty. And Luz is at a double disadvantage. The hotheaded Latina stereotype Antoine brought up is alive in the courtroom. There is no margin for error; and although the law says that Luz is entitled to the benefit of the doubt, she is unlikely to get it. Not a brown girl accused of killing a white man. Not with a knife through the heart and not a scratch on her.

"No," Abby says finally.

"Why not?"

"Because I don't think it would be helpful."

Luz nods. "Mr. Estrada told me you would say that."

Abby looks at Luz in surprise. "What?"

"He called me," Luz says, "after Will came to see him to get my file. He asked me some questions about my case. I told him about the manslaughter deal, that I wasn't taking it. He explained to me about the law of self-defense."

Abby holds up her hand, trying to ignore the whining of the breast pump. "What does Mr. Estrada telling you about the law have to do with—"

"He asked me about you," Luz says, speaking over her. "I guess he knows who you are. That you had a big case once and—" she shrugs "—I don't know. I told him you came back early for me. To try my case."

Abby swallows. "What did he say?"

"That you are a holy terror." Luz takes in Abby's shocked expression and smiles slightly. "He said that you would fight like hell for me."

"That's right," Abby says, angry all over again, "and you are making that very difficult by lying to me. Is it because—is it because you think—" she breaks off. "Will told me you disapprove of me. Of—" she gestures to the tubes and cones and cloth velcroed to her upper body "—my choices."

Luz stares at her blankly. "Why would I disapprove?"

*Because you think I'm a bad mother.* Abby opens her mouth to say the words and closes it as Luz says, "You came back for me, right?"

Abby feels her throat close up and swallows again, hard, against the sudden ache in her throat.

"Mr. Estrada told me that there are certain things about my case that wouldn't help you in the fight," Luz goes on. "Some things that would be better off with just him and me knowing." She looks down at Cristina, smoothing the dark hair on her head. "I trust him," she says. "But, he said in the end you would see what is best. That you would understand the situation. He told me to trust you. So if you want to know those things now, I will tell you. Do you want to know?"

What Abby wouldn't give right now for ten more minutes. Fifteen. To think. To digest. To plan. But no, Luz is waiting for her and the clocking is ticking. Slowly, Abby shakes her head. "Just answer the questions I ask you."

Now back in front of the jury, Abby makes sure to smile and exude calm.

"Good morning, Captain Aronson."

"Good morning, counsel."

"You told the jury that when you asked my client if there was someone you could call for her—a friend—that she said no?"

"That's correct."

"But there was someone—there had been someone she was calling all along, right?"

Abby sees a flash of fear in Aronson's eyes, but he inclines his head politely. "I'm not understanding your question."

"Mrs. Rivera Hollis had been calling you to confide the problems she was having with her husband."

Shauna stands, and without looking at her, Abby holds out her hand, five fingers spread. "I haven't asked my question." She turns back to Aronson. "Would records from your cell phone show calls between you and Mrs. Rivera Hollis in the months leading up to the night of Sergeant Hollis's death?"

Shauna is speaking now, objections flying every which way. Assumes facts not in evidence, badgering, speculation.

"Overruled." Dars, leaning forward in his leather chair, is clearly keen to get the story himself. "Did you talk to the defendant on the phone about her husband on other occasions?"

"I— Yes." Aronson has paled visibly and his hands, which had been resting on his lap, now grip each other.

"How many times?" Dars has now apparently decided to take over the questioning.

"I'm not—I'm not sure."

"Alright, ballpark then. More than ten?"

"I— Yes."

Dars raises his eyebrows and nods at Abby, her signal to resume. The courtroom has gone very quiet, the row of reporters leaning forward like greyhounds at the starting line; the jurors, to a person, staring fixedly at Aronson.

Abby picks up Luz's note. "You also met with my client, alone, on several occasions?"

"Sidebar, Your Honor." Shauna isn't yelling, but in the stillness of the courtroom her voice clangs.

Dars beckons them forward as he steps down, joining

Abby, Will, and Shauna in a tight circle around the court reporter.

"This is trial by ambush," Shauna says, visibly struggling to keep her voice at a whisper. "Those cell phone records and witness statements should have been turned over weeks ago."

"We don't have cell phone records or witness statements," Abby says.

"I imagine not." Dars crosses his arms, the sleeves of his black robe closing like drapes. "No need, is there, Ms. Rosenberg, when you can bluff, knowing your client has already told you everything."

*More like a client who tells me nothing until the last possible moment on instructions from yet another lawyer trying to seize control of this case.* And had she known, Abby damn sure would have gotten those records as corroboration knowing she would never have to turn them over on a hostile witness. She can't help but look over at Will, who is determinedly not meeting her gaze.

Shauna isn't giving up. "She can't hide behind the attorney-client privilege to make baseless insinuations of some kind of—of improper sexual relationship."

Dars looks at Abby like she's delivered an unexpected present. "Is that what you're doing?"

Abby keeps her eyes on Dars. "I'm not insinuating anything. What matters are the communications between my client and Captain Aronson about Sergeant Hollis."

"And that's hearsay," Shauna says.

"I'm not offering it for the truth. It goes to my client's state of mind."

"Her state of mind weeks or months before she killed her husband—how is that relevant—"

"You've made it relevant," Abby snaps. "You've argued from the beginning that this was premeditated—"

But Dars has heard enough. "The government's objection is overruled."

"Your Honor—" Shauna starts.

Dars wags a stubby finger in Shauna's face. *Bad girl.* "This is your mess, counsel. How in God's name you failed to ask your own witness these questions yourself is beyond my comprehension. Now step back."

When everyone has resumed their places, Dars says, "Ms. Rosenberg, please continue."

"Did you meet with Mrs. Rivera Hollis alone?"

"Yes." Aronson looks like someone who has just been told he has brain cancer after complaining of a mild headache: his eyes are glazed with shock and his voice is flat. From now on, Abby hopes, he will go blindly wherever she leads him.

"Captain, you described Sergeant Hollis to the jury as a quote 'gentle giant'?"

Aronson blinks. "I— Yes."

"That's not how Mrs. Rivera Hollis described him to you, was it?"

"No."

"She told you when he got drunk she became afraid of him?"

"It wasn't a lot of times."

"That's not my question," Abby says, keeping her voice polite. *Oh, look, you spilled your milk.* "Do you need me to repeat it?"

"I— No. I mean, yes, that's what she said."

"My client was afraid because when Sergeant Hollis became drunk he hit her and kicked her?"

"Yes."

"My client was afraid because when Sergeant Hollis became drunk he would get on top of her and the only way she could get him off her was by submitting to have sex with him?"

"Yes."

"She asked for your help?"

Aronson's voice is low, so low Abby can see the jurors leaning forward as they strain to hear. "She told me not to talk to him about it. That it would make it worse."

Abby ignores this. "You told her you would get Sergeant Hollis counseling."

"I did get him counseling. Anger management."

"It didn't work, did it?"

"Objection, calls for an expert opinion."

"Sustained. Next question."

"When my client called you in the early morning hours of October 14, asking you to remove Travis Hollis from their home, that was a highly unusual event, wasn't it?"

"Yes."

"At the same time, given what you knew, you weren't entirely surprised, were you?"

Aronson passes a hand over his eyes. "I didn't think it would come to that."

"Within two minutes, you were in your car, headed over to the Hollises' house, within six minutes, you were inside the house itself because you sped and ran red lights to get there. That's eight minutes, total, from getting the call to getting inside the house."

"Yes."

"You were concerned," Abby repeats and lightly stresses the last word, "not just by what Mrs. Rivera Hollis told you, but by the nasty names Travis Hollis called his wife before he took the phone out of her hand and smashed it?"

Aronson holds her gaze. "Yes."

"You did not make a call to any law enforcement officer under your command, though, until you arrived at the scene, did you?"

"No."

"And you didn't think to call 911 until you were inside the house, did you?"

"No."

"You were hoping you could handle the situation yourself, weren't you?"

Aronson clenches his jaw. "Listen, I have dealt with more than fifty domestic disturbance calls over my career. Never did I call in any help until I assessed the situation myself. Not one ended up like this. If I had known—"

Abby cuts him off, "You let eight minutes go by before you called anyone for backup. A lot can happen in eight minutes, can't it, Captain?"

"Objection, vague."

"A domestic confrontation, that you knew was escalating, it can turn dangerous, even deadly, in eight minutes?"

"I didn't know she was going to kill him," Aronson says. His eyes are hard now, glittering.

"What you knew," Abby responds pleasantly, "was that my teenage client and her infant daughter were alone in a house with an angry drunk more than twice her size who had just called her a stupid cunt and smashed the phone."

"Objection."

"Overruled."

"I was concerned, like I said, counselor."

"Concerned," Abby repeats. She smiles. "Mrs. Rivera Hollis was so fortunate to have the benefit of your judgment and advice."

"Your Honor—"

"Withdrawn." Abby nods at Dars. "I'm done."

"Redirect?" Dars inquires.

Shauna, not answering, strides to the podium. She has started talking before Abby has managed to sit down.

"I'll keep this brief," she says. "Did the defendant ever discuss with you the possibility of getting a restraining order, or leaving her husband, or filing for divorce?"

"No."

"Why not?"

"Objection," Abby says, "she's asking the witness to speculate."

"Do you know?" Dars asks Aronson.

Aronson turns to Dars. "I asked her that myself, so yes."

"Overruled."

"When you asked the defendant why, if she was so afraid, she wasn't pursuing any of these remedies, what did she say?"

"She said Sergeant Hollis would never let her go. That he would never let the baby go. That it was till death do us part, like in their marriage vows."

"What else did the defendant tell you?"

Abby feels an acrid taste in her mouth and a growing sense of dread. While she had her twenty minutes with Luz, Shauna had her twenty minutes with Aronson. There is a danger coming at her from this witness that she won't be able to control because she hasn't had enough time to figure out what it is. What terrible thing had Luz not told her because Abby had not thought to draw it out? *Just answer the questions I ask you.*

She stands, wobbling slightly. "The question is vague, Your Honor."

"Rephrase, Ms. Gooden."

Shauna says, "What else did the defendant tell you about Sergeant Hollis?"

"She said that the only way to get away from him would be to kill him."

"Hello, Abby."

The voice comes out of the dark, and it is all she can do not to scream. Files fly from her hands and hit the floor in the seconds it takes before the motion sensor flicks on, washing her office in fluorescence.

Jonathan is seated in her office chair, rocking back slightly, his fingers steepled under his chin.

"Jesus Christ." Abby sags against the wall for a moment, letting the adrenaline drain from her body. She stares at her best friend, trying to summon up anger, but she's too exhausted and her voice comes out flat. "Get out of my chair."

Jonathan comes over to her side of the room as she bends down to pick up the files.

"I'd offer to help but—"

"You'll make it worse."

He smiles. "I figured you'd say that."

The piles reassembled, she moves ostentatiously around him to drop them on her desk, which is its usual disorganized mess. Stacks of other files in no particular order, unopened mail toppling the inbox that Cherise, Abby's secretary, insists on keeping there in the hopes that Abby will one day be shamed by it. Abby sits down in her faux leather chair, heart still hammering, and stares at Jonathan across the desk.

"Sorry to startle you," Jonathan says. "But, no returned calls or texts for two days now? I needed some way to get your attention. Are you holding a grudge from—" He waves a hand.

"No, you were right. It was a horrible idea." She leans back in her chair for a moment and closes her eyes. "But I'm in trial, remember?"

"Yes," he says, "about that."

"What about it?"

"Come on, now, Abby. It's me."

She opens her eyes, stares back at him blankly, not a muscle twitching in her face.

He smiles. "Your lawyer."

"Ah, so this is a privileged conversation." Abby is careful to keep her tone neutral. The last thing she wants to do is talk to anyone about what is happening in Luz's case. About what is happening between Abby and Will, the two of them like drunk drivers fighting for control of the wheel as the car swerves on a switchback. If she tells Jonathan, it will be real.

"Yes, it is." Jonathan has stopped smiling. He leans forward, elbows on her desk. "Now why don't you tell me what the fuck is going on. I was in court this morning before I left to go to your house for my mannying duties."

"Your what?"

"My male nanny duties. With your son. Who is fine by the way, thank you for asking."

"That's good, and I—I am so appreciative," Abby says, trying to make the words sound meaningful. At the mention of Cal, she feels a familiar ache in her breasts, wants nothing more than to be alone with him in the bathtub. "I was on my way home, you know, before you ambushed me."

Jonathan shakes his head. "As I was saying. Based on what I saw in court, there is no way that either you or Shauna saw what was coming with Aronson."

"That was a speed bump," Abby says, her mind sticking with the car metaphor. "But everything's okay now. Everything is fine."

"God, you are a crap liar."

"I'm not lying."

"Really? Then why ever would it be," Jonathan asks, lifting an eyebrow, "that you were doing internet searches earlier this afternoon for a California state bar rule about what happens when attorneys have sex with their clients?"

Abby looks at her desktop screen, which has gone black. She hits the return key but there's nothing to see except the screen-saved picture of Cal in a striped onesie, eyes open wide as saucers, a turquoise seen only in the most faraway and uncorrupted of oceans. She looks back at Jonathan. "You went on my computer—"

"I searched your browser history," he says. "You should make a habit of erasing that, by the way. Easy to do and prevents, well, snooping. The government says they are going to give us password-protected desktops any day now, but I wouldn't hold my breath. Until then—" he lifts his shoulders "—I suggest you be more careful."

"You motherfucker," she says, but she can't help the admiring tone that creeps into her voice.

"What are you going to do?"

"Do about?" She opens her eyes as wide as Cal's.

"You know what."

"Nothing," she says. "I am going to do nothing." She pauses. "And I don't know. Not for sure."

"You are such a bad liar it is almost comical. Do you have any idea how many tells you have? You're like a little kid." Jonathan shakes his head.

"I'm not lying," she insists, knowing that she is only proving his point. She can feel the heat spreading from her face to her neck and she can't meet his eyes.

"You need to disclose this to Paul. He'll pull Will off the case. Probably, he'll have to report him, which is unfortunate, but not your problem. Will made his bed, so to speak."

"No. Dars will have to declare a mistrial."

"And you think this case is trying so well? After today?"

What she thinks is that the case is completely out of control. But that is just as true for Shauna as it is for Abby, and as a general rule, defense attorneys cope far better than prosecutors with chaos. Because of whom they represent and under what circumstances—outgunned, out-resourced, and on the wrong side of the facts—people like Abby have to have plans B, C, and D through Z. Whereas prosecutors like Shauna have only one plan, and more often than not, they cannot cope when forced to deviate. Shauna is more unflappable than most, but Abby doesn't doubt that she nearly shat her pantsuit today in court.

"I need Will. He has to do the direct examination of Luz. He has to be the one to protect her on cross. It won't work if we switch up, not now." She doesn't add that she's never actually seen Will do either of these things because he has prevented her. For all she knows, Will has made as much of a hash of that job as he clearly had with Aronson. But her instincts tell her the opposite. She believes what she said to him that day in the car on the way back from Dr. Cartwright's office. She believes what he told her that night in her kitchen. Will can embody Travis. She can't. And that is a powerful visual. The extreme physical mismatch will drive home the mortal stakes in a way that words alone could never express.

Jonathan says, "That's quite a gamble, isn't it?"

"Everything's a gamble in trial, you know that."

"What about Estrada? What if he breaks?"

"He won't." This Abby has real reason to believe, and for a moment, she is sorely tempted to confide everything. To say that, in fact, she has just come from seeing Estrada in the jail. But it's too risky, even with Jonathan. Instead, she tells the part of the story she can give up easily. By tomorrow, everyone will know anyway.

"Maria Elena had a stroke late this afternoon," she says. "She's in the ICU at King."

Now it is Jonathan's turn to stare. "A stroke?" he repeats. "And she's at MLK? They'll kill her if she wasn't going to die already anyway."

That had been Abby's first thought, too. Martin Luther King Jr.-Harbor Hospital, built in the '60s to treat the city's poorest residents, was under federal investigation for a myriad of problems, including abnormally high mortality rates from routine procedures and sanitation that regularly flunked city standards. It was widely rumored to be headed for closure.

"It happened while Father Abelard was helping her into the car after court," she says. "I guess the EMTs thought it was closest."

"Is she going to make it?"

"I don't think so."

"Is Dars going to give you the day off tomorrow?"

"I don't think so."

"How is Luz?"

Not knowing how to answer that question, Abby gives logistical information instead. "She's at the hospital with Father Abelard and other members of her church. Cristina is with her, of course." And Will, she adds silently. On the phone two hours ago, Will had told her little except that the prognosis was poor and that yes, he would make sure he and Luz were in court in the morning if Dars demanded it. It was while Will was talking that Abby had made the decision to go see Estrada at the jail, a decision she had not shared with him. Not sharing, as a general principle, seemed best right now. With all the men in her life. She thinks briefly of Nic, then firmly shuts him out of her mind before the guilt can smother her.

Jonathan watches her for a moment, his head inclined slightly. "How are things with Nic?"

His mind reading scares her. Jonathan is the reason why she doesn't have many close friends. "Fine. Everything is fine."

"That's another lie."

She doesn't bother denying it. On her phone are six texts from Nic.

When are you coming home?

You need to come home now.

Right now.

Cal needs you.

You can't pretend he doesn't exist.

And then, WHERE ARE YOU???

All unanswered. There are probably more now. She hasn't turned her phone back on since leaving the jail. Dars had kept them late and the last text had arrived as she was headed out to see Estrada. Abby had planned to go home immediately, was in fact on her way to the car when the call had come in from Will and with it a decision that could not be delayed. She had come back to her office just now only to drop off the files and then—Jonathan. With any luck, and God knows she is due for some, both Nic and Cal will be asleep when she gets back to the house.

"You act like nothing's different." Jonathan's voice is cold. "Cal isn't some kind of appendage you can remove and reattach when it's convenient for you."

Abby stands up, putting her purse back over her shoulder, trying to keep her voice level. "You have no right to lecture me about my parenting skills."

Jonathan stands, too. "Why? Because I'm gay and childless?"

"Don't throw that in my face. If you and your rich screenwriter boyfriend want a baby, you can go out and buy one."

"Right, because that's so easy. People are just dying to give their kids away to two gay men. We can't even get legally married."

"You don't want to, is my point."

"Actually, we do—on both counts. We put in an adoption application about six months ago. Average waiting time for gay couples is three years to infinity."

She opens her mouth, then closes it. Jonathan had been over the moon about her pregnancy, had been the first person to visit at the hospital. She thinks of the look on his face every time she puts Cal in his arms, like it's some kind of holy privilege. This is a sucker punch, but she should have seen it coming.

"Don't make this about you, Jonathan. And don't you dare pull this bad mother bullshit on me. I am so sick of you, of all of you, and your 1950s misogyny. I am doing my job. My very fucking important job."

"You have an infant. And you act like you can put him—and his father—on a shelf until your almighty case is over and that they'll still be sitting there in the same place like two stuffed animals when you decide to come back and start playing with them again. They won't be, Abby."

It occurs to her with a chill that Jonathan might actually be talking about her to Nic. Jonathan hadn't hesitated to interfere in similar ways in the past when he was worried about her. But Nic's not a talker. And anyway, she would never give Jonathan the satisfaction of asking. She heads for the door. "I have to go."

Jonathan crosses his arms over his chest. "Why did you have him?"

She stops, her hand closing over the doorknob. "What?"

"Why didn't you terminate the pregnancy?"

*Unplanned, but not unwanted.* That is what her mother had said about Abby and her brother, no matter that they had turned her life upside down. It had been doable, or, at least, manageable, until her husband's untimely death—at which point Roz was broke and alone with three-year-old twins. She left her PhD program at UCLA, never to return.

Roz had made the best of it, was now a well-respected high school principal for an underserved public high school. Abby knew her mother derived great satisfaction from her work. But Roz had never become an art history professor in an ivory tower, spellbinding eager grad students with pixelated slides of Renaissance paintings and enjoying sabbaticals in Italy. In high school, Abby found a draft of her mother's dissertation on Caravaggio in a cardboard box on a high shelf in the closet. It had been written on a typewriter, faded red-inked notes in the margins in Roz's careful script. Flipping through the yellowed pages, Abby had felt a stab of pity followed by revulsion. She had shoved the box back into its dusty place, wanting immediately to rid herself of the knowledge of her mother's beloved dead thing.

She turns around slowly to face him. "When I found out, I was in denial. I didn't know what to do so I didn't do anything except pretend it wasn't happening. And then Rayshon was murdered and I— It did something to me." She had made the mistake of looking at the crime scene photos, one in particular now embedded in her brain. A close-up of Rayshon lying in a McDonald's parking lot, brain matter oozing like the insides of a rotten pumpkin after taking three shots to the head. The grief had been like drowning; every time she opened her mouth for air she breathed water instead. In the end, it had all been for nothing.

Without Cal, Abby would have kept drinking until she was dead or in the hospital. Forget feeling a sense of responsibility: the tiny seed in her body made her so sick she couldn't. Cal's existence forced her to feel something other than an ever-rising despair. She began to look forward to the doctor visits, where she got to listen to the rapid-fire whisper of his heartbeat, had even recorded it on her phone to play back at night.

"Cal gave me a reason."

"A reason not to drink."

"A reason not to give up." She pauses. "It is impossible to describe to you, the way I feel about Cal. I know what you think of me. I know what Nic thinks of me—what everyone thinks of me. That I don't love Cal or that I don't love him enough. But you have no idea. After everything that happened—and, Jonathan, you will never know—my little son saved me. The way I feel about him—" She breaks off. "Cal is the driving force behind my doing this case. I know you don't understand that, but I think—I hope—he will."

She looks away from him, to the framed sketch of Rayshon on the wall, his head touching hers as they bumped fists that miraculous day in court. For the first time in a long time, she lets herself look—really look—at his face, the wide-set eyes, the perfectly shaped head, the hollows beneath his cheekbones that are plainly visible as he smiles at her. Only at her. Pain floods her and she forces herself to stay in the moment, feeling it deep inside of her before looking back at Jonathan. "The situation with Rayshon—it's not like that with Luz."

Jonathan turns to go. "Not for you anyway."

"Wake up, wake up."

Abby opens her eyes to see Nic's face inches from her, bleached white with anger and fear. Her head snaps back and hits the tile, her hands reach reflexively for Cal's body but he's not there, only her naked lap, the skin on her thighs starting to shrivel in the bathwater. "Cal," she says frantically. "Where's Cal?"

Nic grips her by the upper arms, shaking her. "You almost fucking killed him. Goddammit, how many times have I told you not to nurse him in the bathtub. When I came in here—" he stops and squeezes his eyes shut "—you were passed out cold and he had slipped. His chin was in the water." When Nic opens his eyes, they are wet and she turns away, unable to look at him.

"Where is he?" Abby is whimpering now, trying to lift

herself up and look over Nic's shoulder, but he tightens his grip so she can't move.

"You didn't even wake up when I took him away from you." Nic shakes his head in disgust. "What the fuck is wrong with you, Abby?"

She keeps her head turned away, is sobbing now, can taste the snot on her lips. "It was an accident. I want Cal. I need to see Cal." When Nic says nothing, she screams, "Give him back!"

Nic removes one hand from her arm, pinching her jaw between his thumb and index finger hard enough that she knows there will be marks tomorrow she'll have to cover with makeup. "Look at me."

Abby forces herself to meet his eyes, telling herself that Cal is fine. If he wasn't, Nic wouldn't be in here. He would have left her to drown. She has to calm down and get through this, she has to answer Nic's questions so she can get her baby back. So she can see for herself that she has not hurt him.

"Were you drinking? Have you been drinking, Abby, all this time?"

She shakes her head violently from side to side. "I would never. I was just—I was just—" She has to stop to catch her breath, a sob strangling in her throat. "I was just tired, Nicky. I swear to you. But I haven't had anything, not one thing to drink since I found out I was pregnant. I swear to you." She forces herself to stop babbling, knowing that the desperation in her voice makes it sound like she's lying even though she isn't. "You have to believe me," she whispers. "I would never."

"Here is what you are going to do." Nic is speaking very slowly, careful to enunciate each word. "You are going to court tomorrow and you are going to get off this case."

"No—"

"Yes. It's over, Abby. This grand little experiment of yours is over."

She stares at him wide-eyed, so surprised she's stopped crying. "You know I can't do that."

"Yes, you can. Paul did, in the middle of Rayshon's trial."

"Paul was the second chair. He was just—sitting there. And with Paul, it was an emergency. His twins were in the NICU."

"Your son is going to end up in the NICU. Or worse."

"No," she says suddenly and fiercely angry. "I am not going to walk out on my client. I would never do that. Especially to her." *You came back for me, right?* How could Abby make Luz believe that and then abandon her? And then there's Will. But Nic is looking at her with such furious contempt she feels something approaching terror. "Listen to me," she says, "you don't understand. Even if I wanted to, I couldn't. I can't leave Luz alone with Will."

"Why not?" Nic's eyes are boring into hers. Abby tries to twist her head away, but his grip is too strong. Her anger flares again and she tries to get ahold of it, knowing it will only make things worse.

"I can't talk to you about it," she says. The water in the bath has cooled and she is starting to shiver. She is suddenly aware of her appearance, how ridiculous and vulnerable she is: naked, wet hair plastered to her scalp, goose pimples on her arms, a droplet of milk on her left breast. "Please, just let me up. I want to see Cal." The thought of him makes her start to cry again. "I just need to see him, okay? Let me up, Nicky. Please, please."

Nic acts like he hasn't heard her. "He's fucking her, isn't he?"

She shakes her head as much as she is able, too afraid to lie out loud.

"There's a rumor going around the courthouse," Nic says, his voice calm and reasonable, like they are discussing a grocery list. "Do you want to know what it is?"

No, a thousand times no. But she says nothing, knowing that it won't matter.

"The rumor," Nic continues, "is that you went to see Dars in his chambers. That you took off all of your clothes. That you tried to blackmail him so he would get off the case."

For a moment, Abby wonders if her heart has stopped beating. Her mind races backward. The two marshals standing outside the door when she had entered and exited. Jonathan telling her *word is going to get out*. "Who told you that?"

"Is it true?"

She tries to shake her head again but he tightens his grip on her jaw so she can't move.

"Is it true?"

Abby sucks in her breath, forces herself to look Nic directly in the face. "No."

Nic looks at her for what seems like forever. "You're a liar." He shakes his head, then releases her jaw, and slowly gets to his feet. Abby falls back against the tub, shaking uncontrollably.

When Nic gets to the door he turns to look at her. "Cal is asleep in his crib. Don't go near him."

Shauna hits a key on her computer and up comes a picture of Travis Hollis's torso, sliced open and pulled apart, a deep tranche that shows skin, blue beneath the dark hairs, then muscle, bone, organs.

"Zoom in."

Up close and in sharp focus, Travis Hollis's torn heart is suddenly everywhere: on the TV monitors set up on either side of the jury box, on both counsel tables, on Dars's bench.

Will looks at the jurors. Several blanch, all are staring fixedly. He cuts his gaze to the witness, Dr. William Forrester Bridges. A diminutive man with a short, pointed gray beard and rimless glasses, he answers Shauna's preliminary questions with a precise, clipped diction punctuated by short, sharp breaths through his nose.

Luz looks nearly catatonic, her only visible reaction to

list slightly. In the end, she had spent the night in the hospital with Maria Elena, which is where Will had picked her up at 6:30 that morning, curled in a green plastic chair next to the bed. She had not said a word on the forty-five-minute, traffic-choked drive to court, or a word since.

Like an obedient child, Luz had allowed Abby to hustle her off to the ladies' room. She emerged ten minutes later, hair brushed, the worst wrinkles smoothed from her dress, looking just barely presentable but remaining unresponsive to their questions. Abby looks only marginally better. Even Will can tell that she has used too much foundation—it looks caked on—but has nevertheless failed to conceal the shadows under her eyes or what is obviously a bruise on her jawline, a bizarre injury if ever there was one. *I tripped and fell*, she told Will when he asked her. *And landed on your jaw?* he had wanted to ask, but hadn't. People in glass houses.

Dars, who had taken the bench promptly at 8:15, was unmoved by Luz's circumstances. "The jurors are here and I will not have their time wasted," he said. When Abby, who had begun by asking for several days off, pleaded for just one, his voice had risen dangerously. "This medical situation with the grandmother—" he had waved a dismissive hand "—could go on for weeks."

At those words, Will felt Luz sag slightly in the chair next to him, her eyes opening and closing with the slow deliberation of a mechanical doll. She had remained that way, and was, to Will's relief, now somehow managing not to look at the autopsy photo.

Shauna, clear-eyed and smart-looking in her houndstooth suit, is going to make sure the jurors swim in every awful detail, visual and verbal. "Dr. Bridges, are you employed as a regional medical examiner with the armed forces?"

"I am."

"In that role, did you perform the autopsy of Sergeant Travis Hollis?"

"I did."

"What did you rely upon in performing that autopsy?"

"I reviewed the medical records of the deceased, the notes of the emergency room physician, with whom I also consulted, and, of course, my own findings."

"Let's start with Sergeant Hollis's arrival at the hospital. What happened there?"

"First he was intubated, meaning that Dr. Chowdury, the emergency room physician, inserted a breathing tube into his throat to assist with respiration."

"What did Dr. Chowdury do next?"

"Perhaps I should begin by describing the medical problem that presented itself?"

Shauna nods encouragingly, and Bridges turns to the jury. "Sergeant Hollis had a condition called cardiac tamponade. A sharp object had penetrated his heart, causing bleeding into the protective sac that encases it."

"That sounds extremely serious."

"It is life-threatening." Bridges, who has turned to look at Shauna, goes back to addressing the jury. "The buildup of blood in the sac prevents the heart from functioning. Dr. Chowdury attempted to draw out the blood with a needle."

"Was that successful?"

"No. The blood had clotted."

Shauna clicks to an image of the bloodied heart, glistening on a stainless steel tray. At Shauna's instruction, Dr. Bridges uses an electrical pointer to indicate the torn lining and clots of blood. The courtroom is utterly silent except for one of Travis's sisters, who is sobbing audibly.

"What did Dr. Chowdury do next?"

"She paged a trauma surgeon to perform a thoracotomy to open the chest and relieve the pressure around the heart."

Another picture appears on the screens, of a medieval-looking device clamped on a bloodied organ. "Dr. Bridges, can you tell the jury what we are looking at?"

*Or not looking at*, Will thinks. Several of the jurors have averted their eyes.

"A Finochietto retractor. It was placed around the heart as part of the thoracotomy procedure."

Shauna wrinkles her brow. "A what?"

"A steel crank. Dr. Chowdury used it to spread Sergeant Hollis's ribs apart in order to search for the source of bleeding and make it stop."

"Was that successful?"

"No. The wound was mortal."

Shauna gives a crisp nod. "You had occasion to examine the wound as part of your autopsy. What did you find?" She clicks back to the picture of the torn and excavated heart. It isn't any better on the second viewing, and Will feels his empty stomach lurch. He looks over at Luz, who is crying, but silently, tears streaming down her face, a bubble of snot visible in her left nostril. He cuts his eyes to Abby, who starts, then reaches for a tissue from the box on the table and passes it to her.

"The wound was caused by a sharp object, which I later determined to be a steak knife. The hemorrhagic track—that is, the pathway of the knife—extends through the subcutaneous tissue and muscle through the anterior fourth rib, severing it."

"How much force does it take to drive a steak knife through a rib?"

"A significant amount." Another click and a new image, this time of a snapped white bone. "As you can see here,"

Dr. Bridges says, and indicates with his pointer, "the break is angled, not straight, which indicated that there was some type of twisting or turning of the blade."

"Did the knife stop there?"

"No, as I said, it went through the pericardial sac into the heart—" Dr. Bridges pauses. "If we could go back to the last slide so I could explain—"

"Certainly."

Will thinks he would rather be punched in the face than have to look at the gruesome image again—at precisely what it is that Luz has done—but looking away is not an option. Abby is staring stoically, her lips pressed together in a thin line. "The knife penetrated the right ventricle of the heart," Dr. Bridges says, indicating with the electronic pointer, "which is one of the major blood pumping chambers of the heart."

"How exactly did Sergeant Hollis die?"

"As I said, the medical term is cardiac tamponade. The stab wound created massive bleeding. The bleeding compressed his heart and prevented it from beating. At that point, his lungs filled with fluid and his brain swelled until he could no longer breathe."

Shauna clicks to the next slide, which shows two figures drawn three-dimensionally: a tall male and a much smaller female, both with their arms at their sides. The female is holding a knife in one hand.

"What was the trajectory of the wound?"

Dr. Bridges uses the pointer to demonstrate, the rod line moving across the man's chest area as he speaks. "Front to back, left to right, downward and twisting."

"Downward and twisting," Shauna repeats. "Meaning that, in your medical opinion, the knife was used in an overhand motion?"

"Correct."

Shauna clicks on a few buttons and the woman raises her arm over her head, bringing the knife down in an arc-like motion like she is spearing a fish. The man staggers back, then collapses. Shauna replays the image again, this time in slow motion as she intones for the record what the jury is watching.

"Is this animation an accurate depiction of how you believe the wound was inflicted?"

"It is."

"No further questions, Your Honor."

"Mr. Ellet?"

Will stands, buttons his suit coat. His hands are shaking: dosed with a double espresso, he feels jittery and febrile. He nods at Abby, who is now tapping away furiously on her laptop. They have their own slideshow.

Another organ appears on the screen, also in a stainless steel dish. A football-shaped hunk, it is a muddy purple, the surface dotted with yellowy, gelatinous blobs. It looks like a side of beef gone bad.

"Dr. Bridges," Will says, "what are we looking at?"

"The liver of the deceased."

"Is that a normal-looking liver?"

"Objection."

Dars's eyes are fixed on the image. "Overruled."

"No."

"What about it isn't normal?"

Dr. Bridges picks up the electronic pointer and circles the blobs. "These fatty deposits."

Will takes a quick look at the jurors; he's got their attention, too. "How old was the deceased?"

"Twenty-three."

"Measurements?"

"Six feet four inches, 260 pounds."

"What was his blood alcohol content?"

A slight hesitation, then, "Point two six."

"We are talking here about an extreme level of intoxication, are we not?"

"Yes."

"A level that most people never reach, even at their drunkest?"

Dr. Bridges stares back unblinkingly through his rimless glasses, face impassive. "Yes."

Will looks at the jurors. Most of them are still staring at Travis's liver. Before he can help himself, he says, "It's not a pretty picture, is it?"

"Objection."

"Sustained." Dars gives Will a hard stare.

Will looks back at Bridges. "How many shots of hard liquor would Sergeant Hollis have had to consume and in what approximate period of time to achieve a .26 blood alcohol level?"

"Objection, calls for speculation."

"Dr. Bridges is an expert. Under the federal rules of evidence, I'm entitled—"

"There is no need to school me on the federal rules of evidence, Mr. Ellet," Dars says nastily. "The objection is overruled."

"How much hard liquor, Dr. Bridges, to get to .26?"

"I would say fifteen, sixteen shots over a period of several hours."

The stay-at-home moms are wide-eyed, as is the computer programmer. Even the retired nurse—who has probably seen it all—looks disapproving. "Can you explain, please, how the body processes alcohol?"

"Through the liver. The liver breaks down the alcohol

into acid aldehyde, then acetic acid, which is then removed from the body."

"Is processing alcohol the only function of the liver?"

"No. The liver is also responsible for processing the food ingested by the body. That is—should be—the primary job of the liver."

"Should be?" Will raises his eyebrows, looks over at the jurors. "Why wouldn't it always be?"

"With individuals who drink chronically and excessively, fibrosis and scarring can develop within the liver. This scarring leads to decreased blood flow through the liver and a reduced capacity to perform its necessary functions. These fatty deposits on the liver's surface—" Dr. Bridges highlights them again with his pointer "—are a marker of decreased liver function."

Will nods. "So, when a normal person stops drinking, the liver will remove the fatty deposits and metabolize them. But with someone who drinks an extreme amount over a long period of time, the liver's whole job becomes metabolizing the alcohol and it does not perform its essential functions properly. Do I have that right?"

Dr. Bridges shrugs slightly. "More or less."

"Having reviewed Sergeant Hollis's entire medical file, as you previously testified, you are aware that he was referred to the ADAPT clinic in May of 2004, following his return from a yearlong deployment in Iraq?"

"Yes."

"What is ADAPT?"

"Alcohol Drug Abuse Prevention and Treatment. It's an on-site clinic that provides treatment for active service members who may be suffering from alcohol or substance abuse problems."

"How long did Sergeant Hollis receive treatment at ADAPT in 2004?"

"For six weeks."

"Was that Sergeant Hollis's only contact with ADAPT?"

"No. He was referred there a second time, in August of 2005, following an altercation with another service member."

"Where did that altercation occur?"

"In a bar."

"Is it fair to say that Sergeant Hollis was an alcoholic and that the army's attempts to treat his alcoholism failed?"

"Objection."

"Overruled."

Dr. Bridges tightens his mouth. "No, it is not fair to say. In fact, it would be irresponsible to say given that I was not Sergeant Hollis's treating physician. I never evaluated him or met him while he was alive."

Will cuts his gaze to Abby, who zooms in on the chunk of rotting meat they have left on the screen, the yellow bubbles of fat like open pustules. "For a young male, at the age of twenty-three, otherwise in good health, is it normal to see a liver with this degree of damage?"

"No."

"In fact, it is highly abnormal, isn't it?"

Dr. Bridges looks briefly at the photograph, then away. "Yes."

"What behaviors might we expect to see a person with a blood alcohol content of .26 exhibit?"

"It depends on the individual. Some people have a higher tolerance than others. I really couldn't say, specifically."

"Generally, then. Might we expect someone at that level of intoxication to have difficulty controlling his emotions?"

"Possibly, yes."

"To become violent?"

Dr. Bridges isn't going to go quietly. "It depends, counselor. Some individuals become sleepy. Others have trouble walking, experience slurred speech and slower reflexes."

"And some individuals become quite violent, don't they, and at the same time they have a reduced ability to control their violent impulses? They say and do things they would not say or do if they were sober or even somewhat less drunk?"

"Some do, yes. Others become withdrawn."

Will nods. Time to move on. "You testified about the trajectory of the wound, specifically your belief that the knife was used in an overhand motion?"

"Yes."

Will nods at Abby, who pulls up a new slide. Two images appear, similar to those shown on Shauna's slide, but in different postures. The male figure is crouched down like a baseball catcher, the woman, still standing, is now the taller of the two.

"Your theory, Dr. Bridges," Will says, "was premised on the assumption that both parties—that is, Sergeant Hollis and his wife, Luz Rivera Hollis, were both upright?"

"Yes."

"But if we assume a different hypothetical in which Sergeant Hollis was crouched down, his right hand curled into a fist as he gets ready to deliver a punch—" a few quick clicks from Abby and the man's fingers curl into a fist beside his ear then thrust outward toward the woman "—the positioning of the bodies is such that even an underhand quick jabbing motion by my client—" more clicks and the woman's knife hand shoots out, underhanded from her side "—could cause the wound trajectory that you described?"

Dr. Bridges presses his lips together primly. "I don't think that's what happened."

"There is one living witness to what happened, Dr. Bridges, and it isn't you," Will says testily. He needs to slow down, take the edge off. He walks toward the jury box, hands clasped behind his back. "Sir, I am not asking you what you think. I am asking you what is possible." He turns and nods at Abby, who replays the animation. "Is this possible, yes or no?"

"Yes."

Will inclines his head, eyes on the jurors. "You testified earlier that my client would have had to use some degree of force to drive the knife through Sergeant Hollis's skin, muscle, rib, and finally his heart?"

"A great deal of force."

"But any amount of force used by my client would be greater if it was met by an equal or greater amount of force coming from the opposite direction. For example, a train traveling at the speed of, say, fifty miles an hour, will do twice as much damage if it crashes into a train that is traveling fifty miles an hour toward it, as it would if it crashed into a train that is stationary?"

"That's true as far as it goes, but—"

Will holds up his hand, smiles politely. "Allow me to finish, Doctor. So if we assume that Sergeant Hollis was crouched down and moving forward, moving into the knife as it was pointed at him, part of the force necessary to drive the knife deeply into his body would have been generated by Sergeant Hollis himself, isn't that right?"

"I don't agree with your assumption—"

"I am not asking whether or not you agree with my assumption." Will can feel his irritation edging back in; he shouldn't have had all that caffeine. He looks at Luz. She has stopped crying and is looking steadily back at him, the smallest hint of a smile on her lips.

Desire and relief move through Will simultaneously as he takes a step back toward the lectern and fixes the jury with his thousand-watt smile before turning it on the doctor. "I am asking whether you agree with the laws of physics, namely, that two people moving toward each other in a direct collision will generate more force than one body moving toward another body that is not moving at all."

"Yes, the amount of force would be greater."

"And it would be generated by two bodies, not one?"

"That is correct."

"Thank you, Doctor."

Walking back to counsel table, Will makes eye contact with Abby and she nods approvingly. He's done what needed to be done. Now the jury has another story to consider. In this story, it's Travis, not Luz, who is the monster.

# 2006

**Wednesday, July 19, 2006**
**7:30 a.m.**
**Willowick, Ohio**


From: sexxygirljax@yahoo.com
To: travman@hotmail.com

Hey T, ur a daddy! he's almost 9 lbs, gonna be a big man like his daddy. i named him Chance, middle name is Robert, after your dad.

   i can't wait for us three to be a family.


**Wednesday, July 19, 2006**
**1:37 p.m.**
**Ramstein Air Base**
**Ramstein-Miesenbach, Germany**


From: travman@hotmail.com
To: sexxygirljax@yahoo.com

can't wait to see the lil man! but could be awhile. i put in for Xmas leave and was denied. send me some pix.

whose name is on the birth certificate?

T


**Thursday, July 20, 2006**
**6:32 p.m.**
**Willowick, Ohio**


From: sexxygirljax@yahoo.com
To: travman@hotmail.com

who's do you think??? who's been there 4 me this whole time? not you.

Its time to tell the truth, that you love me, that you are Chance's daddy, and that we are a family. i am ok with u paying her child support but she needs to go the fuck back to mexico or wherever she's from and get help from her own family.

**2007**

Wednesday, March 21, 2007
1:30 p.m.
United States District Court
for the Central District of California


Shauna's next witness is another doctor, Lenore Spellman, who is there to tell the jury about her physical examination of Luz at the army base medical clinic. It's a short and extremely unhelpful story: Dr. Spellman found no wounds, bumps, bruises, or abrasions on any part of Luz's body. No physical injuries to suggest that she had been attacked or hurt while trying to defend herself. No physical injuries of any kind.

Asking questions on cross will make a bad situation worse and Abby declines when Dars asks her.

He turns back to Shauna. "Call your next witness."

"The government requests a sidebar, Your Honor."

Dars beckons the lawyers to approach and steps off the bench. They form their usual circle around the court reporter, her hands ever-poised to tap-tap-tap on the stenographer's machine. Dars crosses his black-robed arms over his puffed-out chest.

"Well, Ms. Gooden?"

"Your Honor, this morning's testimony went more rapidly than we had anticipated. Our next witness, Michael Ravel, was on call for 1:30 p.m., immediately following the lunch break."

"Who?"

"Michael Ravel," Shauna repeats, "Sergeant Hollis's closest friend on the army base and the witness to Sergeant Hollis's signing of the life insurance policy—the second time around, that is, when he left everything to the defendant. Mr. Ravel is prepared to testify that—"

Dars says impatiently, "I think I have some idea about what he's going to testify to."

"My assistant has been trying Mr. Ravel's cell phone and put in a call to the hotel where we've put him up at the Olani. When she didn't get a response, we had the concierge go up to his room. He knocked, but there was no response, and there's a Do Not Disturb sign on his door."

Abby looks at Will, who looks back at her, eyebrows raised.

"Is he under subpoena?" Dars asks Shauna.

"Of course."

Dars leans forward, a vein throbbing visibly in his forehead. "Then go disturb him." He jabs his index finger inches from Shauna's face. "This isn't a government paid vacation, Ms. Gooden. Send one of the marshals if you have to. I'll let the jury have a twenty-minute recess, after which he better be sitting in that chair." Dars jabs his finger again, this time at the empty witness box.

"Understood, Your Honor."

\* \* \*

Twenty minutes pass, then thirty, then forty. Shauna has disappeared from the courtroom. When Will comes out to check, he finds her huddled with Jared and another marshal, a short, heavyset Latino guy he doesn't recognize, at the far end of the hallway.

Closing in on their group, he makes sure his heels click loudly on the marble floor to give them plenty of notice before he touches Shauna on the shoulder. But she flinches before looking up, obviously startled.

"The clerk sent me. The judge wants us back inside."

Shauna's lips are set in a grim line. Without a word, she beckons to the others, and they walk back to the courtroom in a phalanx, leaving Will to trail behind and wonder what the hell is going on.

Dars is looking at Shauna with great displeasure. "I gave you twenty minutes and you took fifty-seven. Fifty-seven minutes," he repeats, as if each one is a treasured grain of sand lost forever to the hourglass.

Beside Will, Luz shivers slightly and draws her shoulders in tight. After feeding Cristina, brought by Father Abelard and another member of Luz's church—a middle-aged sweet-faced woman who is now the baby's de facto babysitter—along with the disheartening news that there had been no change in Maria Elena's condition, Luz had lain back in one of the old leather chairs in the attorney lounge and passed out. It had taken both Abby and Will to rouse her, Will repeating her name as Abby shook her by the shoulder. She still hadn't said anything to either of them, but when she emerged from the bathroom, Will was relieved to see that she had made more of an effort to pull herself together: applying lipstick and tying back her hair.

Shauna clears her throat. "On Your Honor's instructions, we sent two marshals to Mr. Ravel's hotel room. When he did not answer to the door, the desk clerk was summoned with a key. The marshals entered and found Mr. Ravel sprawled on the bed, nonresponsive. Emergency personnel were called immediately. Narcan was administered to reverse the effects of what appeared to be an opioid overdose."

"So, he's come around?"

"No, Your Honor. He's dead."

Will tries to look suitably somber at the delivery of the news but it is all he can do not to grab Abby's hand and raise it high in the air. After a nightmarish twenty-four hours in and out of the courtroom, they have caught a break. Ravel could have devastated their careful efforts to portray Luz as the real victim with Shauna using his marginal relevance— witnessing Travis sign a life insurance policy—as a lever to pry open the closed window of Travis Hollis's misgivings and grievances. Ravel would have been Travis's voice from the grave, narrating a story of the marriage in which Luz was an instigator who gave as good as she got, alternating red-hot and ice-cold, and using every means at her disposal to get what she wanted. Now that window was glued shut: the waiflike woman-child safe inside. There would be no sharpening of the edges that Will had worked so diligently to plane—not from this witness anyway.

Abby would have pounded away when it was her turn, probing the dishonorable discharge, the PTSD diagnosis, and portraying Ravel as a drug-addled, memory-ravaged and badly damaged individual who might well have harbored his own feelings for Luz—the beautiful, untouchable wife of his far handsomer best friend, and who was, in any event, way out of his league. But Will had always

worried that it would backfire badly. Dishonorable discharge or not, drug addiction or not, Ravel was a veteran
who had served his country honorably during two tours in
Iraq. He would start with the jury's sympathy and if he did
nothing to squander it, could have made Abby look petty,
even mean by comparison.

Dars swivels his chair and stares up at the ceiling. They
are all quiet, waiting. "Well," he says finally as he turns
back to them, "this is quite a turn of events. But while it
is no doubt a tragedy for this young man and his family, I
see no reason to stop the trial."

"Your Honor," Shauna says, "if we could just have until
tomorrow morning. Our next witness is on a flight from
Ohio and doesn't land until this evening."

Dars frowns but says, "I see no alternative. Madame
Clerk will tell the jurors they are excused for the afternoon
and we will reconvene first thing tomorrow morning."

Abby and Luz are sitting in Abby's office, Abby drinking a can of Ensure, Luz taking sips from a can of a Diet Coke that Cherise had gotten her from the vending machine. Luz's hair is limp, her mascara has clumped, and her nail polish is chipped. Abby, having glimpsed her own wan reflection in the bathroom mirror, knows she looks no better. So much for that post-baby glow that Jonathan had raved about.

"How are you holding up?" she asks Luz.

Luz looks back at her with glazed eyes. "I'm numb," she says. "It feels like what the dentist does before he uses the drill..." She searches for the word and not finding it, gives up, shrugging her shoulders.

"The Novocain shot?"

Luz nods. "But the feeling is—it's in my brain instead." She closes her eyes for a moment, then opens them. "I need to get back to the hospital. Father Abelard texted me that he's waiting downstairs with Cristina."

"I know." Abby had gotten the same text. "I won't make you stay long but I want to go over what it's going to be like with Jackie on the stand tomorrow."

"We've been over it," Luz says flatly.

Abby nods. She and Will had stressed to Luz the delicate balance that must be struck. But Luz never seemed to appreciate the gravity of the situation no matter how many times they have warned her of the consequences if she fails to react in exactly the right way.

"Every time Jackie opens her mouth to answer a question, the jury will be looking to you for your reaction. You can't stare her down and you can't look away. You can't look angry and you can't look catty."

Luz shrugs. "She doesn't mean anything to me."

"You keep saying that, which is what worries me." Denial is not a good thing, not when it could evaporate on sight. Abby leans forward across her desk, trying to close the distance between them. "They are using Jackie to prove that you premeditated in the hours between getting her email and Travis coming home. That you lay in wait. Her testimony is the heart of the first-degree murder charge."

Another indifferent shrug. "That's not what happened."

Abby opens her mouth to say, "What did happen?" then thinks about Mr. Estrada and what Luz had said to Abby the last time she and Abby were alone together. *He told me to trust you. So if you want to know those things now, I will tell you. Do you want to know?*

Did she want to know?

Abby looks more closely at Luz, who is taking another sip of her Diet Coke, her eyes moving around the room until they settle on the picture of Abby and Rayshon.

"That was your big case, right?" she says, and nods toward it.

Abby doesn't look at the picture. "Yes."

"Mr. Estrada told me that everyone thought the guy was guilty—he was like a stone-cold killer or something." Her eyes go to Abby's face. "You don't like talking about it, though, your big victory with him."

"He wasn't a stone-cold killer and no, I don't like talking about it."

"Why not?"

Now it's Abby's turn to shrug.

Luz looks at her. "He died right after, so it's like you lost anyway."

Abby says, not exactly knowing why, "He had a little boy—well, his fiancée, Sheila, was pregnant during the trial. He was excited about it."

Luz looks interested. "What happened to the baby?"

"He lives with his mother. The family got a decent-sized settlement, after everything came out about the LAPD and the evidence tampering."

"What's his name?"

"The baby? Rayshon Jr."

Luz nods. "So Rayshon Jr. will be okay?"

"I think so," Abby says.

"Will Cristina be okay?" Luz's eyes search Abby's

Abby drinks some of her Ensure, sets down the can. "You mean, if you're..."

Luz nods.

"Mr. Estrada and I have done everything we can, I told you."

"Is it enough?"

"I hope so," Abby says. She rubs absently at the bruise on her jaw. "But I don't know."

They are quiet for a moment.

Luz says, "I've never had a real family. My dad left and my mother killed herself. My grandmother—" She shrugs again. "She's never had any idea what's going on with me."

Abby nods. "Dr. Cartwright told us." She pauses. "My father killed himself, too, in a way."

Luz looks at her skeptically. "What do you mean 'in a way'?"

"One night he was driving home from work, he was very drunk, and he drove into a median on the freeway."

"But that was an accident," Luz says.

"A single car accident," Abby says, repeating the words her mother always used, then shakes her head in disbelief. "Do you know how drunk you have to be to drive into a median when there are no cars around you, when all you have to do is drive in a straight line on a flat road?"

"You're still mad," Luz says. "Me, too."

"He had a drinking problem and he never dealt with it," Abby says, knowing she should stop talking. She never talks about her family—not to anyone and especially not to her clients. But this breach feels minor given the weight of all the others in this case, and she keeps going. "My dad picked alcohol over his family. He left my mom alone to raise my brother and me. I grew up hating my father but now—" She stops. "Now I worry that I'm too much like him. He was a trial lawyer, too," she adds after a moment. "Really gifted."

"I grew up hating my mother," Luz says, "but I know that I am nothing like her."

"No," Abby says, "you're not." She thinks that now is the time to steer Luz back to the purpose of this meeting. Instead, almost before Abby realizes the words are coming out of her mouth she says to Luz, "You really don't give a shit about Jackie Stedman, do you?"

Luz looks slightly taken aback at Abby's language, her sharp emphasis on the profanity, but doesn't say anything.

"Why not?" Abby says, then answers her own question as the realization sets in. "Because the only thing you care about is Cristina. And that's always been true, ever since you found out you were pregnant."

"All I ever wanted was to have her." Luz looks at Abby, and the glazed look is gone. "Imagine if this were your baby."

"I do," Abby says, "every day. And then I leave my baby to come here and defend you."

Jackie Stedman is pretty enough: tall, ash-blonde, curvy. But her eyes are a bit small and close-set and she's made the mistake of over-tweezing her eyebrows. As she makes her way to the witness box in her pink skirt suit and heels-dyed-to-match, she holds her head high, taking small, practiced steps. All eyes are on her as she settles in, tucking a lock of hair behind one ear and placing her hands on her lap. She bites down on her lower lip and casts a quick fluttery glance at Dars, who is regarding her with an interest that borders on covetous.

Abby watches Jackie put her hand on the Bible, repeating the oath after the clerk in a soft high voice. Like a little girl's, except for its slight rasp.

A picture appears on everyone's computers screens: Jackie in a full-length strapless turquoise gown, smiling at the camera as Travis, grinning in a white tuxedo, pins a corsage to her left breast. She is beautiful, he is handsome, they are happy and in love. The photograph has a poignancy not lost on anyone in the room. Travis Hollis had no idea about the darkness that was coming for him.

"The prom," Jackie responds in answer to Shauna's question about the photograph. "That's Travis and me in our senior year of high school. My mom snapped that picture out in the backyard of his parents' house." Her voice trembles slightly and she bites her lip again.

"Travis Hollis was your boyfriend?"

"Yes, we had been dating three years at that point."

"Did the relationship continue after high school?"

"We had the summer together, and then 9/11 happened. I had started at community college to get my associate's degree in cosmetology. Travis enlisted in the air force." Another tremor in her voice, another biting down on her lip. "I didn't want him to go—there was already talk that we would be going to war, but he told me—" she straightens in her seat, eyes steadfast on Shauna "—that it was his duty as a patriotic American to defend his country."

To Abby, she sounds as canned as a stumping politician, but the jurors appear to be eating it up.

Shauna nods sympathetically. "Was Sergeant Hollis ultimately deployed to Iraq?"

"Yes. After he completed his basic military training in San Antonio, he was sent to the air force base in Minot, North Dakota. In 2003, his unit was called and he went over there for a year."

"Did the relationship continue during all of that time?"

"Yes, long distance. He was home for holidays, I flew to North Dakota when I could afford to. But mostly we talked on the phone and emailed. We wrote letters, too." Jackie smiles wistfully. "It seems old-fashioned to say that now, but even a couple of years ago, it wasn't as easy to call, the cell phone plans were expensive, and Travis just loved getting my letters."

Abby writes those last words down to use later, then casts a quick glance at Luz, who appears to be listening politely, as if to a speech at the memorial service for a distant cousin.

"And during the deployment?"

"It was harder, of course. Travis didn't talk much about what was happening, but I was following the news and I knew about the IEDs. I knew he was in danger every day he went out on patrol."

More nodding from Shauna. "Was his unit directly impacted by IED explosives?"

Jackie nods. "About six months in, an IED hit the Humvee in front of Travis's. Two of the men in his unit were killed and Travis's friend Mike Ravel was hurt pretty bad with head and back injuries. Travis saw it all happen." Jackie's smallish eyes are bright with tears and her voice cracks. "He was never the same afterward." Tears roll down her cheeks and Dars's clerk hands her a Kleenex.

Shauna waits a respectful few minutes while Jackie dabs at her eyes, blotting carefully so as not to smear her mascara. Abby makes another note, this time to Will. When it's Luz's turn, they need to make sure she looks like a train wreck by comparison. Right or wrong, people measure emotional suffering by physical appearance, particularly when it comes to women.

"Where was he sent when his tour was over?"

"To Fort Irwin, a base out here in California near Barstow. That was in early 2004. We had been talking about getting married and then—" another lip bite "—he started to change."

"Started to change how?"

"He sounded distracted, upset. Like I said, he was coping with the trauma from the war. He mentioned spending a lot of time at this bar near the base. It made me worry that he was drinking too much and not associating with the best people." Jackie is pointedly not looking at Luz, but it is clear who she means.

Shauna decides not to draw things out. "Did there come a time when the relationship ended?"

Jackie nods tearfully. "A couple of months later, Travis said he had met someone at the bar where he was going. She worked there as some kind of barmaid, I guess." Jackie's implication is clear: Luz was, in fact, some kind of prostitute. Abby looks sidelong at Luz, who appears unperturbed, her gaze still trained on Jackie with a polite attentiveness.

Jackie takes a long, shuddering breath. "I asked him if he loved her, and he said he didn't think so, but it was like he had a fever. Those were his words. That she had come over him like a fever and he couldn't shake it. He tried but—" Jackie shrugs her shoulders helplessly.

"When did it happen, the ending of the relationship?"

"October 5, 2004. I remember it was a week before my birthday."

"How did you feel afterward?"

"Just devastated. Travis was—is—the only man I've ever loved. We were meant to be together. It felt unreal to me. I think it felt unreal to him, to tell you the truth."

"Can you briefly describe your contact with Sergeant Hollis over the next year?"

Jackie twists her hands in her lap. "We agreed not to have contact. No calls, emails, letters. But I'm close with his family, and I heard from Travis's mom that Travis got married to her and they went to Germany when he got stationed there. Of course," she adds, "I was relieved for his sake that it wasn't a deployment to another war zone."

"When did you next see Sergeant Hollis?"

"At his father's funeral." Jackie's eyes well with tears again. "Travis's dad died of a heart attack, just dropped to the ground one day out of the blue. That was in October, too, in 2005, right after my birthday. Travis flew home and we—we reconnected at the church, after the memorial service."

Shauna, still in head-nodding sympathy mode, asks, "Can you explain what you mean by reconnected?"

"When we saw each other, it was like no time had passed. He came across the room—there must have been a hundred people—and embraced me the way he used to, in that bear-hug way of his. The attraction between us—there was no denying it, and that night he came over to my place and we—" Jackie's voice drops "—we were intimate with each other."

Shauna is leaving nothing to the imagination. "You had sexual intercourse?"

Jackie nods. "Well, yes. But that isn't all I mean by intimate." Jackie moistens her lips. "Travis was so sad, so deeply pained, and he told me what was in his heart."

"What was in his heart?" Shauna is gamely playing along, but Abby can only imagine how painful it is to stick to the paperback novel romance script. She looks at the jurors, trying to assess how Jackie is coming off and concludes that so far, they are buying it. There's a reason why those dime-store books on the spin rack at Walmart sell millions of copies.

Jackie sighs. "He was miserable in his marriage. He told me—"

Abby is on her feet. "Hearsay, Your Honor."

"Indeed, it is," says Dars dryly, "which is because, as you well know, Sergeant Hollis is unable to speak for himself. The objection is overruled."

Shauna looks to Jackie. "Go on."

"He told me that she was always changing up on him. Like he never knew who it was that was going to greet him at the door."

"And by 'she,' you mean the defendant?" Shauna turns to look directly at Luz and the jurors shift in their chairs as they follow her gaze. The moment stretches out like pulled elastic and Abby braces for the snap, but Luz only stares demurely down at the table, her eyes unreadable under her half-closed lids, her right hand gently worrying at the cross around her neck.

"Yes. Sometimes she was as sweet as could be and other times she was cold, vicious even, in the things she would say to him. She had violent outbursts where she scratched and bit and kicked and slapped him. She saw other men behind his back but he knew about it. He said he had made the worst mistake of his life marrying her and he was going to file for divorce because every day was like a living hell."

"How did you leave things when it was time for Sergeant Hollis to go back to Germany?"

"We both cried like babies. It was only four days that we had together and it had been like a taste of heaven. We stayed in touch by email, and I sent him letters with—" Jackie blushes "—some sexy pictures of me that he asked for."

*You sure did*, Abby thinks. The Jackie speaking to the jurors bears little resemblance to the Jackie in the naked selfies and pornographic emails collected in her binder. Abby had purposefully picked the color—a brilliant scarlet. Jurors, like everyone else, trafficked in stereotypes, however reductive and demeaning. Abby's job was to flip the script and show the jurors that it was Jackie, not Luz, who was the man-eating temptress no female juror would want within a thousand miles of her husband.

Jackie was on to the pregnancy, describing her delight at finding out just before Christmas. "The most beautiful present I could ever ask for."

Shauna flips a page in her binder. Time for some tough questions. "Now, you were seeing someone else at the time, Lance Richards. How could you be sure that you conceived the baby with Sergeant Hollis and not with him?"

"Lance and I used protection," Jackie says. "Travis and I didn't."

"When you told Sergeant Hollis the news over email, he didn't respond immediately, is that right?"

"Yes, and at the time I was hurt by that. But now I realize the situation he was in."

"The situation being that the defendant was also pregnant by him?"

Jackie nods. "I think he was scared. He was going to end the marriage and now everything was so much more complicated."

"But Sergeant Hollis didn't tell you that directly?"

"I'm sure he didn't want to worry me."

"How did you find out?"

Jackie looks down. "On Facebook."

"Can you explain?"

"She posted a selfie of her sideways in a bikini showing off her baby belly." Jackie's voice is contemptuous, and her eyes seek out a few of the younger women on the jury as if for support. Beside Abby, Luz is completely still.

"How did you connect with the defendant on Facebook?"

Another lip bite. "I sent her a friend request and she accepted it."

"Why did you want to be friends with the defendant on Facebook?"

Jackie flushes. "There was a lot I didn't know and it was a way for me to figure out what was real and what wasn't."

"What was your understanding of Sergeant Hollis's intentions toward you?"

"He was going to leave her to be with me and the baby. It's just the situation was so complicated. He was stationed overseas, and all that was going to have to wait until he came back stateside. I got impatient." Jackie's eyes fill with tears again and this time, the clerk hands her the whole box of Kleenex. "If only I had just waited," she says, her voice rising to a half wail. "If I had never sent her those emails Travis would still be alive."

Abby is on her feet, but Dars has already intervened. "That last sentence will be stricken and the jury will disregard." He turns to Jackie, finger wagging. "You are not here to speculate about the events leading up to the victim's death, young lady."

"You referred to sending the defendant some emails," Shauna continues smoothly. "Can you tell the jury what the emails were and when you sent them?"

This time, Jackie is having trouble meeting Shauna's gaze. "I messaged her on Facebook asking for her email address. I said I had something important to tell her about Travis."

"What day was that?"

"October 12, 2006."

"Did she respond?"

"Yes, the next day, October 13, she messaged back with her email address and I wrote to her."

"The same day?"

"Yes."

Shauna flips through her binder and pulls out a sheaf of paper. "The time stamp on the email you sent to the defendant says 3:02 p.m. Eastern Standard Time. Do you know the time difference between Ohio and Germany?"

"They are six hours ahead."

"So the defendant would have received this email at 9:02 p.m. her time?"

"Yes."

Shauna turns to the jury. "The parties have stipulated that an analysis of the computer in the defendant's home shows that the email was opened at 9:58 p.m. in Ramstein-Miesenbach, Germany. A stipulation means you must accept that as a proven fact."

She turns back to Jackie. "Tell me about the email."

"All the communications between me and Travis were in one string back and forth. I hit the forward button, typed in her email address, and hit send."

"You sent a year's worth of emails documenting your affair and pregnancy with Sergeant Hollis to the defendant?"

Jackie lifts her chin. "Yes," she says, and there is a note of defiance in her voice. "I wanted her to know the truth."

Shauna walks up to Jackie holding a stack of paper and places it before her. "Are these the emails you are referring to?"

Jackie picks up the paper and flips through a few of the pages. This time the color spreads from her face to her neck in a mottled rash. "Yes."

"Your Honor, we would move these into evidence."

Dars looks at Abby who shakes her head slightly.

"There being no objection from the defense, the items will be received."

"I'm sorry," Jackie whispers. She bows her head and her shoulders shake as she sobs quietly.

Dars looks at Shauna who says, "The government has no further questions at this time."

"You're sorry?" Abby asks politely, as if to make sure she's heard correctly. She will not be raising her voice, not once during the entirety of the examination. Jackie must be the high-pitched red-faced one. The woman who is not in control.

"Of course, I am." Jackie has stopped crying now, but her face is pink and puffy. It makes her look angry and her tone has an edge to it.

Abby walks from the podium back to the counsel table and stands behind Luz, her hands resting lightly on her shoulders. Luz stiffens at her touch, and Abby, careful not to look irritated, presses down with the pads of her fingers until her posture softens.

"Are you apologizing to Mrs. Rivera Hollis?"

Jackie's mouth falls open. "I— No."

Abby nods. "The emails you forwarded to Mrs. Rivera Hollis about your affair with her husband were accompanied by a message you wrote. I'd like you to read the message out loud please."

Jackie dutifully picks up the top page, but her hands are trembling. There is a pause before she begins to read and Abby can hear the collective movement in the jury box as they lean in to listen. Abby stays where she is, her hands now firmly on Luz's shoulders, forcing Jackie to look in Luz's direction if she lifts her eyes from the page.

"'I am sending you these emails because you need to know the truth. Travis and I were together for six years before he met you and we've been together again since last

October. I had his baby in July. We belong together, always have and always will.'" Jackie looks up. "I was upset when I wrote this next part. I didn't really—"

"Finish reading, please," Abby says and makes sure to give Jackie an encouraging smile.

"'Your baby is a'—" Jackie swallows audibly "—'your baby is a grudge-fuck, ours is a love-fuck.'" Her voice has dropped to an almost inaudible whisper.

"A what now?" Dars says, and when Jackie just stares back at him mutely, he says impatiently to the court reporter, "What did she say?"

They all wait while the court reporter reads back the words in a slow, loud monotone, which has the effect of making the obscenity sound even worse. Dars is all smiles. "Next question," he says to Abby.

"She's not done," Abby says, her eyes still on Jackie. "Keep reading, please."

Dars leans forward and gives Jackie another *naughty girl* finger wag. "And make sure we can all hear you this time."

"'Travis doesn't love you.'" Jackie's voice has gone tinny. "'All that happened was that you tricked him into believing that you were something other than the Mexican whore you really are.'" Abby hears a sharp intake of breath from the jury box. "'He is going to leave you as soon as he can, but you could make things easier for everyone and clear out on your own. Just don't plan on any child support. There's always welfare for people like you.'"

Abby lets the last words descend on the silent courtroom as she walks back to the podium.

"What plans had Sergeant Hollis made to leave his wife?"

"Like I said already, he was going to file for divorce."

"But he didn't, did he?"

Jackie's chin comes up again and her tone is truculent. "He never got the chance."

Abby pretends to look puzzled. "But you said the affair had been going on for nearly a year. Over and over again in these emails, you express impatience at Sergeant Hollis's failure to take any steps to be with you, isn't that right?"

"It was just a matter of time."

"In the meantime, you stalked my client online?"

Shauna is on her feet objecting but Dars waves her down.

"I didn't stalk her. I just made friends with her on Facebook."

"Made friends with her." Abby takes her time with each word as she looks at the jurors. "You pretended to be her friend as a way of keeping tabs on Sergeant Hollis because you didn't believe he was telling you the truth about the state of his marriage?"

"No. You're twisting my words around."

Abby turns to Will, who taps a few keys on the computer. Up comes a color photograph of Luz, eight months pregnant, seated on Travis's lap. They are outside, at what looks like a backyard party: there are plates on the table in front of them littered with the remnants of chicken wings, spare ribs, and potato salad along with cans of Budweiser and Coors light. Luz is looking directly into the camera, her face lit up with a huge smile. Travis's hands are placed protectively over her swollen belly and her hands rest lightly on top of his, her diamond ring and wedding band prominently on display. He is looking at Luz with an expression of naked adoration on his face.

"Mrs. Rivera Hollis posted that picture on October 11, 2006, reminiscing on her pregnancy following the birth of their daughter?"

"I don't know why she posted it."

Abby leaves the picture up on the screen.

"Seeing that picture must have made you angry?"

"No, that was an old picture, and anyway, I knew Travis had to keep up appearances."

"But it was the very next day that you messaged Mrs. Rivera Hollis on Facebook. Then, immediately after she sent you her email address, you replied and attached the history of your—" Abby winces slightly "—correspondence. Is that correct?"

"I thought once she knew the truth, she would do the right thing."

"The truth," Abby repeats. "The truth was that Sergeant Hollis liked getting your dirty emails and naked pictures, right?"

Jackie is scarlet now, but it isn't blushing—she's angry. "That was just one part of our relationship."

Abby picks up the stack of papers that is her copy of the emails and rifles through the pages. "Of course, the jurors will have a chance to read these and judge for themselves, but it seems to me like that was the entirety of the relationship."

Shauna stands. "Is there a question pending, Your Honor, because I'm not hearing one, just a lot of speechifying from Ms. Rosenberg."

"Yes, and the speech is stricken. Move on, counsel."

"The truth is that Sergeant Hollis did not believe that Chance was his son?"

"Not at first but then I proved it to him."

"You took a DNA test, then hid the results from your boyfriend, Lance Richards, and told him that the condom broke one night and that it was his baby?"

"It was the story that Travis and me decided on."

"In fact, it is Lance Richards's name on Chance's birth certificate, correct?"

"Yes."

"And you never actually provided proof to Sergeant Hollis of this DNA test, did you?"

"I did the test," Jackie says fiercely. "Chance is Travis's son."

Abby acts as if Jackie hasn't answered, knowing it will infuriate her even more. "You wrote to my client telling her not to expect any child support from Sergeant Hollis. Did Sergeant Hollis provide child support for you and Chance?"

"Not officially, but he sent me money one time."

"How much?"

"Thirty-five dollars."

Abby lets that answer sit for a moment, then asks, "Where in the chain of emails does Sergeant Hollis say, 'I love you'?"

Jackie's eyes harden. "He told me," she says. "I didn't need it in writing."

Abby nods. "Where in the chain of emails does Sergeant Hollis say, 'I do not love my wife'?"

"He told me that." Jackie's hands have balled into fists, and when she speaks it is as if she is spitting out the words. "He told me."

Abby looks at the stone-cold faces of the jury. "I guess we'll have to take your word for it." She waits a beat, then says to Dars, "I have nothing further for this witness."

Abby, Will, and Antoine are seated around the small table in the witness room. Antoine has brought in sandwiches from Quiznos, and Will, his appetite back, is tearing through his meatball sub, pausing occasionally to swipe at the lower half of his face with a balled-up paper napkin.

Antoine's ability to order the messiest thing on the menu and escape unscathed has always impressed Abby. He's swept his tie over one shoulder, and though his Reuben is drenched in Russian dressing, he manages to confine the drippings to the sandwich paper.

Luz, her legs tucked under her, is seated on the carpet beside Cristina's removable car seat, which she rocks with one hand while taking small bites of her ham-and-cheese sandwich with the other. "Twinkle Twinkle Little Star" is playing low on repeat from her iPod.

Abby gamely picks up her can of Ensure and takes a

swig. Outside, Nic is waiting with Cal so she can feed him. There had been no time to pump, yesterday or today. She has fifteen minutes to finish this can before she has to meet them, and she's dreading it. For two days, Nic has not said a word to her that wasn't absolutely necessary; last night, he slept on the couch. When she had gotten up in the middle of the night to pee, he had opened the door and looked past her sitting on the toilet seat at the empty bathtub, before closing it. *After trial*, she had told herself that morning, blotting her lipstick in the bathroom mirror while doing her best to ignore Cal, who was screaming like someone was trying to murder him. When Abby had tried to nurse him, Nic had said, "I'm warming up a bottle, so why don't you get ready for work" in a voice that said, *Get the fuck away from us.* All morning she has trained her full attention on the task at hand: apply mascara, cross-examine Jackie, choke down chalk shake.

They eat in silence, the mood grim. After Jackie, Shauna had called her final two witnesses, ending on a triumphant note. The first, a mousy-looking woman from Sprint PCS in an '80s dress-for-success outfit complete with a neck-bow, had testified to the ten phone calls between Luz and Estrada that spanned ten months, ending with the final ninety-seven-minute call on October 10. Over Will's objection, Shauna had moved Estrada's billing records into evidence. Without Estrada, there was no context for any of it, but looking at the jury, Will wondered if that made things worse. The absence of information was the absence of an innocent explanation, and there was no getting around the fact that Luz had talked to her lawyer at great length seventy-two hours before stabbing her husband to death.

Then there was Henry Chu, the twentysomething representative from Servicemembers' Group Life Insurance;

with his crew cut and crisp answers. Chu had met with Travis stateside in 2002 to fill out the original $400,000 life insurance policy naming Travis's parents as the beneficiaries. He had also taken Travis's call on September 25, 2006, requesting to change the beneficiary, and duly carried out Travis's instructions, faxing the paperwork to Germany and receiving it back with Travis's and Ravel's signatures a few days later on September 28.

The dates landed like stones and Shauna drove home the timeline by posting it on the computer screens. Luz's second-to-last call with Estrada had been placed on September 24, 2006. Twenty-four hours separated that call and Travis's call to Chu asking to remove his parents as the beneficiaries and replace them with Luz. On cross, Will had done his best. They had introduced Travis's father's death certificate into evidence and Will had gotten Chu to admit that the policy ought to be changed under those circumstances. They had also introduced Cristina's birth certificate, and Chu had stated that, yes, new parents often changed their policies shortly before the birth of children and no, minors could not be named directly and yes, many service members did name their spouses. But the timing. There was no getting around the fact that Travis had made no effort to change his policy after marrying Luz a year earlier, or that nearly a year had passed since his father's death.

Will had asked, "If the named beneficiary is convicted of causing the death of the insured, can she collect the proceeds from the life insurance policy?" Chu had replied no.

"In that circumstance," Will continued, "the proceeds would go to the alternate named beneficiary, Travis Hollis's mother, correct?" To which Chu had replied that would in fact be the case.

But it was Shauna who had the final word on redirect.

"What would happen if the named beneficiary is charged with murder and found not guilty because she claimed she acted in self-defense?"

"There is nothing in the policy that would prevent her from collecting."

"Meaning she would receive the entirety of the $400,000?"

"She would, yes."

When Will speaks now, the sound of his voice is almost startling in the thick silence.

"I've been thinking," he says, "about the jury instructions."

Abby and Antoine look at each other quizzically. Antoine says, as if speaking her thoughts out loud, "It's a little early for that, man. We haven't even put on our case."

"Luz is our case," Will points out, "and she starts this afternoon. We could be done as early as Friday."

"The jury instructions are the least of our problems," Abby says icily, amazed that Will would want to talk about something so mundane. Their entire case is about to rise and fall on Luz's ability to tell her story in a way that will explain how someone with no defensive injuries, tremendous financial incentive, and explosive evidence that her husband had an affair and another baby could have acted without any premeditation or intent to kill. *Twinkle twinkle little star.* She shoots a glance at Luz, willing her to turn off the music.

"And anyway," she adds, "Dars will give all the standard ones, that's what they all do."

"Maybe we don't want the standard ones," Will says. "Shauna's going to ask for the jury to consider every possible formulation of the murder charge—first-degree, second-degree, voluntary manslaughter, and involuntary manslaughter. What if we say no. The jury can convict on first-degree or nothing. No compromise, no middle ground."

*How I wonder what you are.* Abby stares at Will. "That's insane."

"I've been thinking about it a lot," Will says evenly. "First-degree was always a reach. I don't think Shauna's proved it. But the other counts?" He shrugs. "Criminally negligent homicide—she overreacted to the threat with too much force. Manslaughter? She acted in the heat of passion. After the medical testimony, Jackie, and these last two witnesses, there's a real risk of conviction on either of those counts, even on second degree. So I say we give them no choice."

"No, you say we give them two choices, and one of them is to send her to prison for the rest of her life. That is reckless, that is wrong, and we are not doing it." Abby looks to Antoine for support, but his eyes are on Will and from his expression she can tell he's giving it serious consideration.

Will's eyes are on Luz. "Your grandmother is dying. You don't have any other family. If you go down on any count the prosecutor is allowed to argue to the jury, you are going to prison. Maybe for three years, maybe for five, maybe for fifteen, which means Cristina will be taken away and raised by Travis's family. Your best chance to keep your baby is to do what I'm telling you."

*Up above the world so high, like a diamond in the sky.*

"That is not true." But even as Abby says this, she knows there will be no way to convince Will because she hasn't told him about her visit to the jail and she doesn't intend to. She looks pointedly at Luz, wishing she hadn't been so equivocal when Luz had asked her if the legal trick with Estrada would work. "You know that's not true."

Luz is looking back and forth between Abby and Will.

"It could be," she says quietly. "And it is true that I'll be separated from Cristina if they find me guilty."

"This is not her decision," Abby says to Will.

"It is if you and I can't agree."

Abby laughs harshly. "What—you think the tie goes to the client? That isn't how it works."

"You want an acquittal, Abby? This is how we get there."

"Antoine?" Abby looks to him for help, but he's shaking his head.

"I don't weigh in on the legal questions, you know that. You want me to get Paul?"

"No, I don't want you to get Paul," she snaps. As if that was an option at this point. "What I want is for my client not to spend the rest of her life in a cage." Abby turns back to Luz, trying for a softer tone. "Listen to me. We could beat the lesser included offenses. And even if we don't, it's not the end of your life. Cristina will visit you in prison and when you get out—"

"I'm not going to prison." Luz continues to rock the carrier seat in an uninterrupted rhythm, the baby sleeping peacefully throughout. The song ends, starts again. *Twinkle twinkle little star.*

"This is her decision, Abby," Will says, in a more-in-sorrow-than-in-anger tone that makes her want to scratch his eyes out, because whatever the legal rules say it is obviously the right answer. It is Luz's life.

Luz looks at Cristina for a long moment, and then at Will before turning back to Abby. "I overrule you."

Thursday, March 22, 2007
1:30 p.m.
United States District Court
for the Central District of California

"The defense calls Luz Rivera Hollis."

These are Abby's words. They want the jury's eyes on Luz, and so had delayed the moment when Will would have to stand up. One surprise at a time. The jurors are still adjusting to the sight of a baby's crib—complete with a plastic baby doll and white blanket—situated incongruously on the green-carpeted rectangle separating the judge's dais from the defense and prosecution tables.

Known as The Well, it is a sacred space that for security reasons can be entered only with judicial permission. Older attorneys gleefully tell tales of the good old days when the US Marshals would tackle novice lawyers who breached the invisible barrier and strode up to the bench unannounced. Getting permission for this setup had been a headache involving additional security officers, who are now seated in the front row and stationed discreetly along the back wall behind Dars.

Luz walks alone to the witness stand, even more slight-seeming than usual in a man-size white tee shirt and shapeless sweatpants. Her long black hair is tied back in a loose ponytail, the shorter strands lifting and settling around her face as she moves. Bare face. Bare feet. Behind him, Will can hear the murmurs from the packed courtroom. Media coverage, which had escalated when Jackie testified, has reached a whole new level. This was the main show.

Will watches the jurors watching her. For days they've been looking at Luz, but only head-on and chest-up, flat and flimsy as a paper doll. Utterly silent. And now here she is, fully realized in a way that Will and Abby have been doing everything they can to suggest she was on that night.

He sees Shauna tense, imagines her considering some way to object already, and feels some mixture of scorn and pity. *Lady, you have no idea*.

Luz says her name, puts her hand on the Bible, and repeats the clerk's words about the truth and nothing but. She sits down, head bowed, hands in her lap, twisting at her wedding ring.

Will stands, removes his suit coat and drops it over the back of the chair. He can't remember the last time he was this jacked up with adrenaline. His blood isn't pulsing, it's sizzling in his veins. The jurors are looking at him now, their eyes widening in surprise. Behind him, he hears murmuring from the packed gallery.

Will bypasses the lectern in strides longer than he'd usually take and plants himself directly in front of the witness box, shoulders squared.

"What am I wearing?"

Luz looks at him, her eyes dark and enormous. "Wrangler jeans," she whispers, "a brown belt, and a Pearl Jam tee shirt."

"Speak up. Now, why am I dressed this way?"

Luz leans into the microphone. "Because that's what—that's what Travis was wearing the night he died."

"Are these his actual clothes?"

She shakes her head. "He's bigger than you and his actual clothes are—they're evidence."

Black and stiff from having absorbed a geyser of blood. But, of course, Shauna has made sure that the jury knows this already. How many times had Will objected when their positions were reversed? Cumulative, waste of time, unduly prejudicial. Those had been his arguments, rejected by Dars. The jury had seen all of it, even gotten to pass around the horribly crusted plastic-bagged pieces—what is left of the tee shirt that had been slit in two when the doctors cut it off Travis's body.

"How much bigger was Sergeant Hollis than me?"

"Two inches taller and about eighty-five pounds heavier." Luz had measured and weighed Will herself, using—God help him—the scale Meredith kept in their bathroom, the tape measure she stored in her sewing box.

"What are you wearing?"

"One of Travis's tee shirts that I kept." Luz's eyes are glittering now. She swallows and Will can feel it in his own throat, the enormity of what she is forcing down. "A pair of sweats I used to wear when I was heavier. Right after the baby."

"That is how you were dressed the night your husband died?"

"Yes."

Will looks at Dars. "At this time, we ask the court to

permit the witness to step down." Dars's eyebrow goes up, and Will takes a breath. "For demonstrative purposes."

Shauna is on her feet, as Will knew she would be, a mind-numbing list of objections shooting from her mouth. *Improper, no foundation, relevance, prejudice.* Again he looks at Dars, tensing. *You let the government put on their show. Now it's our turn.* All along he has been betting on Dars—that he won't dare refuse because it will allow them to once again raise the issue of his bias—but if Will has bet wrong, it's game over.

"Overruled."

Luz descends the steps and stands rigid facing Will, her face unreadable. He feels a rush of affection, a need to offer some kind of reassurance, but they are firmly in role now and his job is to crush her.

Keeping his eyes fixed on her face, Will backs up to the low swinging door that separates the courtroom from the spectator benches. "Do you know the distance between the witness stand and where I am now?"

"Twenty feet."

"Is that approximately the length of the hallway of the house you shared with Sergeant Hollis on the base in Germany?"

"Yes."

Without moving his body, Will shifts his gaze to the bench. "We seek permission to use the items already entered into evidence. The steak knife, the flower vase, the cordless phone, and the moving boxes. We ask that the government provide these items to the witness to set up in the appropriate places."

That request draws another slew of objections from Shauna. Will says nothing, and after a pause, Dars says, "So ordered."

A silence gathers as Shauna stacks the boxes in front of

Luz and puts the other objects on top of them. Will waits until she retakes her seat, then walks Luz through the steps of setting the scene. In response to curt commands from Will, she silently places one of the smaller boxes close to Will to serve as the tiny hallway table, then puts a vase—they had bought a replica to replace the smashed one—on top of it. After each action, Will says, "Let the record reflect," and intones aloud what she has done. After getting Dars's permission, they repeat the steps in the baby's room: at Will's instruction, Luz identifies the crib, the baby, and the phone, which she puts down on the floor.

When Luz has taken her original place twenty feet away from him and restacked the remaining cardboard boxes beside her, he says, "What are those?"

"The actual boxes we used to move. I was packing to leave Travis. Some of the boxes I had never gotten a chance to open so I was reopening them."

"Why?"

"To see if there were things I could take out to make more space for Cristina's things. That's what I was doing when Travis came home from the party."

"What time was that?"

"A little before three in the morning."

"Why were you awake?"

They have practiced this answer a thousand times, and yet she seems to stumble, staring at Will blankly for a moment before answering in a halting voice. "He hadn't come home. I had fallen asleep around 11:30, but then I woke up around 2:00 and he still wasn't there. Cristina was crying. She was hungry, so I fed her and put her back down, but afterward, I couldn't go back to sleep."

"Why not?"

She lifts her shoulders slightly. "He hadn't returned my

calls since the first one. I had called him starting around 10:30, six, maybe seven times. I didn't know where he was."

"Were you worried?"

"I was—I was a lot of things." She looks down, twists again at her wedding ring. "Worried, upset, scared."

"Because of the email messages from Jackie?"

Her lips tighten. "Not about what was in them as much as what I was going to do. What I was going to say, I mean. When he got home."

"Which was what?"

"That Cristina and I were going back to California. That I had called my grandmother and she had said it was okay to move back in with her for a while, with Cristina, and so…" Luz's voice trails off.

"So that was your plan," Will prompts.

"Yes," she says. "As soon as my grandmother could send me money for the tickets."

"Okay," Will says. "Show me how you were reopening the boxes when your husband got home."

She crouches down on her knees and moves to open one of the boxes.

"No," he says. "You weren't using your hands. What were you using?"

A shock of loose hair falls across her face when she looks up at him. She turns her head and gestures at the steak knife lying in a plastic sheath on the floor beside one of the boxes, caked to the handle in a rust of dried blood. She hesitates. Without access to the actual weapon, they have always used a toy version to practice.

"Pick it up."

She closes her fingers over the handle and stares at it.

"Pick it up," he says again loudly, and she does, then pantomimes sawing through the tape on the boxes.

"Then what?"

She puts the knife down. "I heard Travis outside. He was trying to use his key but he couldn't get it to work in the lock. It used to stick sometimes. He started banging on the door and cursing."

"What curse words did he say?"

"Shit. Fuck. Shit. Fuck. Shit. Fuck."

Will lets the words hang there, waiting for her to go on.

"I ran to open the door because I didn't want him to wake the baby. I think he was surprised when it gave way like that because he kind of stumbled into me."

Will beckons and Luz comes flying toward him. When she pulls open the imaginary door, he staggers and pushes her backward. "Like that?"

"Yes." Will had used his full weight, and Luz is breathing audibly, back on her heels. More hair comes loose from her ponytail, partially obscuring her face, but he can see two scarlet spots forming, one on each cheek. Will has a sudden, almost overwhelming urge to pull Luz into his body, to feel the warmth of her skin. To inhale her. He sees her on the conference table staring up at him, eyes wide, her legs wrapped around his waist.

But she isn't looking at him that way now and he could swear her head is shaking slightly. What had she said to him once, afterward? *You need to be angrier, Will. You need to hate me.*

He blinks. "What happened after he stumbled into you?"

"I told him, 'Travis, you can't stay here. You're too drunk.' He smelled like liquor and he was angry in that way he gets. I didn't want him waking up Cristina."

"Did he leave?"

"No." She pushes back the loose hair, tries to tuck it behind one ear. "He said, 'This is my house. I'm not going anywhere.' He grabbed me. He started shaking me—"

Will puts his hands on Luz's shoulders, pulls her to him, away, and to him again. "Like this?"

"Harder. My head kept hitting the wall."

"Like this?" Will uses more force, jerking her back and forth against an imaginary surface.

"Ye-e-s." He hears a vertebrae crack in her neck, feels her recoil.

"Then what?"

"I pushed him." Luz puts her hands against Will's chest and gives him a surprisingly forceful shove. "And he reached out and grabbed my face, around my jaw."

Will pulls her toward him again, cupping her chin in the V between his thumb and forefinger and pushing down into the sides of her face. "Like this?" Behind him, he hears someone in the gallery gasp.

"Yes." His grip is making it difficult for Luz to speak, and he has to ease up slightly so she can get the word out. Their faces are inches apart now, his fingers on her jawbone, clamping her in place.

"Then what?"

"He took off his shirt and his belt—"

With his free hand, Will pulls his tee shirt over his head and undoes his belt buckle, sliding it through the loops of his jeans. It's the craziest thing he has ever done in court and physically one of the most difficult—it's tricky as hell to hold her still and undress himself at the same time. But strangely, it's a relief; he's hotter than he realized, sweat is trickling down his exposed rib cage. The frozen silence in the courtroom fissures. Will hears rumbling all around him, sees Shauna stir in her seat.

"Your Honor, this is highly improper—"

Will keeps his eyes on Luz. "State of mind. This entire case is about my client's state of mind."

"Overruled."

"Finish what you were saying," Will tells Luz.

"He told me to pull down my pants."

He turns her face a few inches in the jury's direction, forcing her to speak to them. "Meaning what?"

"He wanted to have sex." She tries to look down, but Will tightens his grip on her jaw, stamping the pads of his fingertips onto her skin. She takes a shallow breath and he eases up again to let her get out the rest of her answer. "That's what always happened when he was like that. He would want to and I would—I would let him just to make it not so bad."

"Did you let him this time?"

"No."

"What did you do?"

"I scratched his face."

Her nails rake his cheek and he can feel tiny dots of blood spring up along the trail they leave behind.

"What did he do?"

"He hit me."

Will lets go of Luz's chin and smacks her across the face. It's a clean flat hit, not hard enough to take her down, but nearly, and it's shatteringly loud. Luz stumbles backward, her hand to her cheek. The courtroom erupts in sound and Shauna is on her feet.

This time Dars isn't having it. "That is enough," he bellows. "Do that again, Mr. Ellet, and you will be removed from my courtroom. And to everyone else, you will remain silent or be escorted out."

Will does not look away from Luz. "Then what?"

"I ran to the baby's room where the cordless phone was. When I got in there, I shut the door and locked it." She turns, moves quickly into the space where they have placed the crib, shuts an imaginary door, and picks up the phone. "I called Captain Aronson." Will moves swiftly to close in on her.

"Why didn't you call the police?"

"Travis *is* the police." Her eyes are glittering again and she takes a ragged breath. "They're all— Those are the guys he serves with. I just thought—" She breaks off.

"Thought what?" He has turned to face her, his back to the jury.

"If I could get Captain Aronson to come over he could handle the situation. He understood about it and he was— he was Travis's commanding officer."

He points his finger at her, half turns to the jury. "You were sitting here in court when Captain Aronson testified about the call you made. Did it go the way he said?"

"Yes."

"Not crying or screaming, were you?"

"No." Her voice is lower now.

"I can't hear you."

"I said no." A hard emphasis on the last word. Another ragged breath. "I was trying to stay calm, for the baby and because I didn't want to—to escalate the situation."

He wishes she hadn't used that word; it isn't hers, it's Dr. Cartwright's, and it rings false. "What was the situation at that point?"

"Travis was banging on the bedroom door and Cristina had started crying. Captain Aronson had to repeat himself. He told me, 'Let me speak to Hollis,' so I opened the door to hold out the phone and when Travis took it I kind of slid around him out of the room—"

Will, looming in the imaginary doorway, snatches the phone out of her hand.

"Then what?"

"I heard Sergeant Aronson say, 'Hollis? Hollis? What's going on there?'"

"And then?"

She looks at him steadily. "Travis answered the way Detective Aronson testified."

"'You stupid cunt.'" Will takes his time with each word, staring her down. "Then what?"

"He threw the phone against the crib."

Will hurls the plastic phone, which hits the side railing with a satisfying crack. "Was Captain Aronson still on the line after that?"

"No."

"Where were you at that point?"

"He was coming after me. I was running down the hallway to the front door but then I turned around because I realized I couldn't leave—couldn't leave Cristina there." Luz doesn't need to be told now. She runs the length of the hallway and Will comes after her. When she whirls around, he is right in her face.

"I told him then—" Luz is out of breath, her ponytail a tattered mess "—that I knew about Jackie and the baby. All of the lies—I knew. I told him to get out. To get out of the house."

Will leans in, leering at her. "It's my house," he says. "You get out, you stupid cunt."

Luz's slap is open-handed, right to left, and it stings hard enough to bring tears to his eyes. "I'm leaving you." Her voice rises to a near scream. "I'm taking Cristina and we're going back."

"Your Honor—" Shauna's voice is practically pleading.

"Overruled."

Will puts his hands around Luz's neck. No matter how many times they have practiced, it still surprises him how stem-like it is, how easy it would be to snap. "You're not going anywhere with my baby. You are never going anywhere." Will says the last five words like they are each separated by a period. They are nose to nose now. This close, her eyes are inky black, all pupil. "Start praying," he says in a low voice that is meant to carry.

Shauna is on her feet again, objecting.

"There is no question pending," Will says through gritted teeth.

"Then ask one," Dars says tightly.

Will backs off a few inches but keeps his hands firmly around her neck. "What did you take it to mean when your husband suggested you start praying?"

"That he was going to kill me."

Will tightens his grip.

"Could you breathe?"

"Yes, but it was getting harder."

He feels her throat constrict as she tries to swallow and he forces himself to ease up.

"He grabbed my hair and pulled my head back—"

Will yanks hard on what is left of her ponytail. The hair tie falls out and her neck arches, her chin pointed at the ceiling, the mark on her face like a red stripe where he's hit her. She looks terrified, eyes rolling like a colt caught out in a thunderstorm.

"What did you do?"

"I kicked him and scratched him."

"Show me."

Again she scratches him, leaving a parallel track beside the first one, and kicks at him in the shins with her bare feet. "Did he let go?"

"No. But out of the corner of my eye, I could see—" She tries to wrench free and he jerks her back.

"See what?"

"The flower vase on the table. I got hold of it and I hit him over the head." Luz picks up the actual vase from the make-shift nightstand and cracks it against Will's skull. She's hit him hard and he actually cries out, his hand to the side of his head, and then she is running back down to the other end of the hallway and he is chasing her.

She stops as she reaches the clerk's bench and turns to face him. Will crouches down. He is intensely present in the moment, his physical odor raw and pungent like an animal's, and yet also outside of his body, disconnected from himself and from her, watching from a distance. There are no more questions and answers now, they are in it.

Luz picks the steak knife off the floor. She holds it out, tip first, wavering. "Stay away from me or I'll cut you."

"Fucking bitch," he yells. "Whore. You ruined my life." The last line is unscripted, and it's the one he means the most.

"Stay away from me." She is screaming now, her face contorted, the knife hand shaking.

Will pulls back his fist like he is about to hit the heavy bag at the gym. He lunges, putting his full weight forward and Luz shoves the knife toward him, the thick plastic encasement hitting the left side of his chest. He lets it stick under his armpit; from the jury's vantage point it looks like it has entered his body. He waits a moment, then steps back, letting the knife fall. He's breathing heavily as he sinks to his knees.

Luz is weeping now openly, her hands at her sides. "I was afraid, I thought—I thought if I could scare him, get him away from me, but then—"

"Then what?" Will is trying to get his breath under control, but finds that he is still panting. He lies on the ground.

"There was so much blood. And I could hear Cristina,

she was still crying. I thought I should call for help, so I ran back in her room to get the phone but it was broken from when he threw it and when I came back into the hallway there was even more blood." Luz does not act this part out. Instead, she stands still, her eyes squeezed shut. *"Mi culpa,"* she whispers.

This is not in the script. Will shoots Luz a warning look, but her eyes are still closed. *"Mi culpa mi culpa mi culpa."* She is rocking back and forth, her eyes squeezed shut, her arms hugging her chest. Tears streaming down her face.

"What did you do?"

She opens her eyes and takes a long shuddering breath. "I sat down next to him. He was on his side and I saw his cell phone in his back pocket. I used it to call the desk—"

"The recorded call we heard?" From his prone position, Will has to project his voice to make sure the jury can hear him.

"Yes."

"Then what?"

"I held him." Luz sinks down to the carpet beside Will, raising his head and putting it in her lap. Her hands are warm running over his scalp, itself slick with sweat. "I said, 'Baby, baby. Please don't die. Please don't die, baby.'"

Will lies against her, finally allowing his body to relax and be still. Luz's hair is a tangle, her sobs echoing off the walls, tears running down her face and onto his body. As his chest finally stops heaving, Will feels Luz convulse. He reaches for her hand and she takes it, bending over him, her voice in his ear.

*Mi culpa.*

Friday, March 23, 2007
7:13 a.m.
Riverside, California

Luz says goodbye to Father Abelard at his front door and walks slowly to Will's car, her head down. She is wearing a black dress with short sleeves. It's not the right look: too short, too dark, too informal. Will knows that Abby would have told Luz to go back inside and put on something else, but given the blow Luz has just had to absorb, Will doesn't have the heart to say anything. She gets into the passenger seat and puts on her seat belt.

Will reaches for her hand and squeezes it as he backs out of the driveway, but Luz doesn't return the pressure and he lets go.

"She's dead."

"I know," Will says. "Father Abelard told us. I am so sorry, Luz." The call had come in at around 5:30 a.m., jolting Will out of the deeper end of a fitful sleep. He had assured Meredith that everything was fine, the judge just wanted them all there early, and to go back to sleep. Then he had slipped out of the bedroom to call Abby, shaved and gotten dressed in the bathroom, and left to get Luz.

Luz is silent, not looking at him, and Will adds, "And I'm sorry we couldn't get you a few days off. Abby spoke to the clerk this morning to explain the situation, but the judge was—" He pauses, unable to come up with a euphemism. "The judge is an asshole."

Luz seems not to have heard him. "Cristina and I have no family now," she says. "There's no one left."

"No," he says, "don't say that."

"Why not? It's true." She is staring out of the passenger window.

Will wants to say, *You have me.* But the words are corny beyond belief and in any event, not true. He's not her family. He's her lawyer. Her half-crazed, besotted lawyer. But did that necessarily have to be the beginning, the middle, and the hard end of a relationship that had never stayed within those boundaries in the first place? Maybe this was a sign. Maybe it was time for Will, like Charles, to take a wild, scandalous action and embrace an utterly different way of thinking about the world and his place in it. Maybe that break—with convention, expectation, tradition—was the end of the story, in the same way it had been for Charles and Sarah. At least in one of the novel's three endings.

Deep in thought, Will pulls out of the driveway and heads west toward the freeway.

"She's right," Luz says out of nowhere.

It takes him a moment to register what she'd said and even then, it makes no sense. "Who?" he asks. "Who's right?"

"She said I was going to have to make my own family."

"Abby said that?"

She nods.

"Meaning what, exactly?"

Slowly, she shakes her head. "Nothing," she says. "It was

just a conversation we had. It doesn't mean anything." She turns again to look out the window.

Feeling her attention slipping away, Will says, "I missed you yesterday after court." It had been the first evening that they hadn't met to practice Luz's direct examination in as long as Will can remember. Leaving the office to go home, Will kept thinking he was missing something, had repeatedly checked his pockets for his wallet, his keys, his parking pass, only to realize that what was missing was the time he would normally be spending with Luz. At that point, the endorphins that had been coursing through him since their triumphant performance in court had evaporated. There would be no more practice sessions because the show was over. But maybe it wasn't after all.

"You did?" she says. "That's nice." But her voice is distant, as if she is talking to a well-wisher she barely knows. They drive in silence for a few blocks until they get to the intersection. The light turns green. Straight ahead is the freeway ramp. This is it: the literal fork in the road. Will turns left, heading east again, speeding down the road that leads to Maria Elena's empty house.

"Where are you going?" Luz says, and then, when several turns later it becomes clear, she says, the pitch of her voice sharper, "What are you doing?"

Will waits until he has parked in front of Maria Elena's house to answer. He turns off the engine, and turns to Luz. He strokes her cheek with his thumb. "We have some time before court," he says. "I picked you up early."

She is staring at him now, barely breathing.

"Let's go inside," he says, "Be together."

Luz is shaking her head: short, sharp gestures.

"I know this sounds crazy and I wasn't going to say anything but, Luz, I love you." He reaches for her and she pulls away. "It's not just for now. I am going to leave my wife. I am going to be with you, always. And I know you probably don't believe me, you think it was about—that it was only to—" He stops. "But what I am telling you is the truth." He leans forward to kiss her, pulling her toward him over the gearshift as he slides his other hand up her skirt. He waits for her mouth to open, for her legs to part, but she is rigid, unyielding.

"I love you," he says again in her ear, knowing he sounds desperate but unable to help himself.

Luz's shove sends Will back against the steering wheel with enough force that his neck muscles contract reflexively, causing whiplash. "What are you talking about? You want to leave your wife? You want to fuck me in my dead grandmother's house? You think that's what I want?" The words feel violent, but underneath he hears a strangled sob and then she is weeping, her hands over her face, her shoulders shaking.

Flooded with shame, Will tries again to reach for her, apologizing, saying that he just wants to be close to her, to comfort her. "I know," he says, "it's a lot. Maybe I said too much just now. You need time. But let me hold you," he says, again and again, "let me."

Luz lifts her hands from her face. Her eyes are streaming, her nose is running, her makeup looks like a child has experimented with black and red finger paint, but to Will she is the most beautiful woman in the world.

"I love you," he says again.

"Leave me alone," she says in a fierce, quiet voice he has never heard before. Mortified now and also a little frightened, Will starts up the car again, making a U-turn to head back to where he came from. Luz turns away, making a small place for herself on the far edge of the passenger seat. For the rest of the ride, she never once looks in his direction.

"First," Dars says, "some ground rules before we call in the jury." He seems to have put extra gel in his pompadour today, aspiring to a regal look, his gaze imperious as he looks out over the packed courtroom.

Lawyers from both offices are out in force, but a sizable part of the crowd is reporters. The *Los Angeles Times* and every other local paper has diligently covered the trial. In addition to leading the local news—radio and TV—Will and Abby have fielded calls by CNN, Court TV, and even *People* magazine, which is running Luz as one of their true-crime features. The fact that neither they nor Shauna are permitted to talk to the press has made the feeding frenzy worse; into the void have jumped so-called experts of every stripe: former prosecutors and defense attorneys–turned–law professors spouting nonsense, speculating about the lawyers, their strategies, and most especially about Luz.

Beaten Wife or Cold-Blooded Killer, screamed yesterday's headline in the *National Enquirer*, which was apparently having a slow week on the celebrity muckraking front.

"Number one," Dars says, looking at the lawyers, "there was a last-minute request from the defense for a break in the trial to allow the defendant to mourn her grandmother, who passed away yesterday. That motion is denied. The jury is here and we are not going to stop this trial."

Will sees Luz sag visibly in her chair, and even though he knew this was coming, he is suddenly so angry that it takes all of his self-control not to hurl a stream of invective at Dars. How is it possible to be so inhumane? Then he thinks about his own behavior in the car and his face grows hot. He was no better than Charles, who in the novel's pivotal scene had forced himself on Sarah under the delusion that they were seeking the same kind of intimacy. Depending on which ending of the book one embraced, Charles's decision to indulge his selfish hunger had cost him Sarah's love. Will sighs, more loudly than he had intended, and is rewarded with a withering look from Abby.

"Number two," Dars continues, "and on a related topic. The government has moved to exclude any reference to the grandmother's death. I'm going to grant that motion. We are not going to have this jury contaminated by extraneous matters or moved by undue sympathy."

That last comment gets Will to his feet. "Your Honor—"

"Sit down, Mr. Ellet. You got to put on your little show. Now it's Ms. Gooden's turn."

Will takes a quick glance at Shauna, noting the careful choice of clothes: navy blue suit, white blouse, tasteful pearl necklace and earrings. Light touches of blush and eyeshadow. She looks all business: classy but not cold.

"Number three." Dars lets his gaze settle on Luz. "I've

given a lot of thought to the attorney-client communications here—the ones between the defendant and Mr. Estrada. Now, I've had my law clerk look into this, and it is clear to me that the defendant does not waive the privilege by taking the stand in her own defense. Not based on what we know. The only reason to break the privilege would be that she used her attorney to help her kill her husband and we don't have evidence of that."

Shauna stands. "Respectfully, we might, Your Honor, but Mr. Estrada has declined to provide it."

"So he has." Dars gives a sage nod. "And I put him in jail for it. But the fact remains that without him telling me, in a sealed hearing, outside the presence of the government, a privilege that I extended to him—" here Dars's voice takes on a tone of righteous indignation "—I don't have the basis to make that ruling. Therefore, Ms. Gooden, you may not inquire into those conversations. But you can ask the defendant about the fact that she made those calls, when she made them, how long they were, that sort of thing. The jury has that evidence in the form of his billing records."

Over Luz's head, Will and Abby exchanged a relieved glance.

"Alright then. Mrs. Rivera Hollis, you will retake the witness stand. Let me remind you that you are still under oath."

From the beginning, Will can sense it's going wrong. All wrong. Within minutes, Luz's affect has gone from flat to pissy. At first, she sounded like a bored teenager. Now she sounds like a bitch. He can feel Abby tensing; her poker face mask is firmly in place but she has gone pale, her lips pressed together in a thin, bloodless line.

"That's not what I said."

Will snaps his attention back to Luz, who has crossed her arms over her chest and is glaring at Shauna.

Shauna smiles pleasantly, as if over a minor misunderstanding. "You didn't say to Captain Aronson that the only way to get away from your husband would be to kill him?"

"No. I told him Travis was possessive and jealous and that he could get violent if he thought I was even looking at another guy."

"Why would Captain Aronson say that you said you would have to kill your husband to get away from him if it wasn't true?"

"I don't know. Why don't you ask him?"

Shauna casts her doe eyes at Dars. "Your Honor, please admonish the witness that it is my job to ask the questions and the defendant's job to answer them."

Dars, who has settled back in his chair, appears to be thoroughly enjoying himself. "It sounds like you did just that, Ms. Gooden. Next question."

"You told the jury that before you stabbed your husband, he had attempted to rape you—"

"I never said it was rape." Luz's eyes are glittering.

Clearly surprised, Shauna takes a literal step back. "Did you want to have sex with him that night?"

Luz shakes her head like Shauna is stupid. "It's not about whether I wanted it. He was my husband. What happened between us wasn't rape."

"You had sex to make up after fights?"

Luz is practically rolling her eyes now at the obviousness of the question. "Sometimes."

"But not that time. You were not willing to make up with your husband that night, were you?"

"You saw—" Luz gestures to the narrow pathway where

she and Will had so per
dance.

"Objection," Will says.
voice he's hearing. "Argume

"Overruled."

Luz turns back to Shauna, c
do you think I could have done?"

"You created the situation and the
it, because you were angry." Shauna,
both firm and sorrowful, lands the arro

"You think I got him drunk? You think I made him hit
me?" Luz shakes her head in disgust. "Look at him. Look
at me. What do you think I could have done?"

"I think," Shauna says evenly, "that you wanted to make
him as hurt and angry as he made you. I think your intent
was to provoke him."

Luz snorts. "You don't know anything about my intent."

"I know you were angry."

Will is up again. "Objection. Calls for speculation—"

"Overruled."

"Your Honor—"

Without looking at him, Abby says in a barely audible
whisper, "Sit down and shut up, Will."

"I wasn't angry," Luz says.

Shauna's eyes widen. "Hours before he came home
drunk, you learned that your husband had betrayed you
in the worst way possible by fathering a child with his ex-
girlfriend. Your testimony to this jury is that you weren't
angry?"

"I was disappointed."

Shauna lets her answer hang in the air for a moment
before moving on. Will cannot bear to look at the jurors,
pretends to take notes on his notepad.

Shauna reminds her, "that you were
ur husband when the money came through
ndmother for plane tickets. That could take
eks. What was your plan in the meantime?"

shrugs. "Just take it day by day, I guess. I thought
is would leave after I told him to and we could live
part until it was time for me and Cristina to go."

Now it is Shauna who is crossing her arms, taking on, Will has no doubt, the expression she once used with her own kids when they lied to her face about something readily disprovable. "So let me see if I understand. Your husband comes home, very drunk. You tell him that you are leaving him and taking Cristina with you even though, according to you, he was possessive and was never going to let go of you much less let you take his daughter away. Your expectation was that his response would be to leave the house voluntarily and what? Go stay with friends on the base in the meantime?"

"I don't know. I guess."

"Even though, according to you, when your husband got very drunk, he got violent."

"According to me?" Luz shakes her head in disbelief. "Ask the guy he punched in the face at the bar. Ask his friends. Ask anyone who knew him." Her voice gets louder with each sentence. "When he got drunk and jealous, he got mean, and he wanted to take everybody else down with him."

"But he wasn't going to take you down, was he?"

"I wasn't going to let him kill me, no." Luz's eyes are glittering again, her hand raised, a shaking index finger pointed at Shauna. She is so angry that Will can feel it; for a moment he can feel the blade entering his own body.

"He never said he was going to kill you, did he?"

"No." Luz's tone has gone sarcastic. "He just slapped me, yanked back my hair so my head almost came off from my neck. He just called me a cunt and told me to start praying. That's all." Luz turns to the jury with a frosty smile. *Can you believe this bullshit?* Will, watching the twelve faces, wills her to stop, wills it all to stop.

"But all those things had happened before in your relationship, to one degree or another, right?"

"This time it was different."

"It was different because you decided it was going to be different."

"It was different because I had Cristina to think about."

Shauna nods. "You didn't want her growing up in that environment."

Luz stares at her, shaking her head in disbelief.

Shauna appeals to Dars, who says, "Answer the question."

Luz rounds on him, half rising in her chair, and screams, "I had to protect my baby." The sound of her voice seems shocking even to her, and she sinks back down with her hand over her mouth.

Dars says evenly, "Raise your voice like that again and I will strike your testimony. All of it." He nods at Shauna. "Ask your next question."

Shauna's voice is quiet but firm. "Are you telling us that if it hadn't been for Cristina, you would not have resorted to violence?"

Luz is back to rolling her eyes. "I am not a violent person. I don't go around stabbing people, if that's what you mean."

Will is on his feet but Shauna's question is already out.

"Isn't it true that when you were in high school you stabbed a girl in the bathroom?"

Will is shouting, "Sidebar, Your Honor."

Abby has already started for the bench. When they are gathered around the court reporter, she speaks first, her face the color of ash. "Your Honor, we move for a mistrial—"

"Not you." Dars turns pointedly to Will. "She's your witness."

Will has made the mistake of looking at Luz, who is staring straight ahead, eyes vacant. There is too much saliva in his mouth and he has to stop to swallow. "We move for a mistrial," he repeats. "You ruled weeks ago that her juvenile prior could not be brought up and there's case law stacked to the ceiling that says so. Those are sealed records." He hears his voice shake. "They are never admissible. Never."

Shauna says, quietly, "She just lied. When a witness lies, I have the right to expose the lie."

"She didn't lie," Will explodes. "Jesus Christ."

"That is enough." Dars is looking past them at the jury box and Will follows his gaze to meet twelve wide-eyed stares. Dars turns back and says in a low voice, "The motion for a mistrial is denied." Will starts to say something and Dars puts out his hand, five fingers spread, inches from Will's face. "Shut up. Shut. Up." The court reporter lifts her hands from the stenographer's machine and for a moment they are all silent, waiting.

Dars says, "The defendant did lie. She's been lying. She's a liar. But—" and now Dars is looking at Abby "—I'm going to do *you* a favor here. I'm gonna split the baby. So to speak." He smiles at his own humor. "The question will be withdrawn and stricken from the record. The jury will be instructed that the defendant was in a physical altercation in high school with another student where she used a knife to inflict injury."

Beside him, Will hears Abby's sharp intake of breath.

He says, "That's worse than letting her answer the question. At least then she could explain—"

Dars leans in, his face inches from Will's. "She doesn't get to explain. Now step back."

"Your Honor—"

"I said step back."

Shauna nods once, turns, and briskly walks to her place at the podium, Will and Abby trailing in her wake.

"Alright then." Dars leans forward, his eyes on the jurors. "The question is stricken. But I am taking judicial notice that the defendant was involved in an incident where she wielded a knife against another student while at school at the age of sixteen and inflicted injury. Judicial notice means you are to accept what I have told you as a proven fact." He looks at Shauna. "Move on."

Shauna turns a page in her notebook. "When we left off, you were telling us about your responsibilities as a mother. One of those responsibilities is to provide for your child. At the time you were living on the military base with your husband, did you have a job?"

"I would have found something back in California."

"Did you have any savings?"

"No." Luz, scowling, isn't even looking at Shauna now.

"What you did have, though, was Sergeant Hollis's $400,000 life insurance policy?"

"Not while he was alive I didn't."

"Not while he was alive," Shauna repeats and Will feels the dread curdle in his stomach. "But if he was dead, no one stood to benefit financially except for you."

"The money was for Cristina."

"Your lawyer, Mr. Estrada, arranged that?"

"Yes."

"Before you killed your husband?"

"You're acting like I planned it. I didn't."

Shauna looks at the jury. "You picked up a steak knife and stabbed him through the heart."

Luz leans forward, her voice rising again. "I was defending myself. I was defending my baby."

"You had no injuries. He was nowhere near the baby."

"So what? I'm supposed to wait until he broke one of my bones? Until he grabbed Cristina out of her crib and threw her against a wall?"

Will cringes.

"You took a parenting class before you had your daughter, right?"

Will looks at Abby. *Where is she going with this?* But Abby's eyes are trained on Luz, her face a studied blank.

"Yes."

"In the class, you learned to perform CPR, didn't you?"

"Yes."

"As your husband lay bleeding to death on the floor of your house, did you at any point attempt to perform CPR on him?"

"I was in a panicked state, I couldn't think—"

"I'll take that as a no."

"I called for help," Luz says with a note of triumph, as if she is reminding Shauna of a fact she had forgotten. "Before all of it happened. I tried to get help."

"You called your husband's boss. Why didn't you call 911 right away if the situation was as bad as you are saying?"

"I thought I could handle it with him helping me. That's what I believed." Luz is starting to lose energy, her anger flattening to surliness. "I never meant for this to happen. I never thought it would end up like this."

"Like what?"

Luz gestures to the jury, the judge, then the whole courtroom in a widening sweep of her hand. "I never thought I would be here."

"You never thought anyone would blame you, isn't that right?"

"No one should blame me." Luz has crossed her arms again, is staring at Shauna defiantly.

"But you blame yourself," Shauna says softly, "don't you?"

"No, I don't."

"When you are being honest, you do."

"I'm not lying," Luz says, stubborn as a cornered child.

"Well, you weren't lying yesterday. Do you remember what you said?"

"Not really. Basically, I was out of my mind. Having to relive that night—" Luz breaks off. "You have no idea. You have no idea," she repeats, "what I have had to go through."

Shauna nods sorrowfully as she looks at the jury.

"What does *mi culpa* mean?"

Luz's eyes get hard. "That's not what I meant."

"I am asking you about what you said. To these twelve people. Twenty-four hours ago. What do the words mean, in English?"

Will gets to his feet, putting his hands on the table to steady himself. "Objection, this is badgering. She's answered the question."

"No," Dars says, "she hasn't." He says, slowly and deliberately, "Mrs. Rivera Hollis, what do the words *mi culpa* mean?"

Luz stares stonily back. "My fault."

When it is finally, horribly, and irrevocably over, Abby turns to Will. Having tried and failed to get her to look at him throughout, to connect with her in any way, he now finds he can barely meet her eyes.

"You did this to her," she says.

Friday, March 23, 2007
12:30 p.m.
United States District Court
for the Central District of California

When the clerk calls the case after the lunch break, Will is already standing at the lectern. Abby keeps her eyes on Dars as he strides up to the bench, black robe flowing.

"Alright," Dars says when he has taken his seat, "we are in court outside the presence of the jury, but apparently in the presence of half of Los Angeles." He smirks at the packed gallery. "All of you media people stayed here for the spellbinding experience of listening to us settle the jury instructions." He shakes his head at their collective stupidity and shifts his attention to Will and Shauna, "I've got the twelve of them back there waiting on us—" he jerks his thumb over his shoulder at the deliberation room "—and I don't intend for this to take long. I will instruct them, you will give your closing arguments, and they will start their deliberations this afternoon.

"Now, my practice is to give the standard Ninth Circuit

jury instructions. Ms. Gooden has been kind enough to submit the instructions that apply to this case; I've looked them over and they seem appropriate. I take it the defense has had a chance to look through them, as well?"

"Yes, Your Honor." Will looks at him steadily.

"Do you have any objections to the instructions proposed by the government?"

"We do, Your Honor."

Dars raises his eyebrows at this unpleasant surprise. "And what is your objection?"

"We would ask that the instructions on the lesser in-cluded offenses be removed. The government charged Mrs. Rivera Hollis with first-degree murder. That has been the government's theory—their only theory. They aren't en-titled to have the jury instructed on anything else—not second-degree murder, not manslaughter, not criminally negligent homicide. They haven't offered any evidence to prove those crimes."

Abby watches as Shauna's eyes widen. She stands. "Your Honor, it is standard practice to give these instructions. The law is clear. The government needs to show only a scintilla of evidence for these lesser crimes to apply." She holds up her hand, forefinger and thumb less than an inch apart. "And furthermore, it is beneficial to the defendant because—"

"They can't even meet the scintilla standard," Will in-terrupts. He turns to Shauna. "And with all due respect, the government has no business telling me what is in the best interests of my client."

Abby's eyes move to Dars. "Well," he says to the packed gallery, "I guess you are getting a show after all." He turns to Shauna. "Madame Prosecutor, are you intending to argue any theory to the jury other than first-degree murder?"

Shauna shakes her head. "Mr. Ellet isn't entitled to a preview of the government's closing argument and neither is the court."

"That's the wrong answer." Dars winces slightly, as if in sympathy for Shauna's misstep. "Luckily for you, I am a big believer in second chances. So let's try this again. Are you going to argue any theory to the jury other than first-degree murder, yes or no?"

There is a pause and then Shauna says, "No."

"I thought not."

Shauna says, "Your Honor, this is sandbagging. And it is reversible error to grant their request. I am asking for the rest of the day to research this issue so that I have a chance to submit a brief arguing—"

"There will be no delay of this trial," Dars says. "I know the law."

"Your Honor, if I may," Will begins.

"You may not, Mr. Ellet. Sit down. We all know who's running the show here." Dars turns to Abby. "This has your fingerprints all over it. The whole trial, you've been the puppet master pulling on the strings, but not every puppet performed the way she was supposed to, did she?" He looks meaningfully at Luz, whose hand is on the cross at her throat, then back at Abby, his eyebrows raised. "So here you are, with this eleventh-hour stunt." He leans as far over the bench as he can, his eyes fixed on her. "After I bent over backward to give your client a fair trial." He smiles toothily. "But therein lies the problem, doesn't it, Ms. Rosenberg? I have been so fair that you don't have a single appellate issue and you know it. So now you are trying to create one."

Abby has gone cold inside. She glances briefly at Will,

who now looks as alarmed as Shauna. He says, "Your Honor, that's not—"

"Shut up, Mr. Ellet." Dars looks at Abby. "I want you at the lectern with your client. Now." He snaps his fingers as if she's a misbehaving terrier. "Get up."

Abby and Luz get to their feet and walk to the podium, Luz first, her back straight, her arms stiff at her sides. At the lectern, Abby puts her hand on Luz's arm to turn her toward Dars.

"Ms. Rosenberg, have you told your client to pursue this legal strategy?"

Stunned, Abby realizes that she has become the new Estrada. For a brief moment, she and Shauna lock eyes. "You are asking about a conversation that is protected by the attorney-client privilege," Abby tells Dars. "I can't answer."

"Don't you dare play games with me." Dars has gone scarlet. "Answer my question or I will hold you in contempt."

"No." Adrenaline is coursing through Abby's body as her mind sends opposing messages. *Tell the truth.* But she can't. *Don't say anything.* But she'll doom Luz.

When Dars speaks his voice is low, dangerously so. "You will tell me and you will tell me right now or I will hold you in contempt. You can have the cell next to Mr. Estrada." He motions to Jared. "Mr. Marshal, stand up." Jared rises, an incredulous look on his face. Beside her, Luz reaches for Abby's hand.

The idea of being jailed, of being away for Cal for even one night, possibly days, has an immediate impact on her body. Abby's breasts ache and then suddenly she feels the wetness seeping through the blouse she is wearing under her jacket. As her panic rises—jail, leaking, Cal—she forces herself to keep her eyes fixed on Dars. Luz's hand, hot and dry, grips hers.

"Your Honor." Abby's words separate and stretch, like a recorded voice on the wrong speed as she tries to think her way out. "If you send me to jail, you'll deprive my client of her attorney. That's grounds for a mistrial."

"That's a baseless motion." Dars inclines his head in Will's direction. "She still has him."

"You just said yourself—" Abby shuts her eyes, trying to summon the exact words "—that I run the show and Mr. Ellet is a puppet. A puppet can't be effective without a puppet master. The Constitution guarantees my client an effective lawyer, not just any lawyer."

"He is perfectly capable of giving a closing argument," Dars retorts. "A law student can give a closing argument."

"He's not prepared to give *this* closing argument. I'm giving it," Abby says. "It isn't a moot court competition— my client's life is on the line. Mr. Ellet is not prepared and you have made it clear, repeatedly, that you will not delay this trial—not for any reason, not grave illness, not death. If you prevent me from representing Mrs. Rivera Hollis, she will suffer extreme prejudice as a result. Any guilty verdict will be reversed on appeal." Abby looks quickly at Will, who has, amazingly, managed not to visibly react. Because what she has just told Dars is a lie. Will is giving the closing argument—or was. He had practiced it not twenty minutes ago for Abby, Antoine, and Luz in the witness room.

Dars looks at Jared. "Mr. Marshal, please approach Ms. Rosenberg."

Abby wants to fall down but she keeps her voice loud and strong. "The defense moves for a mistrial. Because the grounds for the mistrial were created by the actions of the trial judge, the government cannot retry my client without subjecting her to double jeopardy."

"You have an answer for everything, don't you, Abigail?" It is all Abby can do, after everything that has happened, not to gasp at this lapse. Momentarily, Dars has forgotten his place high above her on the dais. He has said her name, an intimacy that calls up their past relationship as courtroom equals, a relationship that now exists only when they've been alone. Dars looks at Jared for a moment, then shakes his head slightly. Then he turns back to Abby. "You may come to find out, though, that you've been too clever by half."

Shauna stands up. "Your Honor, respectfully, the government believes that a contempt charge is unnecessary. The court should simply reject the defense's objection. Lesser included offense instructions are appropriate in this case, it's that simple."

"Not so fast, Ms. Gooden." Dars's eyes are on Luz now. "The defendant will address the court." Dars leans forward again, his head tilted slightly to one side, as if attuned to an inner signal. Abby moves away from the microphone and Luz steps forward.

"How old are you, Mrs. Rivera Hollis?"

"Nineteen." Luz's voice, too, is clear and strong. She meets his gaze and holds it.

"How much schooling have you had?"

"I have a GED."

Dars nods. "We've been using a lot of fancy lawyer terms here today. Lesser included offense, double jeopardy, scintilla of evidence. Do you understand what has been said here by the lawyers and by me?"

"Yes."

"Alright. Tell me in your own words what you understand to be happening." Dars settles back in his chair like the most patient of examiners.

"The prosecutor wants the jury to be able to convict me for other kinds of murders that aren't first-degree. My attorney says, no, it's first-degree or nothing. You are the one who decides because you are the judge."

"That's right," Dars says approvingly. "But here is what you also need to understand. Your attorney—" he leans forward and points at Abby " thinks that if the jury is faced with a tough enough choice—all or nothing, as you say—they won't convict. That's a risk by someone who likes to gamble. Someone who likes to win. But now what she's gambling with is your life. Do you understand that?"

Luz keeps her gaze trained on Dars. "Yes."

"Alright." Dars settles back once again into his chair, fingers steepled under his chin. "If Ms. Rosenberg bets right, all glory to her. She gets to humiliate the government, she gets her picture in the paper." He nods at the rows of reporters, scribbling furiously. "Ms. Rosenberg likes that, as I'm sure you know. But if she bets wrong, you will go to prison for the rest of your life. Under the law, there is nothing I can do about that, even if I wanted to. Because the penalty for first-degree murder in federal court is life in prison and we have abolished parole. What that means is that you will never get out. You will never hold your baby outside a prison visiting room. And Ms. Rosenberg, well, she'll go home to her baby. Her life, it won't change much at all. Do you understand?"

Abby's ears ring like there is a fire alarm going off in her head.

Luz says, "But if the jury finds me not guilty, I go home to my daughter and no one can take her away from me."

Dars turns his gaze to Abby. "It appears that your client

grasps what is at stake here. Is there anything you would like to say before I rule?"

Abby looks at Dars, then at Luz. "Your Honor, I need a moment to consult with my client."

Dars inclines his head.

Still holding hands, Abby and Luz walk a few steps from the lectern out of earshot of the microphone.

"Lean in as close as you can." Abby is watching the gallery, hundreds of stares fastened on them. Luz does as she's asked, her forehead touching Abby's so they are eye to eye and the world narrows to the two of them. Abby takes a breath. "Luz, listen to me, I leaked right through my blouse the minute the judge told me I might be separated from my baby. And that would only be for a few days. We are talking about the rest of your life. You know Mr. Estrada and I have made arrangements—"

Luz shakes her head. "Travis's mother could still—"

"But it would be harder. We are creating a legal barrier."

"No." Luz's gaze is cold and steady. "Not one day. I will not be separated from Cristina for one day."

"You are making a terrible mistake."

"The judge said you were a gambler."

"He's wrong. If I were in your situation I would never, ever do this."

Luz looks at her for a long moment. "You wouldn't be in my situation." She lets go of Abby's hand. "This is my decision."

Back at the lectern, Dars again asks Abby if there is anything else she would like to say. Abby looks back at him for a long, shimmering moment. "No."

A silence falls. Abby focuses on keeping her breathing under control. Beside her, Luz is utterly still, her eyes on the judge. Dars's gaze sweeps the courtroom, taking in the

journalists, Travis's mother and sisters, the rows of spectators, Shauna, Will, and Abby before finally coming to rest
on Luz. Everyone is silent, waiting.

"The court finds that the defendant understands the stra-
tegic legal decision made by her attorney and is in agreement with that decision. The government's request that the
jury be instructed on any charge less than the charge of
first-degree murder is denied. The court will take a twenty-
minute recess before the reading of instructions and closing argument. We are adjourned."

Friday, March 23, 2007
2:00 p.m.
United States District Court
for the Central District of California

It is the stuff of nightmares. The final exam administered without warning or any time to prepare. Except here a failing grade is a life sentence.

Abby has always excelled by putting her nose to the grindstone, outworking everyone else. She turned in her papers early, found herself with spare time on tests, sought out every extra credit. Never once had she left anything to chance. It was that relentless preparedness that had gotten her into UCLA, then Harvard Law School.

She is wholly unprepared to give this closing argument. All along, it had been Will's job. Abby had listened, offered comments, but never done the work of learning it. Hearing Shauna's seamlessly interwoven story of law and fact had been terrifying. There is enough evidence, more than enough. Emails from Jackie, calls to Estrada, changes to the life insurance policy. The incident where Luz had wielded a knife *just a few short years ago*. Her chilling switch in demeanor on the witness stand.

In the end, that argument had hit hardest. "The defendant was a completely different person when it was my turn to ask her questions," Shauna reminded them. "It wasn't just that she was rude and inappropriate. That's a problem, for sure, but it wasn't *the* problem." Shauna took a beat here to look each juror meaningfully in the eye. "The problem was that she lied to you. Over and over and over again. And she was *mean*. I submit to you that the person you saw in those moments was the real Luz Rivera Hollis, a cold-blooded killer who will stop at nothing to get what she thinks she's entitled to. All on her own, she drove a knife through her husband's skin and bone to tear open his heart. She's guilty and she knows it." Shauna had leaned in, her hands on the jury rail. "She said it herself. *Mi culpa.* My fault." She paused, letting the words sink in.

Facing the jurors now, Abby is focused on all the wrong things. The chill of her still-clammy skin. The wasting of the short time she'd had to prepare. In the bathroom stall, she'd removed her soaked nursing bra, wrung it out, patted herself down with paper towels, and blotted the stains on her blouse as best she could. Then she'd sat on the toilet shaking uncontrollably, her arms wrapped around her body, her teeth chattering. Finally, she had stood, put the wet bra and blouse back on, buttoned up her jacket, and checked her reflection briefly in the mirror. Passable, but barely.

She is thinking of Cal's face, his eyes fixed on hers, tiny fingers resting on her breast, the sound of rushing water filling the bathtub as they sat alone together in the dead of night. What would it be like, never to hold him again outside a clamoring visiting room that smelled like buttered popcorn from a vending machine? To see, over the years, that pure look of adoration cloud and cool as the visits became less frequent, then stopped altogether? To know that Nic had moved on and was raising her son with another woman? She closes her eyes. *Put it away.* Then it clicks as she realizes, *no, don't.*

"Some of us are mothers." Abby makes sure to make eye contact with the jurors who are. "All of us—" she scans the other faces "—have a mother. All of us have an opinion about what it means to be a good mother."

She takes a breath. "Our definitions may differ. Some of us may think that a good mother should stay home with her baby if she can afford to. Then again—" Abby tilts her head, raises her eyebrows appraisingly as she adopts an inquisitorial tone "—those moms get questioned, too. 'You haven't gone back to work yet?'

"Breast-feed-or-bottle-feed-cry-it-out-or-co-sleep?" Abby runs the words together and shrugs her shoulders wearily. "There is nothing like the judgment we visit on mothers." She waits a beat, looking at each juror in turn, then walks back to the defense counsel table and stands behind Luz. This time, when she puts her hands on Luz's shoulders, there is no resistance.

"Now you are being asked to judge this mother. To pass the ultimate judgment on her. To decide whether she is a murderer. In passing that judgment, you may be inclined to make a series of smaller judgments because it makes the ultimate judgment a little easier. That eighteen is too young to get married, the way my client did. That eighteen is too young to get pregnant, the way my client did. That once married and a mother, at nineteen, it was my client's responsibility to get out of her abusive relationship for the sake of her daughter. That the situation in which she found herself was a situation of her own making.

"You can't take any of these shortcuts, though, to find my client guilty of first-degree murder."

Abby looks down at Luz for a moment and smooths a piece of flyaway hair, before returning her hand to Luz's shoulder. "There is no relationship in this life more sacred, more formative, and more vital to our survival than the relationship we have with our mothers. No other relationship even comes close.

"I think we can all agree on that." Abby nods once, sees one of the stay-at-home moms nod back ever so slightly. "And I think we can all agree that in the end what makes a person a good mother is her ability to protect her child from harm, from grave injury, from death.

"My client told you she was afraid her husband was going to pick up their tiny baby and throw her against the wall. Think about that." Abby raises her voice. "Think about that. Her child's fragile skull slamming against a flat hard surface and smashing." Abby walks rapidly to The Well, reaches into the crib, picks up the doll by her plastic arm and hurls her across the room. The doll hits the side of the jury box with a sharp crack then slides sideways, her painted face now looking over her back, one leg askew.

Abby hears a few gasps from the gallery, a thrum of murmurs. "Think about that," she repeats fiercely. "Wouldn't you expect a good mother to do anything she could to stop it from happening? Wouldn't any one of you? My client acted in defense of her own life and of the life of her child. She did a terrible thing. She took her husband's life, and that's why she feels guilty. *Mi culpa.* My fault. Ms. Gooden wants to rest the government's case on those two words. But feeling guilty and being guilty are two different things. This wasn't a choice. My client had no choice."

Abby takes a long, steadying breath. She had not let herself look out into the gallery before, but she does now. It is packed, not a sliver of space on the benches. There are people standing shoulder to shoulder along the back wall. Some she recognizes, from her office and Shauna's, or the press gaggle. But many are strangers drawn by the celebrity of the case, hungry to experience the drama firsthand. To a person, they are staring at her, waiting for what is coming next.

Slowly, she walks to the jury rail and leans over it, just as Shauna had done. "Some of you may have doubt. I understand that. You may doubt that it is a pure case of self-defense. You may believe that my client acted out of jealousy. You may believe this is a crime of passion. Or you may believe that my client acted in self-defense, but that she overreacted. You may believe that she used too much force. That she didn't have to kill her husband."

Abby looks at each juror in turn. "But here's the thing. My client isn't on trial for manslaughter or criminally negligent homicide. Even if you believe, beyond a reasonable doubt, that my client is guilty of something as serious as second-degree murder, you cannot convict her. There is one charge before you and one charge only—cold-blooded, premeditated, first-degree murder. That's it. She's either guilty or not guilty of that single count. You have no other options."

Abby puts her hands together. "Please understand. I am telling you that my client is a good mother. That she killed so that she would not be killed and her daughter would not be killed. But I know that our perspectives may differ. So I will end by reminding you of the law that you swore to follow.

"You may not like the law. It may seem unfair, even unjust. You may want to compromise. You can't. When the only choice is first-degree murder, the only verdict is not guilty."

"How's the waiting?"

Abby looks up. Antoine, standing in the open doorway of her office. "Awful. But I'm thinking—"

"Jury's coming back Monday, at the earliest."

She nods, waving him over as she staples another set of documents, stacks it with the others, and puts them inside a large manila envelope. "Dars will send them home in a few hours and then it'll be the weekend."

Antoine shuts the door, crosses the room in two strides, and takes a seat in the chair opposite Abby's desk, his own manila envelope in hand. "Doing some work in the mean time, I see. Catching up with your neglected clients?"

She shakes her head. "Estrada."

"He alright?"

"As good as can be expected. Thinner. Not in any danger, though. The other guys like him. It's useful having a jailhouse lawyer." Abby seals the envelope, puts it in her purse. "And you know, now that the case is over, he's getting out. Dars doesn't have any basis to hold him anymore."

"So what—you're being a Good Samaritan and helping his lawyer with the release paperwork?"

She shrugs. "Something like that."

"How's his family been holding up?"

"There really isn't any. He and his wife divorced about fifteen years ago. They had one child, a daughter. She was killed in a car accident during her senior year in high school."

"Huh. Did you ever think Estrada was going to break?" Antoine is looking at her intently.

"Not after— No." She takes a second look at Antoine. "Why? What is it?" She nods toward the envelope in his hand. "What's in there?"

"The report on the hard drive. Travis's emails."

Abby reaches for the envelope and pulls out a thick pile of papers. Lines and lines of numbers. Charts. "What am I looking at, Antoine?"

"Report's at the end."

"Just tell me," she says impatiently.

"What do you know about read receipts?" he asks.

"Read *what*?"

"There's an email tracking system you can use. Shows you when your emails have been opened and read. And if they've been opened and read multiple times."

"Okay."

"So our expert, he looked at Travis's emails from Jackie. There's a couple hundred, dating back from October '05 to a couple of days before he died."

"We know that already. Shauna gave us all of them."

"Yeah." Antoine leans forward, elbows on his knees,

and laces his fingers together under his chin. "Thing is, each email from Jackie was opened twice. First time it was opened, read, then marked as unread, so the second time it showed up in the inbox just like it was new. With each one, it looks like the first read and the second read happened within hours of each other. Or at most, a day."

Abby stares at him, her impatience replaced by creeping dread.

"Our guy looked at all of Travis's other emails. Thousands of them. Only Jackie's have two read receipts."

"She was his girlfriend. He read them twice." But even as she says it, Abby knows it isn't true.

"I checked the time stamps on the read receipts against Travis's schedule," Antoine says. "Travis was out on patrol for every first read."

She shakes her head. "He wouldn't give Luz his password. Not when he was having an affair."

"His user name is travishollis. His password is his birthday. I'm thinking she guessed on the first try."

"No one's that stupid."

"Please. Jonathan's been reading your email for years."

"No, he—" Her eyes widen. "Oh, God."

Antoine shakes his head. "All it takes with most people is knowing them well—a few guesses and you're in."

She stares at him.

"What I am telling you," he says patiently, "is that Luz was reading about Travis and Jackie in real time. She always knew. Jackie's email to Luz wasn't a surprise at all. She knew about it all—the baby, the affair. For months."

Abby is shaking her head.

"Almost a year."

Abby closes her eyes. "What's the time lapse between

the first email from Jackie to Travis and the first call from Luz to Estrada?"

"Two months. Luz's first call to Estrada was on December 8, 2005."

She nods. Had it been closer in time, Shauna would have been suspicious, but Luz had waited. "She didn't call Estrada until—"

"She found out she was pregnant," Antoine finishes. "Then she called him nine more times. Meanwhile—"

"Meanwhile legal documents were being signed and executed." No confrontation with Travis until after Cristina was safely delivered from Luz's body. No confrontation with Travis until after Luz's name was on the life insurance policy.

She thinks of Mr. Estrada, then again to what Luz had said. *He told me to trust you. So if you want to know those things now, I will tell you.* But Abby had not wanted to know. She had had another chance to find out, when she had met Luz in her office, ostensibly to talk about Jackie. Abby still had not wanted to know. She had never wanted to know.

"Jackie's email to Luz," Abby says slowly. "Luz couldn't have known about that, much less planned it."

"No, but she could have planned *for* it. She's keeping up with their correspondence, and Jackie's making threats. Luz knew Travis wasn't going anywhere, which means she knew Jackie was going to get fed up at some point and tell all."

"The Facebook posting on October 11."

Antoine looks at her blankly.

"The memory picture of Luz sitting on Travis' lap at the picnic when she was pregnant with Cristina." Abby looks back at Antoine, who is now nodding slightly.

"Oh God. Luz was using Facebook to—"

"Make Jackie crazy-mad."

"She set this whole thing in motion."

Abby looks at Antoine for a long moment. "You've been sitting on this report for days, haven't you?"

Antoine looks back at her, expressionless.

She nods. "You didn't want to pollute my mind with the inconvenient fact that my client is a cold-blooded, pre-meditated—"

"No, I don't like those labels, never have." Antoine shakes his head. "But one thing I do know, is Cristina, that's her life. If Luz thinks something isn't good for Cristina, something's going to jeopardize her being Cristina's entire world, she is going to see it as something to get rid of."

The brutal truth of that statement cuts through Abby like a frigid wind. "So you hid the report because what, you thought I couldn't handle it?"

"I didn't think you needed to handle it. There's been a lot going on. And this would not have helped."

"You should have told me."

"I'm telling you now. Abby, you did your best. Better than your best. And like I said, my money is on you. My money is always on you. But if our girl goes down, I hope you remember that we had this conversation."

She takes a deep breath, picks up the report again. "Is this the original?"

"Yes."

"You make any copies?"

"No."

Abby swivels in her chair, bends down, and feeds the report to the shredder. They both listen as the machine whirs to life, watch as it sluices out paper spaghettini.

A wave of dizziness comes over Abby, similar to what

she felt in the early days of her pregnancy. Like a carsick passenger, she straightens, keeping her eyes fixed on the horizon line, in this case the blank wall space directly in front of her. Images move in and out of focus: Cal's face on her screen saver, Rayshon's picture on the wall, Nic's eyes on her, staring up from the couch when she'd tiptoed from the house that morning in stockinged feet, holding her shoes.

"Hey. Abby. Look at me."

Slowly, she turns back to face Antoine, his face swimming, then coming into focus.

"Guys like Travis Hollis, they need a killing."

She presses her locket into the base of her neck. "Do you think that justifies what she did? Oh, my God, Antoine. Look at what she did."

"You would have done it," he says. "For Cal."

They look at each other for a long moment, interrupted by the ringing of her office phone from a blocked number. Abby's heart stops. She picks up the phone.

"Hello?"

"The jury—" the clerk begins, but Abby cuts her off, her eyes on Antoine.

"They have a question?"

"A verdict."

Abby looks at the clock, then back at Antoine. "A verdict," she repeats, and in an instant, Antoine is out of his chair, phone in hand, texting, then out the door. "But," she says helplessly into the receiver, "it's been less than an hour. Don't they even—don't they even want to take the weekend to think it over?"

There is silence on the other end of the phone.

"I've never had a verdict that fast," Abby babbles, "and not— I mean, it's a murder trial. This can't be—this can't be…" She puts her hand over her mouth to smother the final word. *Good. This can't be good.*

A pause, and then the clerk says, almost apologetically, "It was just the one count, you know?" And then, "Judge Ducey wants you here right away."

Luz is curled up on the floor in the corner of Jonathan's office—he had offered it to her before heading out for court on one of his own cases. Cristina is asleep in her pop-out car seat. As Abby gets closer she realizes that Luz is asleep, too, her arm flung over Cristina's body.

Abby kneels down, brushes Luz's hair off her face. "Luz," she says softly, "you have to get up now."

Luz blinks, and Abby forces herself to wait while her eyes focus. "What is it?"

"We have to go back to court. The jury decided."

Luz pushes herself into a sitting position. "But you said it might be days. You said they were going home for the weekend." Her fingers wrap around Abby's forearm, the nails digging in.

"I was wrong."

Abby tries to keep her gaze steady as Luz searches her face. "You think it's guilty. That's what you think."

"I don't know. But we have got to prepare for the possibility that—"

"No."

Blood beads appear on the soft skin above the inside of Abby's wrist as Luz bears down. Abby takes a breath. "Luz, we have to talk about Cristina and we don't have much time. Father Abelard is in my office now, he's going to take care of her until—"

"No."

The blood is sliding down Abby's arm now, dripping

onto her stockinged knee. "We have your signature on the guardianship papers. The other paperwork we needed to go to court for and we didn't have time. But Mr. Estrada is getting out any minute now. Once that happens, we'll deal with the rest of it."

Luz is shaking her head. "Even if it is guilty, there will be an appeal. I can stay out on my bond. I've never violated."

"There is no bail pending appeal. Not for this kind of crime. The prosecutor will ask the judge that you be taken into custody immediately." Abby hates herself right now. This conversation should have happened days ago. But in the ensuing madness—Maria Elena's death, Luz's disastrous performance on cross, Abby's near-jailing, the barreling toward closing argument—explaining the consequences had dropped out of her mind. There hadn't been time to think. To tell her client, *If they convict you of first-degree murder, you will not be walking out of the courtroom afterward. You will never go outside again.*

"Luz," she says, "I need you to—"

But Luz has thrown herself on Abby, and she now has to struggle to stay upright. Then Luz smacks Abby's face, her wedding ring hitting her mouth. "No, no, no." Luz's voice is a strangled whisper, then a scream. Cristina starts to cry, then wail. The sound temporarily distracts Luz and Abby grabs hold of her shoulders, pinning her to the wall, their faces inches apart. Abby's lip is stinging and she tastes blood in her mouth.

"Stop it." Abby has to raise her voice above the baby's crying. Luz is struggling to get free, and Abby tightens her grip. Finally, Luz stops fighting. Her body falls forward, chin to her chest, and suddenly Abby has to use all of her strength to hold Luz up, her arm tickling as the blood continues to slide down.

"Look at me." But Luz won't. Cristina continues to wail.

Abby's eyes are burning and her throat aches. "Listen to me now," she says, and she is talking to both of them. "Listen to what I am telling you. I'm going to the bathroom to try to fix what you did. You have a few minutes."

She tilts Luz's face upward and presses her uninjured cheek to Luz's forehead like she's checking for a fever. "This was your decision. I let you make it. I let you make it," she repeats as Luz begins to cry and Cristina screams.

Downstairs Will waits with Antoine, his mind going in a thousand directions at once. It's hard to think, hard to see almost. He presses his palms against his eyes, blinks a few times. The lobby is bustling with lawyers and secretaries, some headed home early, but when they see Luz and Abby step out of the elevator, they go quiet, instinctively clearing a path for them.

Outside the weather is as insipid as always: bright yellow sun, not a cloud in the blue sky. They walk, Abby and Luz in the middle, Antoine and Will on the outside. Luz's head is down, her shoulders slumped, fingers twisting the gold chain where the cross hangs on her neck.

"What happened to your lip?" Antoine asks Abby.

Abby fishes in her purse, presses a crumpled tissue to her mouth. Her lip has started bleeding again. "Nothing happened. Everything is fine."

Will turns to look, then quickly looks away.

At the courthouse, it is far worse than he expected. News trucks double-parked, Court TV, CNN, Fox, MSNBC, all the local affiliates. "What about the Spring Street entrance?" Will asks Antoine.

"It's the same. But I called Jared and he's meeting us at the corner."

And sure enough, Jared is standing at the corner of First and Main with six other marshals. "Alright," he says. "Let's go."

Abby takes Luz's hand, nods at Will to do the same. Antoine falls back as the marshals press in on all sides, taking hold of Will's and Abby's upper arms. As they approach the steps, Jared raises his voice. "Step back, let them through. Step back."

The gaggle moves, but just barely. Then come the questions, like shots fired from a semiautomatic weapon.

"What does it mean that the jury came back so fast?"

"Did you kill your husband?"

"Who will take care of Cristina if you go to prison?"

"Are you afraid of going to prison?"

"Step back," Jared bellows. He and the other marshals aren't escorting Abby, Will, and Luz so much as propelling them up the stairs. There are flashbulbs going off, explosions of light and sound. Will watches as Abby shakes her head slightly so that her hair falls over her face and hunches her shoulders, concealing as much as she can. But they aren't looking at her. Everyone is craning to see Luz, saying her name over and over. "Look down," Will says to Luz, shouting over the noise, "keep your head down."

But Luz stares straight ahead, looking neither right nor left as the questions fly. "Was it for the money? Did you do it for the money?"

"Luz, look over here."

"Luz, can you answer the question?"

"Luz, are you a killer?"

Friday, March 23, 2007
3:51 p.m.
United States District Court
for the Central District of California

In the crush and heat of bodies, the din of voices, and the frog-march up the courthouse steps, Will focuses on holding tight to Luz's hand, limp in his own. It is the first physical contact they've had since his awful mistake that morning, which incredibly, had been only hours ago. This is the longest day of his life.

Inside, security officers wave Abby and Will through the attorney line, but Luz has to be stopped, her shoes removed, the contents of her purse examined. The marshals encircle her to create a pocket of space but the crowd pushes back, swollen in the lobby's contained entryway, voices echoing off the marble walls and eighteen-foot ceiling.

As they wait on the other side of the metal detector, Will looks at Abby again. He notices for the first time that she is wearing a different blouse than she had been that morning and she's taken off her stockings. Showing up in federal court with bare legs is almost as bad as showing up drunk, and he briefly wonders whether she's gone back to her old habits. Abby looks like she's been in a fight. There is congealed blood on her lower lip and an angry red mark on her cheek. Will swallows, instinctively touches his own face, but it has been long enough that there is nothing there anymore.

"Are you okay?" he says in a low voice.

She turns to look him full in the face. "What do you think?"

Dars's courtroom is on the second floor but the escalator is mobbed. Jared hustles them into the judges' elevator, the three of them squeezed together inside a circle of marshals. No one speaks. Luz's hand is hot inside his own, her eyes trained on the ground.

The doors open and they step out. More madness. Will tries not to look but he can't help himself. Thank God there are no cameras or microphones allowed in federal court. But the crowd is so dense and loud it is like being surrounded by locusts, an insistent incessant buzzing coupled with a physical pressure of bodies, smells of perfume, cologne, cigarette smoke, and body odor. Jared and his cohorts storm through, forging a knife's edge path. Will, Abby, and Luz clasp hands, following behind in single file.

Inside the courtroom, Dars is on the bench, the clerk below him, Shauna at her place at the counsel table. Waiting on them. The noise level is lower and subsides altogether as the spectators turn to look at them. Side by side, still holding hands, they walk down the aisle through the short swinging doors that cordon off the gallery, Will and Abby like grim parents about to give away their child.

At the defense table, they let each other go. Will pulls

back Luz's chair and gently pushes it forward once she is seated. He and Abby take their places on either side of her.

The clerk calls the case and Shauna, Abby, and Will make their appearances. Will is surprised to hear how normal he sounds, but then again, all he has to say is his name.

Dars says, "We are here for the reading of the verdict."

Hearing the words, Will feels a kind of shock, and he realizes he has been engaged in magical thinking, believing somehow that this wasn't actually happening. Dars leans forward, his eyes on the crowd. "Now," he says, "this case has generated a lot of emotions, a lot of interest. But let me make myself clear—I will not tolerate any outbursts. Not from the victim's family—" he looks meaningfully at Travis's mother and sisters, who are holding tightly to each other's hands, then brings his eyes to Jackie, who is seated next to them, her baby in her lap " —not from counsel, and not from the defendant." His eyes shift to Luz, then back to the gallery. "Not from anyone. If you cause a disruption in my courtroom, you will be forcibly removed." He nods once. "Alright. Madame Clerk will bring in the jury."

The clerk rises from her seat and disappears through the side door. Everyone waits, the silence thickening. Will and Abby retake Luz's hands; Luz's feels boneless. Will wishes she would look at him, but she doesn't. He wishes there were something he could say to comfort her, but there isn't. He looks over at Abby, who also refuses to return his gaze. She is staring down at the table, pulling her locket back and forth across the chain of her necklace.

The side door opens again and the jurors file out stone-faced. Not a single one of them looks at Luz. Will watches Abby watching them, hears her sharp, quiet intake of breath. Luz's head is bent down, her eyes trained on the table.

Luz will not survive prison. Will knows this with a sudden terrifying clarity. She will take a metal slat from her cot and file it down to a fine point, embed a razor blade in a toothbrush, sharpen a pair of scissors on a stone in the rec yard. She will make a weapon and she will use it on herself.

Will looks at the jurors, now seated, willing them to look back at him. None do. They are about to kill her and they don't even realize it. He wishes there was a way to make them understand, to send them back to deliberate with the weight of this knowledge.

"The foreman will rise," Dars says, "and remain standing."

The stay-at-home dad gets to his feet. He is wearing khakis and a light blue button-down, hands behind his back. He looks ludicrously normal.

"Has the jury has reached a verdict?"

"We have, Your Honor."

Dars nods. "Alright. Please provide the verdict form to the clerk."

The foreman brings his right hand forward, holding out a piece of white paper folded like a letter. The clerk takes it, walks back to her seat, then turns, standing on tiptoes, to pass the paper to Dars. Everyone waits while he unfolds it and scans the contents. Time slows down, stops.

Dars refolds the paper and hands it back to the clerk, who returns it to the foreman. Dars looks at Luz, his face expressionless. "The defendant will rise."

Luz's lips are moving. Abby whispers something to her and she stops. They stand, Will and Abby still gripping Luz's hands as they pull her gently from her seat. Her body sways slightly, then stills.

Dars swivels in his chair to face the foreman. "What is your verdict?"

The foreman clears his throat, looks down at the piece

of paper as if to double-check, and looks up again. "On the sole count of the indictment, murder in the first degree, we find the defendant, Luz Rivera Hollis, not guilty."

There is a collective gasp from the spectators and Will raises his fist in triumph, realizes too late that he has yelled, "Yes! Yes! Yes!" like a rabid fan who has just seen his favorite player leap sky-high to pull a spiraling ball out of the thinnest of air. But his hoarse cries have been absorbed in the general uproar and no one has heard him. He puts his hand over his mouth to stifle a sob. Tears are running down his face.

Dars brings down his gavel. His face has gone red and he is yelling, but Will is no longer listening. Luz has let go of his hand, her face buried in Abby's neck. Abby has one arm wrapped around Luz's body, the other cradling her head, five fingers pressed like a white starfish over Luz's dark hair. He will never forget how he feels, the wave after wave of shuddering elation and relief. His wild bet—his and Luz's—has paid off.

Will wants to wrap his arms around both of them. But as he reaches out, Abby lifts her battered face, rests her chin on the top of Luz's head, and gives him a look that cuts him dead.

Friday, March 23, 2007,
4:30 p.m.
United States District Court
for the Central District of California

The euphoria of the verdict quickly gives way to logistical problems. Abby, Will, and Luz cannot leave the courthouse without getting mobbed, so Abby quickly confers
with Jared, who hustles them out of a side entrance and
back into the judge's elevator. This time, they go all the
way to the thirteenth floor to wait it out in an actual judge's
chambers. The judge and his law clerks are away hearing
a case in San Francisco, and his judicial assistant kindly
offers to take them in.

There they sit, waiting. Luz falls asleep almost immediately, curled in the fetal position, her hands clasped together
under her chin. Abby, determined not to let Luz out of her
sight, sits beside her, fielding congratulatory calls on her
cell phone and trying to tamp down her impatience at the
fact that they are temporarily trapped in the building. The
media, as it turns out, has tremendous staying power, doing

man-on-the-street interviews and buttonholing anyone who looks like they might at some point have had something to do with the case while they wait for the stars to arrive.

There is a television in one of the law clerk's offices, and Jared keeps it on low. It's a slow day for national news and Luz's case leads every broadcast. The same pictures are shown again and again: of the three of them harried, heads down, walking to court before the verdict, professional photographs of Abby and Will taken before they started at the federal public defender's office—Abby regretting that she'd forgotten to smile in hers while Will, of course, looks as movie-star perfect as ever—snaps of Luz pulled from her Facebook page, including some that had been shown at trial. Mainly it was those pictures that dominated: Luz on Travis's lap with her protruding belly, Luz and Travis on their wedding day, a beaming Luz holding Cristina in the hospital.

"You're famous," Jared says to Abby. His voice is flat, almost accusatory. "They're calling you and him—" he jerks his head toward the office next door, where Abby has exiled Will "—the best lawyers money can't buy."

Abby looks up warily. "I can't get Nic to text me back," she says. "Have you talked to him?"

Jared looks away. "No."

Abby tries calling. "We won!" she says into his voice mail. "I'm so excited to come home." She pauses, lowering her voice. "I know it's been hard and—and—I'm sorry for everything. I love you, Nicky. Give Cal a kiss for me."

But there is still no word from Nic an hour later when they are finally allowed to leave, taking the judges' elevator to the basement. From there, Jared drives the four blocks back to the federal public defender's office in a van marked POLICE US MARSHAL, Will seated up front, Luz and

Abby in the back. Abby has had to wake Luz up and she is groggy, her head lolling against the seat, eyes half-open. No one speaks.

At the deserted elevator bank, Abby says quietly to Will, "Walk away." He starts, a shocked, pained expression on his face. She says it again, her voice low and warning, and he turns away, heading back to the lobby.

Father Abelard is waiting in Abby's office with Cristina, still in her car seat and sucking peacefully on a pacifier. Jorge Estrada is there, too, sitting in one of the client chairs opposite Abby's desk in a gray suit and silver tie with blue stripes—the same suit he was wearing the day Dars sent him to jail. Luz goes immediately to Cristina, picking her up and speaking to her softly as she undoes the buttons on her blouse, then settles in the corner while Cristina nurses.

Father Abelard looks at Luz and Cristina, then at Abby. His eyes are wet. "A miracle," he says.

Estrada shakes Abby's hand. "Congratulations, counselor."

Abby looks him in the eye. "To you, too. We are grateful."

Estrada releases her hand and steps back, looking her over. "Everything okay?"

The cut on Abby's lip is already starting to scab. Almost guiltily, she puts her hand to her mouth to touch the crusted edge.

"Everything's fine," she says. "And you?"

"Never better." Estrada smiles, a broad genuine grin "I'll get everything filed on Monday." He nods at Luz. "We'll go to court together."

Luz stiffens visibly. "No. I don't want to go back there."

"Luz, honey, it's county courthouse in Riverside, no big thing. When Ms. Rosenberg visited me in the jail, she and I worked out the details, and she tells me you already signed the papers. The judge needs to see us, but it's just a formality."

Abby says quietly, "Court on Monday is about you and Cristina. Keeping everyone safe. The criminal case against you is over. No one can bring it back." Luz nods, turning her attention back to Cristina as Abby exchanges a few more pleasantries with Estrada and Father Abelard. When Luz has finished feeding Cristina and has changed her diaper in the ladies' room, they depart, Father Abelard with his hand on Luz's elbow, Estrada following behind carrying the baby in the car seat.

At the door, Luz turns back to look at Abby, her black eyes enormous. She has scrubbed off the smudged makeup and brushed the tangles from her hair. Her face is naked, impossibly young. "Thank you," she says.

"You're welcome."

Luz looks at Estrada. "You were right about her," she says to him.

"You were right," Abby says to Luz. "And you—" she pauses "—you made me understand what this case was about."

Luz looks at Cristina for a long moment, then lifts her gaze again. "She's my everything, you know?"

Abby nods. "I know."

Friday, March 23, 2007
6:30 p.m.
Weilands Bar & Grill
First Street, Los Angeles

When Paul, Antoine, and some of Abby's other coworkers—
a few of whom had driven back to the office after hearing
the news on the radio—appear in the doorway minutes later
cheering loudly and demanding to take her out to Weilands
for drinks, she hesitates. She should go home now. But Nic
was being such a jerk. Yes, she'd messed up, but she had
apologized and given the circumstances—that, against all
odds, she had gotten an acquittal and given her client her
life back—Nic should find it in his heart to be magnani-
mous. At the very least, he should call her back.

"Come on, Abby, I'm buying," Paul says.

"Well, maybe just one," she says. "But then I really have
to go home."

She texts Nic again, the fourth time since the verdict.
Be home by 7/7:30. Like the others, it goes unanswered.

"You should go home," Jonathan says on the short walk to the bar when Abby tells him.

"Fuck Nic," she says angrily. "Father Abelard said it was a miracle. And you know what, Jonathan, it was. Luz has her life back. A chance to start over with Cristina." She looks at Will, walking several paces behind them, hands in his pockets as he talks with one of the other newer hires in their office, then says in a low voice, "In spite of him."

"I'm not sure that's fair," Jonathan says mildly. "He was the one with the winning strategy in the end."

"And I was the one who executed it. What he did to her—" She shakes her head in disgust.

"What he did to her." Jonathan repeats the words slowly. "Well, I guess that's one way of putting it."

"I would think," Abby says, staring straight ahead, "given the last few days, that I am entitled to celebrate a little with people who are actually happy for me." When Jonathan doesn't answer, she gives him a sidelong glance. "Wipe that Mother Superior look off your face. It's one drink."

"It's never one drink with you." Jonathan sighs. He's wearing the glasses she likes, the ones with the tortoise-shell frames, and his best suit, the Calvin Klein charcoal she loves. He had told her that he'd dressed up for her; remembering that, she feels less annoyed. Their friendship has been strained and severely tested, but now that the trial is over she is confident things between them will go back to normal. "I know I've been really difficult," she says. "And I know how much you've done for me. And Nic and Cal. I'll make it up to you, I promise."

"You can start," he says, "by ordering a club soda."

But she hadn't ordered a club soda, and it hadn't been just one drink. Midway through the third, vodka on the

rocks, her hand reaching for the communal basket of gar-
lic fries, a young man appears at her elbow. He's white,
early twenties at most, in bicycle shorts and a helmet. He
looks strangely familiar. Abby squints, tipsily trying to
place him, and out of the corner of her eye, sees Jonathan
push back his chair.

"Are you Abigail Rosenberg?"

"I am," she says as it dawns on her how she knows him.
From the courthouse.

The young man hands her an envelope that is so stuffed
the flap can't close. "You've been served."

And just like that he is gone, making his way through
the crowd and out the door.

At her side now, Jonathan is pulling some twenty-dol-
lar bills out of his wallet. He throws them down on the
table, picks up her briefcase and her bag, and grabs her
arm. "Let's go."

Abby follows blindly after him, the warmth of the alcohol and camaraderie replaced by an icy fear. It's late
now and overcast, the sky starless. Abby leans against
the brick wall of the building and pulls out the paperwork
with trembling hands. Court forms. A temporary order, ex
parte, granting sole physical and legal custody of Macallan
Rosenberg Mulvaney to petitioner Nic Mulvaney. Stamped
and filed today. She drops it like it's on fire and Jonathan
bends to pick it up, scanning the contents as she pulls out
the next document. *In re Macallan Rosenberg Mulvaney*,
petition by the biological father seeking—Jonathan takes
it out of her hands. More paper. A declaration under penalty of perjury, notarized and signed by Nic. She tries to
read but the words are moving like inchworms across the
page. *Immediate and irreparable harm—fell asleep in the
bath on several occasions with infant.* Jonathan snatches it

away from her. "We are not doing this here. We are walking to my car. We are driving to your house."

She trails behind, panting with near-hysteria and the effort of keeping up with Jonathan's long strides in her high heels for two endless asphalt blocks.

In the parking garage, they climb the stairs to the third floor and Jonathan hits a button on his key chain, unlocking the doors to his black Audi sedan. When they are inside, the doors shut, Jonathan turns on the overhead light, pulls out the paperwork, and starts reading from the beginning.

Cold sweat breaks out on Abby's forehead as her stomach churns. "I think I'm going to be sick," she says.

"Use the trash can by the elevator," Jonathan says without looking up.

She opens the car door and runs, vomiting into the foul-smelling bin until there is nothing left but a string of spittle hanging from her lower lip. Pulling a tissue from her purse, she wipes clumsily at her mouth, accidentally tugging at the scab, which immediately starts bleeding again. She fishes deeper into her purse before finally locating a mini-pack of Cal's wet wipes. Tearing it open, she pulls one out and presses it hard against her lip.

Back in the car, Jonathan passes her a box of Altoids and Abby takes three, sucking hard. It takes a second wet wipe to staunch the bleeding and she focuses her mind on succeeding at that task as she waits for Jonathan to finish reading. When he does, she reaches for the paperwork, but he shakes his head firmly before turning the engine on and pulling out of the parking space.

As soon as Jonathan parks in front of her house, Abby is out of the car, running to the front door. The living room is terrifyingly tidy: the playpen and the bouncy chair are gone. She goes into the bedroom and flips on the light switch. The crib and the changing table are gone. Empty hangers rattle in the closet when she opens the sliding door. Nic's shoes are gone. She rakes her hands through the half-full bureau drawers looking for any sign of Cal— his striped socks, his Elmo blanket, his onesies. Gone. Abby sinks down onto the floor and pounds her fists into the bed. Nic had made it that morning, as he always did. Sheets so taut you could bounce a quarter off them. Abby starts pulling off the pillows, pulling off the bedspread, then the sheets. She is crying, then wailing.

Jonathan comes in, stands behind her, and pulls her to her feet. His hands grip her shoulders as he speaks. "I need you to listen to me." His eyes search hers. "Can you do that?"

Abby forces down a sob and nods her head.

"Nic went to court earlier today and convinced a judge he needed a temporary custody order for Cal, effective immediately. These orders are hard to get and they don't last long. On Wednesday, there will be a hearing in front of the same judge where you can tell your side of the story. That's three business days from now."

When Abby gasps, Jonathan holds up his hand. "Until then, you can see Cal, it just has to be supervised."

"Supervised?" she repeats stupidly.

"It looks like you can spend unlimited time with Cal as long as it is in the presence of a responsible third party." Jonathan pauses. "The order lists a CPS social worker. And me. You can go with either of us to pick him up and you need to stay with one of us the whole time you're with him."

Abby looks at Jonathan. She had expected sympathy but his gaze is clinical. His coldness makes her stomach drop. "You knew," she says. "Oh, my God, you knew he was going to do this."

"I didn't know," Jonathan says evenly, "but I thought it was a real possibility."

"You've been talking to Nic, you've been helping him. You Judas motherfucker—" she struggles away from him but he holds on "—how could you do this—"

Jonathan cuts her off, "I haven't been helping him. But he told me. About what happened in the bath. He was angry, but mostly he was terrified. Ever since, I have been trying to talk him out of it." Jonathan's mouth is set in a tight line. "I warned you, Abby." He shakes his head in disgust. "Goddammit, you should have seen this coming."

Abby, forcing herself to keep looking at him, stifles a sob.

"When we go to court, you will have the opportunity to argue that the order is unnecessary. That Cal isn't at risk when he is alone with you."

"Of course he isn't." Now she is yelling. "I'm his mother. This is insane."

"Be quiet and listen to me. From now on you are going to practice being the most reasonable person in the room. Because that's who's going to win in court. Right now, Nic is coming across as pretty fucking reasonable. You, not so much."

"What if we get this—this thing reversed," she asks shakily. "Then what?"

"The court will order some kind of joint custody pending review of Nic's petition for permanent custody. That could take weeks or months. It's hard to get sole custody, especially for the father. He would have to prove that you are unfit."

"Of course I'm not—"

"You, in the meantime, will take the rest of your maternity leave. All of it. And you will allow Child Protective Services to inspect your home. You will submit to a custody evaluation from a psychologist. You will cooperate with them. You will play nice. You will be nice. To everyone. Including Nic. You should assume from now on that everyone is watching everything you do, even when you are alone. You will not drink. We've been here before, after Rayshon, but you have a lot more to lose now. You've never actually hit rock bottom, but if this isn't it, then I don't know what's below it. So not one sip. Nothing. Don't give the Child Protective Services people any more ammunition than they have already."

The doorbell rings and she starts. "Maybe that's Nic. "

She turns to leave and Jonathan tightens his hold on her. "Stay here."

He walks out of the bedroom, shutting the door firmly behind him. She hears muffled voices, a man and a woman, then Jonathan's voice pitched loud enough for her to hear, "Let's talk outside." The sound of the front door closing, then silence. She stands there, frozen for a moment, then realizes from the sudden overwhelming ache in her breasts that she needs to let down. Her breast pump, is it in the car? She shuts her eyes, trying to remember. Jonathan had taken her bag along with her briefcase when they left Weilands. She's almost certain. She opens the door, walks out into the living room, then stops when she looks out the glass door.

Jonathan is standing on the porch, his back to her, talking to two uniformed police officers. The man, middle-aged, paunchy, his sandy hair cut close, is nodding intently. His partner, the woman, her dark hair in a slicked-back bun, is writing something on a notepad. She looks up. For a brief moment they make eye contact, and then Abby turns, walks back into the bedroom, and turns off the lights. She stands in the corner, shaking, her back pressed up against the wall.

A few minutes later she hears the front door open and close. Jonathan reappears in the bedroom. He pushes the heap of bedclothes aside, then gestures for her to sit next to him on the bare mattress.

"They don't have a warrant," he says.

"A warrant? For what? There isn't anything here." She looks around, then adds bitterly, "Especially now."

"Not for any*thing*. For you."

She gapes at him.

"They don't have enough to arrest you." Jonathan takes off his glasses, massages the bridge of his nose.

"Arrest me?" She repeats the words hoping they will make sense, but they don't.

"A report has been made, an allegation of child endangerment."

"What?" She claps her hand over her mouth, feels the sting of that stupid cut.

"If they had enough evidence they would charge you. But they don't. They can't prove intent."

Her lip is bleeding again. Jonathan reaches across her body to take a Kleenex from the box on the nightstand and hands it to her.

"It only took a couple of minutes to figure that out," he continues. "I told them that I was your lawyer and that you had nothing to say to them. We exchanged business cards. And then, as politely as I could, I suggested that they get the fuck off your property."

She reaches for Jonathan's hand, holds it tightly, and leans against him, breathing in his comforting, familiar smell: like linen that has dried in the sun. For the first time in weeks, Jonathan responds with his familiar warmth, leaning into her and rubbing her back with his free hand. *Don't cry*, she tells herself. *Be reasonable.* She concentrates on her breathing, tries to think of a winning strategy. She will explain. She will make the best argument. She will get him back. She will get them both back.

In the darkness, lost in her thoughts, Jonathan's voice startles her. "Abby, was Cal going to drown?"

She turns to look at him. Jonathan's gaze is cold. His words are like a reckoning, allowing her to see, finally, why he has been so hard with her and how far she will have to crawl before she can climb out of a hole that is spreading wide and deep like an abyss.

"Will Ellet, what a surprise." Estrada comes around from behind his paper-piled desk, hand extended. His smile is friendly enough but his eyebrows are raised and his look is questioning. They shake. "Have a seat."

There had been no traffic this time and Will had managed to get to Estrada's strip mall office in eighty minutes. Leaving work, he had told his secretary he had a client visit scheduled at the Riverside County Jail. A lie, but a plausible one. Part of the job for the LA-based federal public defenders involves handling cases from one of the satellite offices in Santa Ana and Riverside on occasion.

Will is dressed for court, has in fact, two court appearances later that afternoon back in Los Angeles. Estrada, too, is wearing a suit and tie.

"You look well, sir," Will says. Estrada does, in a neatly pressed suit, thick gray hair freshly cut. He looks relaxed, as if he has been away on vacation, which Will suspects he has been. When Will had driven out last week and the week before, the office had been closed.

"You look like you haven't been sleeping."

Will smiles, trying not to show his irritation at the fatherly smile of concern. "Stress at work, you know how it is."

"I would have thought," Estrada says, "that they would have given you a break."

Will rubs his jaw. No one had offered him a break, but his caseload hadn't exactly been punishing, either. That wasn't what was keeping him up at night, causing him to lose his appetite, and making him snappish, even cruel, with Meredith.

"The thing is," Will says, trying to keep his voice casual, "I haven't been able to get in touch with Luz. She's changed her cell phone number and she's not staying with Father Abelard anymore. I went by Maria Elena's house and it's up for sale."

Will pauses, waiting for Estrada to say something. When he doesn't, Will continues, "She's been through so much, as you know. And I'm—I'm concerned about her. I want to make sure that she's okay. That she and Cristina are okay. So I thought maybe, since you were her lawyer, too, at one point, that you might have some contact information, maybe her new number or an address." His voice goes up at the end, and he forces himself to smile, hoping to mask the tinge of desperation.

Estrada picks up a paper clip from his desk and begins prying it apart. "You haven't spoken with Ms. Rosenberg about any of this, have you?"

Will has a ready answer for this. "Abby is on maternity

leave. And she's been, well, there have been some issues with her—her domestic situation."

"So I read. Unfortunate that someone inside the LAPD leaked that report when they had no intention of charging her."

More like hundreds of cops vying for the honor, Will thinks. After the Rayshon Marbury case, Abby has been about as popular with the LAPD as a low-flying seagull at a beach picnic.

Will, too, had read the coverage, finding it impossible not to take great pleasure from it. Joan of Arc, Feet of Clay? was the headline on one of the legal rags. He must have read the first sentence a dozen times: *In acquitting her client of first-degree murder charges and reuniting her with her baby, Abigail Rosenberg may have sacrificed the well-being of her own child, according to a report made by the child's father, who has obtained temporary sole physical and legal custody following an emergency filing in court.* The gossip in their office was off the charts, though Jonathan and Paul remained tight-lipped. Will had made no attempt to contact Abby himself. Not after the way she had treated him. And anyway, provoking her—or being perceived as passing judgment was begging for trouble. People in glass houses.

To Estrada, he says, "Well, there's an ongoing case of some kind in family court, and I haven't wanted to bother her."

Estrada has the paper clip undone now, in a horizontal line balanced between his two index fingers. He moves it to the left, then to the right in abbreviated half circles.

"Luz and Cristina are doing well," he says finally. "They're safe. Luz is—" he pauses "—recovering."

Will tries to keep the excitement out of his voice. "So you've—you've heard from her?"

Estrada smiles. "Son, I live with her. It's all legal now."

Will feels the blood rushing to his face. He lunges over the desk, hands grasping Estrada's tie to pull him forward so that their faces are inches apart. "You married her? You—you're sleeping with her?" Estrada's hands are on Will's forearms, his grip surprisingly strong, but Will hangs on, jerking him closer, and hears the sound of fabric ripping. "You perverted old man, you sick fuck."

Estrada pushes Will away, sending him backward. Papers fly everywhere and Will stumbles, nearly falling before grabbing ahold of the desk edge. He is beside himself, shaking with rage.

"I didn't marry her, I adopted her." Across the desk, Estrada is removing his ruined tie and massaging his neck, but his eyes are fixed on Will, as if the look alone will keep him in place. "She's my daughter now. Cristina is my granddaughter." When Will just stares back, bug-eyed, Estrada says almost wearily, "Sit down."

Will drops heavily into his seat and Estrada retakes his own seat in the battered leather chair. "I've known Luz for quite a while," he says, "through Father Abelard. I'm a member of his church, too, and I do pro bono work for some of the members. Usually, it's helping people fill out medical forms, insurance forms, reading over rental agreements, fighting evictions. Every once in a while, one of the members, or their kid, gets into trouble, and they ask me to handle that, too."

"Luz's juvenile case," Will says hoarsely. "I know."

Estrada nods. "With the white kids, it's all about counseling and second chances. With the brown and black kids, it's all about 'find me the nearest juvenile hall.' I've seen prosecutors and the police throw away too many people in my community. With Luz," he says, and shakes his head, "I just wasn't going to let them do it. Not after everything that had already happened to her."

"She hurt that other girl pretty badly," Will says.

Estrada nods. "For a while there it looked like maybe she'd have to do some time for it."

"But she didn't."

"That's right." Estrada is picking up the pens that have spilled from their holder and is putting them back one by one. "It helps to have an older gentleman like myself, a fellow parishioner and quasi-pillar of the community, on the record as representing her for free. And I talked to the victim's family beforehand, explained Luz's situation. Turns out they didn't want her to get thrown away, either. Because they understood, you know, that there is a bigger issue with what is happening to our community and it's not going to be solved by locking up our children."

"Luz kept in touch with you after?"

Estrada shrugs. "Not regularly. I would see her from time to time at services but then of course she moved away. I always told her, though, that if she needed help she could come to me. The attorney-client relationship, you know, it never really ends."

Will thinks of the billing records, the calls in the months and days leading up to Travis Hollis's death. "Did you think she was going to kill him?"

"You know better than to ask a question like that."

Will says, too eagerly, "I believe her. I've always believed her when she told me it was self-defense." As he says the words, it occurs to Will that Luz has never told him that, has never told him anything about what she was thinking the night that Travis died other than to reject Will's various attempts to explain it for her. But the man sitting across from him knows what happened, or at least enough of what happened that he went to jail over it, and maybe, it occurs to Will now, not only to protect Luz.

They sit in silence for a moment, Will with his hands clasped together trying to regroup, reminding himself of his goal. Estrada has picked up another paper clip, is fiddling with it. Will keeps waiting for him to say something, but Estrada seems content with the silence and finally Will breaks it. He tries again for the aw-shucks grin, the one that until recently he had slipped on comfortably on so many occasions over the course of his life and to such great effect. "Look, sir, I just need to see her. Just— I need to see for myself that she's okay."

Estrada stretches the paper clip, pressing it flat on the table. "Is that why?" he says.

Will feels his face flush. "I just want— She's my client. You said it yourself, the attorney-client relationship never really ends."

"I have reason to believe," Estrada says, "that your relationship with Luz went beyond attorney and client."

Will tries to hold his gaze, looks away.

"Luz has a history of problematic relationships with men," Estrada says quietly, "Sergeant Hollis being the most extreme example. It's not surprising, given how she grew up, with no father, no real parenting. I'm trying to be that for her now. A parent. Technically, she's an adult but she's still a teenager, you know. She and Cristina are alone in the world."

"What makes you think you'll have any better luck with Luz than her grandmother did?"

"Maria Elena was a good person and she did her best, but she was overwhelmed and outmatched. Back then, Luz was at a different stage in her life, less open to thinking differently about her own behavior, particularly around romantic relationships. Part of it is breaking these cycles, don't you think? These relationships aren't healthy—for either party."

"So you're the hero in this story, is that it?" Will says bitterly. "What a bunch of bullshit. You're just exercising another form of control over her and congratulating yourself all the way to a $400,000 payday."

"That money is in a trust for Cristina," Estrada says sharply, "not that it is any of your business. And no, I don't see myself as a savior. Far from it." He looks at the picture of the girl behind him on the credenza with the long dark hair, smiling against the sky blue background. "My motivations are selfish. I'm long divorced. My own daughter is dead. It's a lucky, lucky second chance for me. To be part of a family again." Estrada leans forward, elbows on his desk, hands clasped, the paper clip momentarily forgotten.

"But I'm not the only one who has a second chance here." Estrada inclines his chin toward the platinum band on Will's left hand. "Go home to your wife. Move away with her, maybe somewhere closer to her parents or yours. Forget all of this. It's over now."

Will closes his eyes against the hot and sudden tears.

Tuesday, June 19, 2007
12:30 p.m.
Elysian Park
Los Angeles, California

"Thank you for meeting me."

"The pleasure is all mine." Paul dusts off the park bench carefully with his palm before sitting down beside Abby and Cal. As usual, he is immaculate: dark suit, white shirt, red tie. Not a crease or a wrinkle, not even a stray piece of lint. "It's good to get out of the office every once in a while and be out in nature. Or," he says, and smiles wryly, "what passes for nature."

Elysian Park has its own dry, dusty beauty. There are wide dirt trails etched into steep hills that surround it, offering spectacular views for those willing to make the trek. A two-lane asphalt road runs through the park's valley with picnic areas on both sides just like the one they are occupying. On the weekends, they are thick with families, some white, some Black, but mostly brown. The fathers tend to the barbecue, filling the air with the rich smell of roasting meat; the mothers tend to their smaller children while the older ones run around whooping and screaming as the ice-cream truck drives slowly back and forth, playing its endless jingle.

But today is a Tuesday and school has not yet let out. The park is deserted, save for a few nannies and stay-at-home moms who push their toddlers in strollers and baby buggies. Now Abby is one of them.

"You look well. And this guy, do you mind if I—" Paul smiles and reaches out, and Abby holds up Cal for him to take. "Wow, he's gotten so big."

Initially, Cal squawks, but he quiets down, even rewarding Paul with a gummy smile after Paul tickles his stomach and makes goo-goo noises that sound impossible coming out of his mouth. He sees Abby staring and says, "I did this with my twins, too, when they were younger."

Cal grasps at Paul's watch and Paul takes it off and dangles it. Cal grabs the clasp and puts it in his mouth. When Abby reaches over and gently removes it, he starts to gnaw on her finger.

"He's teething," she says.

"So I see."

For a moment, they sit quietly watching Cal, but he soon tires of the gnawing and lets out another squawk, looking expectantly at Abby. Paul hands him back and averts his gaze while she lifts up her tee shirt and undoes her bra to nurse him. It is a warm day, nearly eighty degrees. Cal is wearing a pale blue onesie; Abby is in shorts and flip-flops. For the first time in years, her legs are tan.

When Cal is settled again, Paul says quietly, "He's a beautiful baby, Abby. You're doing a great job."

She blinks in surprise, then tries her best to look as if

the compliments are stray pleasantries. "Thank you," she says primly.

"How is everything?"

"It's okay," she says. "We're doing okay."

"Funny, I ran into Nic as I was leaving court to meet you," Paul says. "Just talking shop. I was asking him about his weekend and he mentioned that the three of you had gone on a short trip."

"Jonathan and Quinn just bought a place in Seal Beach. They're planning to use it as a rental property but they want to redo the kitchen and downstairs bathroom, so in the meantime..." She shrugs, then says quietly, "It was just the weekend. We're not—we're not reconciled."

Paul nods. "But maybe," he says.

"Maybe." She says the word carefully, testing it out, and then concludes, "But maybe not." She isn't sure if it is possible or even if it is what she wants. More important, far more important, was the improvement in the custody situation. She has the seal of approval from Child Protective Services and the judge's written sign-off. No more supervised visitation. Fifty-fifty custody, which given Nic's work schedule and her lack of one, has turned into more like eighty-twenty.

"So," Paul says, "this is your meeting. You want to talk about work?"

She nods.

"You're welcome back anytime, Abby, but you know you have at least a month left if you want it. More, I'm guessing, because you never take vacation."

"I should have come to you," she says abruptly, "during the trial. I should have told you what was happening. You think that, right?"

Paul turns to stare out into the street. They sit silently

again, listening to the occasional passing car. Finally, he says, "I said at the outset that you and Will were a team. *The* team. I didn't put myself on it. I decided to trust you. Both of you."

"Which you think now was a mistake."

"You made some decisions. You both did. Decisions that were not wise." Paul continues to look out onto the street, his face expressionless. "Will and Meredith are moving back to Oklahoma. He gave his two weeks' notice. He's got a visiting professor gig to teach military law at U of O, starting in August. Did you know that?"

"No," Abby says. A pause and then she adds, "but that's good. For him, I mean. And Meredith." One of her arms is starting to ache under Cal's weight and she shifts position slightly, just enough to relieve the pressure without unsettling him.

"You want to know what I think about the trial." Paul leans forward, elbows on his knees. "If I had known even the bit that I do, which is far from the full story, would I have intervened? Yeah. Would things have been different? Yeah. But maybe things being different would mean that Luz would be in prison right now. The bottom line is that because of what you did, because of what Will did, and because of what Luz did, she walked. She walked away."

"A miracle," Abby says flatly.

Paul shakes his head. "That's not what it was."

Once again, Abby is caught off guard. She responds, lightly, "Mr. Estrada called me a holy terror."

Paul chuckles. "That's good. I like that."

Another silence falls. Cal finishes and Abby cradles him with one arm while taking a white cloth from her diaper bag, then puts his body against her chest so that his chin is resting on her shoulder. She rubs his back, smells his delicious baby smell, and waits for him to spit up.

Paul shakes his head. "Mr. Estrada. The man is impressive. Not many attorneys would sit in jail like that for a client."

"No," Abby agrees.

"But you would," Paul says. "You would sit in jail for as long as it took. Until the last dog died. You almost had to." Paul nods, as if to himself. "That was some very good lawyering, under tremendous pressure. You can't teach that."

"I got lucky," she says. Hearing the familiar sounds from Cal, she takes him off her shoulder, carefully wipes his mouth with the bottom of her tee shirt, and cradles him again. Cal's eyelids flutter, then close.

Paul shakes his head. "It's got nothing to do with luck. You are a fine trial lawyer, Abby. Exceptional, even."

Abby's vision blurs. She blinks hard several times and tries to say "thank you," but the words strangle in her throat. She looks down as Cal, awake after all, opens his eyes and looks up.

* * * * *

# Acknowledgments

This book was years in the writing and benefited tremendously from the editorial advice, expertise, love, care, and encouragement of many people.

To my Los Angeles writer's group: Reyna Grande, Jessica Garrison, Ann Marsh, Sonia Nazario, and Lisa Richardson: you were there with Abby from the beginning. I am thankful and honored that I got to be part of this group. Your generosity and support over the years made me believe I was a writer. You inspired me to keep going even during the hardest times.

To my colleagues and friends at the Office of the Federal Public Defender in Los Angeles: I am grateful for my seven years with you. Maria Elena Stratton and Sean Kennedy: the fearless client-centered bosses who always had my back. To Dennis Landin, who generously supervised me during that very intense first year, in addition to all of his other responsibilities, and to the intrepid and unflappable

Callie Glanton Steele, who taught me to stand up at crucial moments. To my trial partners over the years: Michael Proctor, Michael Schafler, Jill Ginstling, and Myra Sun. To Reuven Cohen, who made me laugh until I cried—and who never got to finish smoking that cigarette. And, especially, to Guy Casey Iversen, the greatest trial lawyer I have ever seen, including on TV. Guy, your ability to see the world in four dimensions and exceptionally high level of emotional intelligence gave me so much: courtroom skills, confidence in myself, and even a freshly laundered tee shirt to blow my nose into when I was crying uncontrollably. Michael Garcia, on that same note, thank you for your huge heart and clean white handkerchief. I know it was never the same afterward. To Alonso Garcia, an exceptional investigator.

To all the hardworking public defender mothers out there who inspire me every day, including and especially Eda Katherine Tinto—there has been no string of acquittals like yours, not before and not after.

This book benefited immeasurably from early and careful readers. John Jay Osborn, Chris Flood, and Reyna Grande, your exhaustive edits made it so much better than it was. Payton Lyon, for educating me about military life, David Frankel, for educating me about medical matters of the heart—all mistakes are mine. To Jenny Estevez, Jessica Garrison, and Melissa Segura for telling me the truth. To Alafair Burke, for lifting up an aspiring novelist, and to Cathi Hanauer—it was high praise coming from you. Jane Dirkes, you are a generous reader and an even more generous grandmother and friend.

I am lucky to have a loving and indefatigable champion in my agent, Emma Patterson, who has known Abby for many years and was the driving force in bringing her to life. I am thankful my novel found a home at Hanover Square

Press, and for a wise, insightful editor, Peter Joseph, who understood immediately what I was trying to do. Peter, Grace Towery, and everyone on the Hanover Square team got me from Mile 18 to the end of the marathon.

Finally, to Matt Dirkes, for our beautiful children, Carter and Ella, and our imperfect but lifelong partnership, and to my parents, who led by example and always told me to shoot for the moon.

# Discussion Questions

1. In the beginning of the book Abby cuts short her maternity leave with her son, Cal, to defend another young mother who stands accused of murdering her husband. Luz says she acted to defend herself and the life of their child. Abby says that she has a unique power to tell Luz's story because "I understand it in my bones." Do you think Abby is right? Why or why not?

2. The story is told from alternating perspectives: Abby's and her trial partner Will Ellet's. The reader is kept guessing as to Luz's interior thoughts and motives. What do you think about that storytelling decision?

3. How did you feel about Abby's decision to go back to work early? Would you have felt the same way if Abby was Cal's father rather than Cal's mother?

4. On cross examination, the prosecutor says, "You told the jury that before you stabbed your husband, he had attempted to rape you." Luz answers defiantly, "I never said it was rape." Given how Luz has described the relationship with her husband, what do you make of that answer?

5. Will and Abby fight for control over Luz's case. Early on, Will convinces Abby that he should be the one who has the primary relationship with Luz, handling her all-important testimony. Why did Abby agree to cede control to Will? Was this decision a mistake?

6. Antoine, the investigator who works with Abby and Will on the case, hides information from both of them until after the trial. Should Antoine have told her about it?

7. Abby's supervisor, Paul, appears at the beginning and at the end of the book. During the trial, though, he does not intervene. What did you make of his explanation for this decision in the final scene of the book?

8. Abby's partner, Nic, makes a shocking decision after a frightening event involving Abby and Cal. Do you think Nic did the right thing?

9. The trial judge is not a good person. But was he a good judge? Why or why not?

10. Do you think Luz is a good mother? Do you think Abby is? Why or why not?